BLOODLINE

Sharon Francis

ISBN 978-1-8381173-8-2

Cover design by: Megan Saunders

PROLOGUE

The ping of Vicky's mobile sent her swinging into a lay-by, impatient for information, but it was only spam. Nothing new from her mother or Tony. She glanced at the dashboard clock, fingertips drumming the steering wheel as she mentally recapped the morning's events. The mere memory of the timbre of her mother's voice on the phone sent a fresh pounding of blood through her veins.

As she had stumbled around, struggling to pull herself together, Tony hadn't wavered. 'Take my car and leave Jamie to me,' he'd said, 'Get to the hospital. Go see your dad'. Normally she would have relished the opportunity to drive Tony's Audi, he was so precious about it, but today all that mattered was getting where she needed to be.

She had been travelling forty minutes already, racing through the suburbs into countryside, until a near miss had shocked her into a more sensible pace. It would probably be another forty before she arrived, although a short cut could skim time off. It was a narrow, winding route, but there was usually less traffic. Decision made she turned back out on to the road.

As she drove out, her eye was drawn to another vehicle mirroring her move some fifty metres behind. She hadn't registered it when she pulled in or seen it arrive. Continuing, her attention flicked from the road ahead to the car behind her and back again. Was it the car she'd almost rammed earlier? Had it followed her for some unknown reason? No, that was a blue car, something Japanese. This one was silver, unremarkable, but something about it bothered her. When she sped up, it stuck with her; when she slowed down to allow it to overtake, it dropped back. Its persistence rankled.

Determined not to miss the turnoff, she checked every signpost, glancing behind at intervals to see if the silver hatchback was still there. It was. Squeezing the brake, she focused on the rear-view mirror as the vehicle edged closer, trying to make out the face of the driver, but it decelerated, dropping back, and she couldn't even tell if they were male or female. Vicky huffed, returning her attention to the road in time to realise her exit was close ahead. She'd be relieved to leave her shadow behind.

The left turn led into a wide sweeping corner, narrowing as it wound past a group of stone cottages, squat front doors nestled right up to the road. A quick glance in the mirror revealed a clear view behind and she felt her shoulders relax. A muddy Land Rover approached at speed, and she pulled in, two tyres mounting the daisy strewn bank, to allow it through.

She bumped out of the mud, back onto the tarmac, rear tyre spinning clods of mud into the air. As she pulled away, the silver car appeared in her side mirror, skulking cat-like in a gateway and a shiver ran through her. This was no longer irritating. Now she was scared.

Vicky increased her speed, swiftly moving through the gears. She should have stayed on the main road. Here, in the middle of nowhere, she felt isolated and vulnerable. She accelerated further, trying to put distance between them, only withholding momentarily as she approached a sharp right-hand bend, but her pursuer was not only matching her speed, but gaining, compelling her on faster. She held a line as close to the bank as she could, conscious of the possibility of oncoming traffic around every curve, while her maverick stalker followed the central channel, regardless of risk. The gap between them shrank with every second, until Vicky could no longer see the front of the vehicle in her rear-view mirror. Her muscles tightened in anticipation of impact. At the same time, her logic denied the madness. What reason could they possibly have to hit her?

She swung the wheel sideways to negotiate an upcoming corner, but misjudged the arc and, catching the offside bank, slid sideways. The silver car was still on her. The Audi spun in the road, front wheels mounting the low ridge, meant as a barrier between road and steep drop into woodland. There was nothing she could do. The speed and the angle brought the back end of her vehicle up into the air as the front dropped away, and she gripped the wheel, knowing she was going to roll.

The car became wedged between towering oaks, their rusty leaves shuddering with the force. The driver's side glass was gone, lost on its descent, leaving yawning access to the interior and the door was crumpled. Vicky was half within the vehicle and half lying, at what should have been an impossible angle, in the leaf mold on the forest floor. There was pain, briefly, but mostly Vicky felt a cold, creeping numbness spreading slowly from her extremities to her core.

She still couldn't comprehend what had happened, but she knew she was fading. Her thoughts turned to Tony and Jamie, her darling boy, such a little boy to be without a mother.

A shadow fell across her and she tried to reach out, a plea for help, but she was incapable of movement and no sound passed her lips. Shallow, short breaths were all her broken body could manage.

The onlooker bent low, looking first at Vicky, then into the empty car, and swore, kicking out at the Audi's tyre in frustration.

As the person hurried from the scene, hope went too. A final breath escaped Vicky's body like a sigh and her vision faded to black.

CHAPTER 1

Nine Months Later

A hoarse whisper cut through the layers of sleep, wrenching Tony from his unconscious state. He lay awake, still and silent, wishing he could return to the blissfully soothing oblivion. Listening to the urgent entreaties of his son, he tried to ignore the persistent pummelling of his shoulder.

'Dad! Daddy! Wake up, Dad!'

The tone became more impatient, until he could no longer resist.

'Come on, Dad! You said you'd help me.'

Without opening his eyes, Tony flung an arm out and grabbed the boy, rolling him over and tickling him. 'Help you? I'll teach you not to wake your dad up early. Will that help you?'

The boy giggled, arms and legs flailing. 'No. No. Dad, stop it.'

Tony ceased the attack and lay still, watching as his son calmed and his breathing normalized, hair stuck up at angles, a shock of dark against the cream pillowcase. 'So, what am I supposed to be helping you with?'

'My homework. You said we could do it before lunch if I got you up in time.'

'Did I? Ok. What time is it?'

The boy shrugged, 'I don't know.'

Tony pushed up onto one elbow, peering bleary-eyed at the alarm clock, before falling back onto the pillow, the little body next to him bouncing with the force. 'It's six thirty for goodness' sake.'

'Is that early enough?'

The question was asked with childish candour and Tony observed his son's wide-eyed hopeful expression. It was like looking at a miniature version of the wife he missed so much, making it impossible to stay annoyed for long. 'Yes, Jamie, too early.'

'Do you want me to come back later?'

'No, no. You're here now and I'm awake, so we might as well get up. What is it you have to do?' He ruffled the boy's hair.

'Lots of stuff. It's in my homework diary.'

Tony made a face. 'Lots? You're seven years old for crying out loud! Don't they work you hard enough in school?'

'Mrs Bates says it's important and if we don't do it we're holding everybody up and that's not fair,' he stated, forehead furrowed in concentration. 'She says, parents can't expect teachers to do everything. I heard her tell Miss Fallon.'

'Did she now?' Tony smiled ruefully, Mrs Bates was either very inexperienced and had not yet learnt little ears were everywhere or was clever enough to know overheard messages would promptly be reported home.

Jamie nodded.

'OK, tell you what. We'll go through your homework book after pancakes. Sound good?'

Jamie was already shuffling off the bed. 'It's a deal!'

In the lull which followed, Tony lay back, studying the stippled ceiling. He wondered how he would have coped with losing Vicky, if it wasn't for Jamie. Many were the days he woke paralysed by loss but had no choice except to carry on. Jamie was a distraction, but also a constant reminder: his sparkling brown eyes and wide smile a carbon copy of hers. Every day was an exercise in dealing with life as it arrived. Some days were easier than others.

An ominous crash from downstairs jerked him from his thoughts and he flung himself from under the covers.

Dust motes of flour pirouetted in the early sun pouring past the kitchen blind, the air heavy with the smell of hot oil and sweetness. Jamie was sitting at the breakfast bar, smattered with syrup. Still chewing, he reached for a battered notebook, but Tony interceded with a damp cloth.

'Hold your horses. Mrs Bates will go loopy if you turn up with a sticky book on Monday.'

Jamie obediently splayed his fingers to be wiped, but cringed away, dodging the cloth with his face, snatching up the book as soon as he was freed.

Tony slipped onto the stool next to him, drying his hands on his trousers. 'Right, what have we got?'

Jamie shuffled onto his knees, making himself the same height as his father and studied the pages like an intricate blueprint. 'For numeracy, I have to learn my five times table.' He broke into a sing song chanting of numbers, 'You can sign to say I've done it now.'

'Right. That was easy.' Tony scribbled his name. 'Next?'

'I have to find three interesting things from nature.'

'What for?'

Jamie scowled at Tony's ignorance. 'We've got to write about them, like where we found them and why they're interesting. We'll probably draw them in art, or maybe make a collage.'

'Ok. So, do you want to go out to the garden and find some leaves or something? You'll have to put your wellies on.'

'Everybody will have leaves.'

'All right, I'll have a think about it. What else?'

Jamie returned his attention to the book. 'I have to draw my family tree, like the one we did for the Queen.'

Launching from the stool, he ran to the hallway, returning moments later with his schoolbag, half open, contents threatening to erupt with every step. He pulled out two stapled sheets, folded in four, then ditched the bag before unfolding them and flattening them with his hands. On one side was the family tree for the Royal family and the other a basic tree template. He snatched up a pen.

'Do I write Jamie or my whole name?'

'Oh, I think you should write your whole name.'

He voiced the words aloud as he wrote. 'James Antony Viscount, born ... When was I born?'

'Well, you're seven, aren't you? See if you can work it out.'

He chewed his tongue, concentrating, counting on fingers, before filling in the year and looking to Tony for confirmation.

'Spot on. Now, me.'

Jamie moved to the space above his own name. 'Antony, like me?'

'Yes.'

'What about middle names?

'No, I'm plain old Antony Viscount, and I was born in nineteen eighty-four.'

Jamie laid his pen down and stared at him. 'That's a hundred years ago if it starts nineteen,' he accused.

Tony laughed. 'I feel like it sometimes, but it's only thirty-six years actually.'

He thought about it a moment before filling in the box. 'OK.' His pen moved to where his mother's details belonged and stalled. He turned to Tony in anguish. 'Do you think Mummy would mind if I write her name down?'

'Of course not, why would she?

He shrugged. 'I don't know, but I can't ask her, can I?'

Tony's chest ached at the angst on his son's face. Vicky's death had been incomprehensible to him: how on earth did a small boy compute the loss of his mother. 'I know she's not here, but she'll always be your Mummy and she'll always be part of your history.'

Jamie bent and wound his pen between star-fished fingers, 'I know she is still my Mummy, but sometimes I can't remember what it's like to have a Mummy and a Daddy.'

'I know.' Tony pulled him onto his lap. 'Things have changed a lot for you and me, haven't they? And, after a while, we get used to things being different, even if we're not happy about it. And sometimes we forget some of the old bits, but we always remember the important parts.'

'Like how she sang *You Are My Sunshine* when she tucked me in?' His voice was a mouse version of itself.

'Exactly like that.' He wanted to hug the boy until everything was better, but he never could, not really. He could soften the edges, but Vicky was never coming back, no matter how they longed for her. Rapid blinking cleared his vision and his gaze fell onto Jamie's homework diary. 'I've had an idea.'

The upbeat tone alerted Jamie to a change of atmosphere, and he sprang up straight like a meerkat, prepared to be excited. 'What?'

'How about we leave this and go and find some

interesting things from nature at the beach instead? We could call Marco & Ruth and see if they'd like to come. They live nearby.' Many friends had fallen away following Vicky's death, not knowing what to say or put off by Tony's pendulum swings from anger to despondency and back again. Marco had doggedly stayed in touch; inviting him out; wittering on about sports and work and whatever was in the news; distracting him from self-pity. Usually, Tony used Jamie or shifts at his restaurant, The Olive Branch, as an excuse, but nonetheless he appreciated the constancy.

'And Max?'

He should have known the smelly old dog would be the most important member of the household. 'Yes, and Max.'

Jamie's face came alive. 'Can I hold the lead?'

Tony ruffled his hair. 'That's a definite possibility.'

Jamie shot from Tony's lap, in a hunt for his shoes while Tony texted his friend. It took only moments to arrange but, before they could leave, the house telephone rang. 'Hold on, Jamie. That'll probably be Marco reminding us to bring something.' He held the handset to his cheek with his shoulder so he could tuck keys into his jacket pocket at the same time. 'Hi.'

'Hi, Tony. Matt Bridgeman here, police liaison. '

Tony's heart and stomach clenched in unison. He had been fielding this call for days.

'Sorry to bother you at the weekend, but I thought it might be a good time to catch you. Could we get together for a chat?'

'Is it something we can do over the phone?'

Matt ignored the reluctant tone. 'There are a couple of issues I need to go over with you to bring you up to speed. It won't take long but would be easier face to face.'

Tony frowned, annoyed he hadn't checked caller ID before picking up. 'It's a busy week, I'll be going straight to the restaurant from school most mornings.'

'How about now, or later this morning?' Matt was not to be deterred. 'I won't keep you long.'

'Jamie and I were about to go out to meet friends.'

'Perhaps your friends could keep an eye on Jamie for half an hour while we chat?' He paused. 'It is quite important.'

Tony sighed, he could muster no further excuses and perhaps it was better to just get it over with. 'I'm sure that'll be fine. Can you give me forty minutes to drop him round and get back?'

Ending the call, he dropped the handset onto the worktop with a clatter, staring into space as he contemplated the conversation. Issues? What issues? No doubt it would be another debate about how Vicky died; why Vicky died; on that road; on that day, as if it mattered. The result was the same.

The door clicked as Jamie swung from the door handle, drawing Tony's attention. The boy was solemnly studying his father's care-etched face. Tony forced a smile. He didn't want to upset him.

'Slight change of plan.' He winked, breaking the tension. 'Let's get you to Marco and Ruth's.'

As Tony pulled back onto his own drive, Matt's car was already parked to one side and Tony breathed deeply. He felt guilty for disliking Matt. No doubt, he was a nice enough guy. He had gone out of his way to be friendly, but to Tony it was what he represented - the official finalisation of Vicky's life. Matt was the ticking of boxes and crossing of 'T's which confirmed she was gone for good.

He wished he'd asked for more information; found

out what the 'issues' were. He presumed they were going ahead with the inquest, but as far as he could see, it was an open and shut case. Vicky had been speeding, beset by worry for her father. It seemed painfully ironic now; Vicky was dead, while her father was alive and well, with nothing more seriously wrong than an inflamed gall bladder. Tony wondered if Neil felt guilty, blamed himself, for making such a meal of something so trivial, worrying Vicky out of her mind. He hoped so. Still, it would be recorded as an accident which, in law, it was. It was Vicky's choice to drive down country roads at ninety, regardless of the provocation. Neil would have to endure his punishment as long as he lived – the loss of his daughter, a harsh toll indeed.

'Hi, Tony. Thanks for making the time to see me.'

'That's fine, come in. I'll put the kettle on.'

Tony led him through the hallway, into the kitchen, straightening jumbled shoes with his foot as he passed. He pointed to the high stools by the breakfast bar. The top was cluttered with cutlery and small stacks of Lego floating in milky moats. 'Take a pew and I'll clear this away.'

He flicked the switch on the kettle and busied himself clearing a section so Matt could make use of the space. Matt kept the conversation light, as he flicked open the case on his lap, pulling out files. He shuffled them awkwardly, locating one and replacing the others before placing the case next to him on the floor. Tony joined in, wishing Matt would get to the point, but the chat continued, until cups of steaming coffee were settled between them. Matt's attitude abruptly switched to professional mode and Tony clamped his lip in readiness for what was to follow.

'Thanks for fitting me in today. I know you could do without me raking it all up again, but it's important you have all the facts, so when all's done and dusted, you're not left with questions. And, of course, if Jamie has questions in the future, you'll be able to fill in the gaps. OK?'

Tony felt too fragile to answer and nodded curtly, swallowing a rising wave of anxiety.

'Right.' Matt flipped open the file, revealing several pages, fronted by a typed sheet of bullet points. 'You know we have to hold a closing inquest, yes? We've just been waiting for completion of the investigation, so all the evidence is in place to present to the coroner.'

Tony remained mute, aware Matt was studying his face. He felt like a bidder at an auction, afraid to move a muscle in case he inadvertently committed himself to something.

'The investigation has now been closed. Of course, there is always an opportunity to reopen a case, if further information should come to light, but at the present time, we are confident all details that could be gathered have been. If it's all right with you, I'd like to read through our final report to give you a chance to clarify anything that's unclear. We don't want unnecessary shocks at the inquest.' He paused, eyes narrowed, as he continued his perusal of Tony's expression, looking for some sign he was engaged. His voice briefly took on a softened tone, displaying something more than mere efficiency. 'Are you up to it?'

Tony was focused on resisting the automatic stress responses in his body; refusing to allow the rush of adrenalin racing through his bloodstream to drive the rate of his breathing, despite his head swimming with lack of oxygen as his heart rhythm stampeded. Everything about him was frozen, his face expressionless, his emotions caged. He released the reins just long enough to nod his head and grunt for

Matt to continue. 'Go on.'

As Matt's voice relayed the contents of each of the documents, Tony was on another plane, only the occasional word piercing the veil. As Vicky's personal information was repeated, he shifted his attention to a moth flitting around the light. As the route Vicky travelled on the day of the accident was detailed, his gaze locked on to the flickering reflection of his coffee, dancing a jig on the ceiling. He looked down at his mug, clasped tightly with both hands, the hot ceramic scalding the soft skin of his palms. A report about the mechanical inspection of the car instigated inner chastisement, *you took better care of the car than you did her,* and he adjusted his grip on the cup, pressing his wrists to the burning heat, the steam curling up, bringing a prickling damp to his throat and chin. There were so many things he wished he had done differently. He would have worked less; spent more time with her and Jamie; fretted less about the trivial things; never let her get into the car alone when she was so distraught. A single word cut through his defences, and he was instantly back in the room.

'Witness?'

Matt paused mid-flow. 'Yes.'

'What witness? What are you talking about?' He stared as if Matt was talking fluent Martian.

Matt nurtured a steady, calming tone, guiding Tony back to a safe, controlled level. 'A witness came forward some time after the collision, in response to house-to-house enquiries. It would seem he was some distance away, walking his dog in the fields above the woodland, but the elevation of the ground meant he had a fairly clear view of fragments of the road. He didn't actually see the accident, but he witnessed events leading up to that moment and heard a crash.'

Tony pushed himself up onto his feet, his hands

pressing down hard on the worktop in fury. 'Then why the hell was she down there a day and a half before you found her? Did he not think he should report it? Did he not think he should call for help?' He grabbed a handful of hair in despair. 'Jeez! She might still be alive if help had got there sooner. What the hell ...'

Matt rose to his own feet, reaching to place a hand on Tony's shoulder, encouraging him back into his seat, his voice firm. He followed his line of sight, forcing him to make eye contact, 'Tony. Tony. No! No, his coming forward earlier would have made no difference whatsoever. Vicky died on impact. The medical report is clear on that point. Please, sit down. Let me go through it with you. Come on, sit down.'

Tony flopped back onto his stool; breath ragged in his throat. 'He should have done something, surely?'

'Yes, he should,' Matt conceded, 'but he says the noise didn't suggest anything like as serious an event as it was, and because there was a second car at the scene, he thought he didn't need to get involved.'

'Involved...?' Exasperation made him weak, his limbs leaden.

'I know, I know. What can I say? People keep themselves to themselves these days and I believe he really thought he would be surplus to requirements. He's an old guy who didn't want to get in the way. It was weeks later before he heard the full story. Someone told him in passing at the pub. Until then, he had no idea it was so serious, that someone had died. When we finally got to him, he was more than happy to co-operate and, as it turned out, was a valuable witness.' Matt withdrew his hand and sat back, eyeing Tony carefully. 'Can I carry on?'

'I'm OK.'

'Good.' He took his time over a sip of coffee, allowing Tony breathing space before he continued.

'The witness reported seeing two cars. They appeared to be racing, at high speed, for some distance...'

Tony shook his head, completely confused. 'Racing? Vicky wouldn't have been racing.'

'Obviously this is just the opinion of the witness. We can't guess what exactly was going on now. Suffice to say, it was news to us there was a second car, so we had to investigate further. One vehicle he described matched your car, but to date we've been unable to trace the second vehicle, partly because the description was somewhat lacking – a silver hatchback, and partly because we have little to no corroborating evidence to back it up. It's like looking for a needle in a haystack.'

'Then what makes you sure it exists? This guy, the witness, he could have made it up or be talking about completely different cars, or the wrong day even.' He shook his head, perplexed. His mind was resigned to the idea Vicky had driven off the road because she was speeding and distracted. The idea someone else was involved muddied the waters, sent him spiralling.

'The witness could confirm the date and time to within half an hour, because of his movements that day, which we were able to corroborate, and also tied up with the post-mortem results. Added to which, scene investigators had identified two sets of tyre tracks where the car left the road, which fits his version of events. Prior to his coming forward, one set of tracks had been disregarded, as we assumed they had occurred separately – it hadn't rained for days and the site was almost a hairpin bend, so they could have been pre-existing. The tyre tracks related to cheap tyres, mass produced, so of no help whatsoever. We're in a position now where, unless another witness appears, or the driver of the silver hatchback comes forward, we have nowhere else to go.'

Tony felt adrift. 'I don't know what to do with this

information. I don't know how to feel about it. It feels like it changes things, but at the same time it doesn't, does it?'

'I know this is upsetting. That's why I wanted to make sure you were up to speed before the inquest. At least now you can ask questions, try and make sense of it, outside of the confines of a court room. Is there anything else you wanted to know?'

Tony shrugged, 'Is there anything else to know?'

'I will finish running through the report with you, but no, I think you pretty much have the full picture.'

The remaining information was reeled off, random facts, anonymous, detached, and Tony was unable to relate the deluge to the loss of his wife. His mind whirled with new, shocking pictures of her racing through the countryside, in pursuit or pursuing someone else, and it made no sense. He was dazed by it all.

Matt took his leave, while a shadowlike Tony thanked him and shut the door on the outside world. Left alone, he turned from the door and sat on the bottom stair, staring at the repeated pattern of the floor tiles, temporarily losing himself in it. He had expected the meeting to be difficult, to be a challenge, but this was something completely different and, to be frank, it had thrown him.

CHAPTER 2

With the luxury of time and space, Tony might have reconciled this new version of Vicky's last minutes, but the dull clunk of the lounge clock reaching the hour reminded him of his promise not to be long, so he grabbed his jacket and keys and left, mind still reeling.

As expected, Marco and Ruth had been happy to step in with Jamie, and had even added an invitation to lunch, guessing the meeting would be stressful enough for Tony, without him having to worry about preparing a meal straight after too.

When Tony finally got there, Marco walked out to meet him. 'All ok?' He asked.

Tony nodded and was glad not to be pressed for further details, but that was just like Marco, always ready to help, but not to pry.

'Jamie's playing with Max in the garden, having been thoroughly spoilt by Ruth. I don't want to incriminate anyone, but there may or may not have been cake,' Marco said. Ruth smiled an acknowledgement, as they rounded the house to join her in the small lawned area at the rear.

'Ah, good, you're here. I'll get the gravy going while you two have a chat.'

'Thanks, Ruth. I appreciate it.'

She waved away his thanks and headed inside. 'Nonsense, I've enjoyed hearing all his little stories of school. The things they get up to.'

'I probably don't want to know.' Tony laughed after

her.

Marco and Ruth kept conversation light and flowing, and, for a while, Tony's thoughts were deflected away from the morning's baffling meeting. He enjoyed the first home cooked meal he hadn't had to make himself for months.

They finished with a walk in the sunshine, away from the crowded front, on a quiet, fern edged track, a few metres back from the cliff edge. Marco detached Max's lead, the dog panting with exertion, tongue dangling from a wide canine smile.

Tony relished the keen breeze on his skin and the salt air purifying his lungs. Jamie was ahead, collecting objects in a bucket for his project, gabbling to Ruth. Marco whipped a fern around like a fencing foil, parrying the undergrowth, until Tony called a halt, checking his watch.

'Much as I hate to say it, we ought to be getting back. This young man has homework to finish.'

'Homework?' Ruth adjoined, horrified, as they turned to backtrack. 'At the weekend?'

'I don't mind,' Jamie reassured. 'I've got to draw my family tree. Dad's going to help.'

'Ooh! I love family trees.' Her voice rose with excitement. 'There's nothing like digging up information and rifling through old documents. If you need help, let me know. I've traced both our families back to the eighteenth century.'

'Thank, Ruth. To be honest, I think we've only got to fill in a few rows, which shouldn't be too difficult, but if we get stuck, I'll give you a call.'

'Lord, the number of graveyards I've been dragged through over the years.' Marco was less excited.

'Not half as many as the cricket pitches I've been dragged to.' She poked him in the chest.

The couple bickered good-naturedly all the way

home, Max disappearing to explore, then emerging from the bushes. Tony and Jamie were silent observers, tired after their exertions, but content.

Back at the car, Tony ushered Jamie into his seat and double checked the seatbelt. 'Thanks. It's been a really fun afternoon.'

'Any time, and don't forget, if you need help with that homework, I'd love to get involved.' Ruth leaned in the open window. 'Call me, Jamie, will you?'

He nodded, too tired to agree or argue.

Tony also climbed in, and Marco stepped back onto the pavement, leaning down next to his wife, one arm loosely circling her waist. 'I think a night at the pub might be long overdue. I'll give you a call.'

'That would be great.' He was surprised to find he actually meant it.

Max magically appeared at Marco's heel, and Jamie waved with renewed vigour until they turned onto the main road.

By the time Tony had finished parking, Jamie was raring to go, batteries recharged, but Tony was flagging, familiar quicksand grabbing his ankles as soon as he walked through the door. The morning's debris was a reminder there was no one to clean up behind him; no back up. He set Jamie to work on his homework, while he headed to the kitchen sink.

The day's events seemed to have wiped away any sentimentality the boy had about the family tree and Tony only wished he could forget so easily. Instead, his thoughts were constantly interrupted with startling new images of Vicky racing some unknown stranger down narrow lanes.

Jamie jotted in his mother's name without a qualm and demanded further information immediately. Tony suddenly became aware of how inadequate his own knowledge actually was. He stood, leaning back against the sink, drying a dinner plate with a tea towel, as he thought about it.

'My Dad was Robert, and my Mum was Fiona, and my Mum's surname before she married was Smale.'

'When were they born?' Jamie fired at him, the end of his pen darting from between his teeth to the paper and back again, with the rapidity of a chameleon fly-catching.

'Do you know, I can't remember. Sometime in the early sixties I think, or late fifties.'

'I can't write that, can I?' Jamie accused.

'Guess not. The problem is my parents died when I was still young, and I don't really know.'

'Did they have a car crash?'

'No. Nothing like that.' Tony kept his tone light. At the moment Jamie seemed to think car accidents were the only cause of early demise and he didn't want to broaden the remit of his paranoia. 'I was much bigger than you when it happened, but I never asked them stuff like when or where they were born. My Aunty Trish looked after me, she would know. Shall I give her a ring?'

'Yes, please.' He laid his pen down expectantly.

Tony threw the tea towel onto the draining board and retrieved the telephone handset from the hallway, dialling as he walked. Jamie watched hawk-like, slumping, with an exaggerated sigh, as it became obvious no one was going to answer.

'I'll try again later.'

Jamie was not to be deterred. 'What about Nanny and Grandad and Aunty Sarah? Do you know about them?'

'Sorry, buddy. I'm a bit useless, aren't I? Nanny is Diana and Grandad is Neil, but I have no idea when their birthdays are. Why don't you give Aunty Sarah a ring?' He handed him the handset. 'I'll make sandwiches for tea.'

Jamie pressed the handset tight against his cheek. Tony turned to the fridge, pulling out packets and tubs, one ear on the conversation in the background. There were a lot of 'Oks', but little else.

'No luck?' The griddle pan spat viciously as he flicked bacon into it.

'No. Tom says the goat's on the lawn eating the washing, so she's out chasing the rat-bag before everybody's pants get munched. She'll phone when she comes back.'

Tony chuckled. A statement like that from anyone else might raise an eyebrow, but it was typical of Sarah's household. 'Never mind' He continued to prepare the sandwich, buttering bread and flipping bacon. 'I'm sure we'll soon get to the bottom of this old family tree. It'll just take a little time.'

CHAPTER 3

On Monday morning, Tony's mind was still full of the previous day's conversation with Matt. He hadn't slept well because of it, and his head ached. Thankfully, Jamie had been whisked away to school early, accompanying his friend Charlie to breakfast club, thanks to Charlie's mum, Adrienne. Recently divorced, she was often glad to exchange babysitting duties and had proved useful to Tony on several occasions.

Tony parked in the bay behind The Olive Branch, but having locked the car with a fumbling hand, he didn't feel ready to start the day.

'Caffeine.' he muttered under his breath; the failsafe which bolstered him through many of life's challenges.

He scuttled through the cobbled alleyway, leading past a couple of highbrow boutiques onto the High Street. The pavements were buzzing already, the promise of sunshine drawing the public out early. He waited for a gap in the footfall and trotted across the road to the dark windowed coffee shop on the far side.

Stepping past the threshold was like entering a new atmosphere, pleasantly cool and mellow. The low hum of voices overlaid a quiet backing track of easy listening tunes, providing a welcoming, distracting backdrop, inviting him to get lost among the conversation and the small knots of bodies around the counter. The fragrance of various beverages revived him a little, his brain perking up and, after placing his order, he stood back to make use of the hiatus, to examine the facts with a clear mind.

Vicky wasn't racing anybody. The witness was a blind fool. No doubt he was thinking of a different car, or a different day. But then, the police had checked his version of events, the timeline and it all fitted. A convincing witness, Matt had said. So, who was in the other car? Why were they racing? Had there been some sort of argy-bargy earlier? Vicky always drove too close to cars in front. He'd mentioned it to her many times; not that she listened. Perhaps she wound somebody up and they retaliated. No, it was more likely there was no other car or, if there was, it just happened to be in the same place at the same time and had nothing to do with Vicky at all. Coincidence. That was it - simply coincidence. Two cars on the same road, on the same day, going fast, for whatever reason, but completely unconnected. Except he knew Vicky's reason – her father. The witness had put two and two together and decided the cars were together. Matt had said the guy was a long way away. Maybe his perspective was skewed. Who knew what state his eyesight was in, and didn't Matt say something about the pub? The guy was probably three sheets to the wind. The police may have confirmed his whereabouts on the day, but they couldn't check how drunk he was. Besides, he surely would have come forward earlier if he was properly compos mentis. A crash like that couldn't be ignored; the noise must have been horrendous. Even from miles away you would surely realise the magnitude unless your brain was completely stewed.

A hand on his arm and a soft, querulous voice pulled him out of his reverie. 'Tony?'

He turned his attention to the woman next to him, his frown changing from one of concentration to one of perplexity as he failed to recognise the face which greeted him. She was short, little over five feet tall, he would guess, and very slight, like a tiny exotic bird. Her eyes were a rich molten chocolate, and he was sure he had never met her before. He would have remembered.

'Yes?' He studied her a moment longer, smiling politely; trying to place her, 'Sorry, do I know you?'

The playful smile behind her eyes leaked to her lips and he could not help but trace the metamorphosis as it crossed her face. 'No,' she gesticulated to the counter with her head, dark hair bouncing with the movement, 'but if you don't claim your latte soon, they are going to throw it away. They have been calling your name over and over.'

He was fixated by every word, the attractive drawl and precise pronunciation suggesting a European origin. As her speech ended, the penny dropped, and he blushed profusely. 'Oh, sorry!' He turned to the frustrated barista, apologising again and collecting his drink, before returning his attention to the woman, lifting his cup in acknowledgement. 'Sorry about that, miles away. Clearly, I need caffeine even more than I thought I did. Thank you.'

He shuffled around the counter, his elbows suddenly out of all proportion as he manoeuvred past tables and customers to the exit. A young woman with a buggy and toddler in tow was tangled in the doorway, struggling to fit her appendages through the gap and he stood back self-consciously, holding the door wide. By the time she had freed herself, the striking stranger from the queue had caught up with him and waited to one side to leave. He waved her ahead, hoping his show of gallantry would override the bumbling first impression he had presented.

'Thank you. Enjoy your coffee, Tony.' She emphasized his name, a kittenish smile playing across her face.

She caught his gaze, holding it a moment longer than necessary and he was aware of colour rising to his cheeks, but he enjoyed the attention and automatically responded to the flirtation. Leaning down, he read the name scrawled on her cup in black pen and tripped alongside her, nonchalantly allowing the door to swing shut behind him. 'I will. Nina? You, too!'

She made to cross the road diagonally, flashing an infectious grin over her shoulder, hair swinging with the momentum, as the tide of pedestrians magically parted ways for her. A lightness temporarily lifted him out of the morning's quagmire, until a secondary wave of awkwardness washed over him when he realised his route was in the same direction and he followed her across. As she mounted the pavement on the other side, she spotted him and raised her eyebrows. 'Are you stalking me now?'

There was a mirth in her tone, but, as Tony jostled with other pedestrians, clumsy ineptitude returned with a vengeance, and the witty rejoinder he longed for evaded him. 'No, no, I work here.'

His gaucheness seemed to amuse her further and she chuckled as she walked away. 'Have a good day.'

She became one with the stream of bodies ebbing and flowing down the pavement, disappearing into the distance. He watched until he could no longer pick out the glimmer of her hair from the crowd.

Having slid into the quiet of the still closed restaurant, he leaned against the door, relieved to be away from the busyness and the noise outside, his nerves salved by the sanctuary of a place long familiar. The ladder backed chairs and oak tables, draped with crisp white cloths; the tulip vases and single stem gerbera and even the neat pine trays holding the condiments, were part of his history; all had stories behind them, which transported him back to a simpler time, a cherished time.

The brief exchange with Nina had left him strangely unsettled and he examined the memory as he sipped from the cardboard cup, steaming liquid scalding his gums.

'Morning boss. Who's the chick?'

The wiry bar manager, the essence of cool in his trim black uniform, blonde hair slicked back, popped up from the welcome lectern, a damp cloth in hand, almost causing Tony to drop his drink. 'Good grief, Lewis. You almost gave me a heart attack.'

'Nah.' He threw the cloth from one hand to another like a cocktail shaker, before bending to wipe the window ledge, chuckling. 'If anything's going to give you a coronary it's chatting up a sort like that first thing in the morning.'

The impertinent comment was par for the course for Lewis, but today it permeated Tony's skin and he scowled, and tutted.

As he pushed through the swing door, into the staff room, he heard Lewis muttering under his breath. 'Somebody's touchy today.'

Tony slammed his cup down, sending a micro-shower of droplets onto the weathered pine laminate table. Give him his dues, Lewis was right, Tony's nerves were jangled, and he felt off-balance, but he was not clear why. Manhandling the stiff door of his battered locker, he pulled out chef's whites and jiggled his arms into the sleeves, fastening the buttons across his chest. He didn't care about making a fool of himself in front of an attractive woman. That was such a regular occurrence he was immune to the humiliation he might have experienced had it been the first time. So eager had he been to impress on his first date with

Vicky, he had made a show of studying the label on the wine bottle, and promptly tipped merlot across the table and down the front of her white blouse. She had been magnanimous, merely saying she preferred hers in a glass, but he had spent the whole evening apologising, until she kissed him and told him to shut up. It was a moment he would never forget, a precious moment they had laughed about together, but now it was his and his alone.

He moved through into the kitchen before he made himself feel too wretched. Work had proven a useful distraction and he was happy to use whatever tactic helped. A cloud of heat enveloped him, the crash and bang of pans and dishes drowning out the voices in his head. He checked in with the busy workers, exchanging banter, listening to gripes, before heading to his own corner.

'So, Ian, what do you need from me today?'

The Head Chef leaned back from his workstation and shouted through the food pass to Lewis, still busy, furnishing a polishing cloth, a pencil tucked behind his ear. Ian's deep Scottish burr travelled to every corner of the room. 'Lewis? How's the diary looking?'

Lewis yelled over his shoulder, 'Fifty-three covers across the evening, quiet lunchtime, but if it stays sunny the beer garden'll lure'em in. We'll be doing high teas all afternoon.' The phone rang and he made a beeline for it.

Ian turned to Tony and shrugged. 'He's generally right. Check the fridges and top up the usuals; cheesecakes, pecan pie, and best add scones to the list. Otherwise, it's up to you, you can do something fancy, if you really feel the need.'

Tony laughed. The team had worked together so long it operated like clockwork. Whatever else he had to worry about, his business was not one of them. 'I might rustle up something a bit swish. I'm in the mood.'

'Knock yourself out.' Ian was his usual pragmatic self.

Tony gathered a halo of ingredients around him. He was comfortable here, with the ringing of steel on steel in his ears and tantalising aromas wafting past his nostrils. The staff were good people, who worked hard and pulled together. When Vicky died, they'd stepped up to allow him the time and space he needed and now an easy routine had developed. He owed them a great deal.

With mixers waltzing in the background, he set to making pastry, his mind drifting back over the morning's events. Why had the meeting with Nina disturbed him so much? She was an attractive woman, that was for certain, but there were plenty of those in the world. He didn't usually feel the need to pick things over with a fine-tooth comb, after the fact. He'd often participated in innocent flirtation in the past and it had never affected him like this.

He tipped scone dough onto the floured surface, manhandling it into shape, working out his frustrations. The difference was Vicky. In the past, those flirtations had been mere window shopping. Vicky had always been there, an almost physical presence in the background of his mind, laughing at his graceless attempts to impress a woman, but now she was dead, it was different, it felt like betrayal.

The atmosphere bubbled up around him as the hours passed, a new sense of urgency emerging when the doors opened, and the public arrived. The familiar faces of waiting staff appeared and disappeared at the pass, exchanging banter, laughter oiling the machine. A gentle lull alerted him to the arrival of mid-afternoon, and he began to clear away, knowing the time to collect Jamie was imminent.

When he returned to the staff room, chores complete, he felt like a different person to the one which had arrived, refreshed, calmer, the efforts of the day ironing his cares away. Perhaps he would let Jamie loose in the park, or, even better, take the football. He grabbed his jacket and made for the exit with a renewed sense of purpose, striding straight into Lewis, heading in the opposite direction, waving a scrap of paper like a flag.

'Hey, boss, message.'

Tony took the note and studied the spider scrawl, frowning. 'What's this?'

'A message from another one of your women.' One eyebrow was raised to his hairline, challenging a repeat of Tony's earlier churlishness. 'Trish.'

'Trish?' The only Trish knew was his aunt and she never phoned him at work, in fact, she rarely phoned him at all.

'She said to tell you, if you bothered to pick up your messages she wouldn't have to phone you at work. Apparently, it would be nice to see you, once in a while, even when it's not a special occasion.'

He grunted, non-committal. Their relationship was a difficult one, having been thrown together after his parents died. He had reacted to the loss with a powerful adolescent anger at the world she had been unequipped to handle. She had resolutely accepted him into her home and resented his being there every second of every day.

'She said she got your message at the weekend and has something important to give you. She's expecting you and Jamie for lunch on Sunday, no excuses.'

Tony pursed his lips. That sounded like Trish. 'Is that

right?'

Lewis chortled as he walked back into the restaurant. 'I wouldn't want to argue with her.'

Tony pensively watched Lewis leave, his mood dipping as he contemplated spending Sunday lunch with his maiden aunt. On the other hand, he was intrigued about what she could have for him. Presumably, if it was in response to his message, it was something to do with his ancestry.

He checked his pockets for his car keys and headed for home.

CHAPTER 4

Jamie sat in the back of the car, legs swinging rhythmically against the upholstery as he shuffled in his seat. He was uncharacteristically clean and tidy, best check shirt and neatly creased navy shorts as crisp and fresh as they could be after thirty minutes travelling in a muggy, airless vehicle. His hair was stuck to his forehead despite the draught from the air vents, and he wriggled with discomfort as he tapped away on a Gameboy, his eyes darting a path around the tiny screen as he followed a miniature creature on an adventure.

'Are we nearly there?' He sighed, without looking up from the game.

'Won't be long.' Tony shot a glance at him, tutting at the speed of the lorry in front. 'Listen, we don't have to stay long. I know it'll be a bit boring for you but try to be good. Aunty Trish doesn't like nonsense. We'll have lunch and then get straight off home, ok?'

Jamie huffed dramatically. 'Why hasn't she got a dog?'

'I don't know, she doesn't want one I suppose. Not everyone who lives in the country has a dog.' This was a return to an earlier and, Tony had thought, exhausted topic of conversation.

'Well, I would have one, and I'd take it for a walk every day as soon as I got back from school, even it was raining.'

Tony replied with a grunt.

After a drawn-out pause, Jamie continued, determined to be disgruntled. 'Doesn't she even have a cat?'

An opportunity to overtake the lorry appeared and Tony accelerated away, foot to the floor. As he left the vehicle behind, finally able to make progress, he relaxed a little and grinned. 'No, no cat. Not even a rabbit. She's a lonely, grumpy old lady without even a hamster for company. That's why we're going to see her and we're going to be nice and polite and good as gold, so we cheer her up. We can do that, can't we? Just for a little while?'

'I suppose.' He didn't sound sure. He let the console fall to his lap as his brain became otherwise occupied. 'Does she know if she stops being grumpy, she might get some friends? At school we have a friendship bench and if someone doesn't have anyone to play with, they go and sit on it. Then other people come and ask them to join in their game. Pippa is always on the friendship bench because she's always grumpy and only wants to play her games. Mrs Bates says, there has to be give and take in friendships and you can't always have everything your own way.'

'A very wise woman, Mrs Bates.' Tony half smiled. Jamie seemed to see Mrs Bates as some kind of oracle.

'Yes, she is. Perhaps she should have a chat with Aunty Trish.'

'I don't think Aunty Trish would want to hear it. People her age are usually very set in their ways, so we won't mention it.' He turned into a short leafy driveway, the car bouncing as the tyres slipped from tarmac to geometric red brick paving. 'Anyway, we're here now, put the game away. Remember, best behaviour.'

As he pulled in front of the closed garage, the glass panelled door opened at the front of the house, as if she had been watching and waiting, and Tony's stomach fluttered unpleasantly. 'Be extra 'specially nice to Aunty Trish, Ok?'

She strode past the front step and stood to one side, arms folded across her chest, the breeze playing with her silver, softly curled hair as she waited. A bright red scarf was knotted jauntily round her neck, a stark contrast to indigo jeans and blue and white striped top, giving her a neat, nautical air. As Tony grabbed his things from the back seat, Jamie unclipped himself and jumped out, flinging the car door shut with a bang.

Trish crouched as he headed in her direction, inspecting him closely, a broad smile and a hint of excitement animating her face. 'Look at you, young man. Goodness how you've grown, but I suppose it would be a bad job if you hadn't.'

'I'm almost the tallest in my class,' he boasted, 'not quite, but nearly. William and Chloe are taller, but they're older than me too, because their birthdays are in September.'

She raised her eyebrows, clearly amused by his open nature. 'Well, that makes perfect sense.'

Standing up right, she tipped her head to one side, encompassing them both with her gaze, 'Come along in boys, lunch is almost ready.' Then, stepped back, holding the door wide for them to enter first. 'My! It is good to see you.'

Tony was taken aback by her enthusiasm. He had not expected such a warm welcome and didn't know how to react, so he bit his lip and went with it.

She led them into the lounge, a room he remembered well, but barely recognised with its current décor. The light flooded in through a picture window, framing the green and leafy back garden. A drooping cherry tree released a flutter of soft pink petals into the atmosphere with every breath of wind. Filled with a pleasant airy warmth, the fresh cream walls and pale wood furnishings made the room feel huge, while a wide tapestried sofa and a multitude of wall hangings, photos and works of art, softened the effect, drawing them in.

She pointed to a stout coffee table, laden with craft kits and comics. 'I've got a couple of things to finish up in the kitchen, if that's ok. You keep yourself busy with these and I'll be back in a minute. There's an old newspaper tucked underneath if you need it for gluing or painting or whatnot. Tony, help yourself to a glass of wine if you like, or there's a beer in the fridge, if you'd rather?'

Tony was completely wrong footed. He hadn't expected such a warm greeting. He could only assume this was for Jamie's benefit. 'No, no, I'm fine. Thank you.' He knelt with his son, who was eagerly shuffling brightly printed boxes and packages, attempting to choose between them. 'Wow, buddy. What have you got there?'

As Trish disappeared into the hallway, he guided Jamie towards the least messy of the kits and allowed himself to loosen up a little, taking in the familiar and yet unfamiliar surroundings. When had she had this work done? Last time he had been here, he was sure the same old dusky pink wallpaper and threadbare carpet of his childhood had covered the walls and floor, and a giant dark mahogany display cabinet, covered in knick-knacks and crockery, had crowded the room. He tried to calculate how long it was since he had visited. The last few times they had met had either been at his home or in a café somewhere, and he was ashamed when he realised he was counting in years rather than months. Family life had become all-encompassing, and Aunt Trish had hardly featured, except for cards and telephone calls at birthdays and Christmas. Perhaps her comments to Lewis were not unwarranted.

Lunch passed pleasantly. The food was good, and she had pulled out the stops, the solid oak table groaning under the weight of steaming dishes. Jamie kept conversation flowing and Trish appeared captivated by his chatter, while Tony played the part of observer. When they finished eating, he helped her carry the dishes to the kitchen, intending to assist with the washing up then make his excuses, but she brushed his offer aside, hurrying him back to the dining room.

'Now, who fancies a stroll up the hill to walk off pudding?' She rubbed her hands in anticipation.

Tony was surprised she was looking to extend their visit, but Jamie was quick to answer. 'I like walking better with a dog, but you don't have one, do you?' His eyes darted around as if expecting a hound to appear from a secret hiding place somewhere.

'No, I don't, but I do have something else to make it fun. Do you like flying kites? Your dad used to love it when he was your age.'

Jamie turned to his father, face aglow with excitement. 'Can we?'

Tony hovered between making excuses for a quick escape, disappointing his son, and giving in, and enduring the discomfort of walking on eggshells for a longer period. He looked from his watch to his son's anticipatory face and back again before facing his aunt and was surprised at the veiled eagerness in her face. It appeared Jamie would not be the only one disappointed if he refused. 'I don't see why not. But we mustn't be too late home. You've got stuff to do for school, haven't you?'

Jamie punched the air. 'Yes!' He jumped from his seat, raring to go.

'All right! Calm it down. Toilet and hands, then shoes on and wait by the door. I'll get your jacket from the car.'

The sun was hidden behind a veil of platinum cloud, but the breeze had picked up momentum – perfect for kite flying. Trish and Jamie huddled together, co-conspirators, scheming as they trotted up the hill, stumbling over hillocks and jumping past obstacles. Tony followed, bemused by this unforeseen friendship forming in front of him. When they reached the top of the incline, the pair knelt down, disregarding the risk of grass stains, and began to unpack the bright, prized diamond, carefully unfurling the string and smoothing out canvas. All their efforts and concentration went into the preparation and launching, ordering Tony into the distance until the string was taut and hollering in stereo when they were ready for him to let go, then hurtling in the opposite direction. After half an hour, Jamie's confidence was brimming, as he single-handedly sent the kite dipping and diving, running one way or another whenever the wind dropped and it threatened to fall out of the sky, chuckling all the way. Trish had sought respite, perched on the back of a bench, ignoring the fantastic views afforded if she were to face in the right direction, choosing instead to revel in Jamie's enjoyment. Tony left him to it and strolled across the gap to the seat. He loved to hear the little boy's mirth and was grateful for the effort she had put in to make their afternoon special.

'Thank you,' he perched alongside her, avoiding eye contact, 'He loves it.'

She coughed a small laugh. 'He's a chip off the old block. Every summer you used to come and stay with me in the holidays. We spent hours up here. Do you remember?'

'Yes and no. I didn't, but when you started unpacking the kite, the colours, it began to come back to me.' Fragments of a long-forgotten past were piecing together in a way that made it feel he was glimpsing someone else's history, happy times.

'It was a long time ago.' Her words were matter of fact. 'It all got a bit lost amongst other things, didn't it? Life took over.' She sighed, 'I loved our picnics, up here or down the bottom of the path there, along by the brook.' She waved her arm in a general direction. 'You spent half your time up to your knees in water. I gave up trying to keep you dry.'

'Who me?' He wanted to deny it, but doors were opening in his mind, and he suspected her memory may be more accurate than his.

'Yes you! And on rainy days I let you loose in the kitchen. Gosh, the creations you came up with. I still think that's where your love of cooking came from. Your mother was far too particular to let you run wild in her kitchen.'

Tony chuckled without replying, still not quite able to grasp the images she was conjuring.

The sweet smell of cut grass hovered thickly around them, held near the ground by the moisture in the air, tickling nostrils. Tony followed Jamie's movements with his eyes, watching proudly as he jerked his arms from below his knees to above his head, forcing the kite into a polka, then swirled in circles, his arms stretched to the sky.

'Green Yorkshire puddings!' Tony announced his eureka moment to the world and turned to meet Trish's gaze for the first time. 'We made bright green Yorkshire puddings!'

Trish studied her shoes for a moment, wistful, 'Yes, we did. They were dreadful, of course, but you were pleased as punch.'

He shook his head at the novelty of the memory. 'I'd forgotten.'

'Like I said, it got lost and life took over… but that doesn't mean it has to stay lost.' She reached out and rested her hand on his sleeve, her eyes fixed on Jamie on the hilltop. 'It saddens me we've not been close these past few years. I so wanted to be there for you when Victoria passed, but the distance between us… it made it difficult. Remember, we both know what loss is. When your mother left us… I think it changed things, between us, didn't it? But I wish it hadn't. You and Jamie are the only family I have in the world, and I wanted to help. I'm sorry I couldn't.'

Tony was saved from having to muster a voice from his constricted throat as a rogue gust of wind whipped the kite from Jamie's hand and away. The little boy dived in panic after it, with no thought or attention to where he was heading - directly toward a patch of stinging nettles. Both Tony and Trish spotted the danger and jolted toward him.

'Jamie, stop. Nettles!'

Jamie's concern for the free-falling kite overrode his senses and he paid no heed to his father's voice, striding out, reaching for the red plastic handle as it writhed at the end of the string, beyond his reach.

'Jamie, stop right now!' Trish's voice boomed with the authority of a sergeant major, drawing Jamie up short in his tracks, only feet from the noxious plants. His head flicked urgently in her direction, but the rest of his body halted statue still.

Drama averted, Tony ran after the kite, trusting Jamie's safety to his aunt. It had floated to a stop many metres away on the far side of a bank of pink flowered shrubs, the handle concealed in rough undergrowth. He lifted his knees high, picking his way through the pink campion and leggy buttercups. Now there was no danger, he was glad to get away from the others and have a few private moments to think. Trish's comments had sent a plethora of emotions broiling inside him and he wasn't sure how to deal with them. He took his time, revelling in the temporary solitude.

By the time he returned to the others, he was calm. Trish was on her knees showing Jamie a nettle, carefully pointing out the fine hairs on the reverse of the leaves, describing the discomfort they would cause if his uncovered ankles had brushed against them. Jamie was listening intently, his head to one side like a bird as he concentrated.

'Come on then. I think it's time for us to make a move. School tomorrow and all that.'

'Is it broken, Dad?' Jamie's face was a picture of concern.

'No, no. It'll live to fly another day. Here you can carry it back down.' Tony handed it over, and Jamie trotted ahead of the adults, satisfied all was well.

Tony and Trish fell in beside each other, watching the boy's antics.

'Well done!' Tony half whispered. 'I haven't seen him follow orders like that ever. I almost stood still myself.'

Trish chuckled quietly. 'Goes with the territory. My Year Two's have to know who's boss or they'd run rings around me.'

'I don't believe anybody runs rings around you. I should know, I tried it.'

They climbed back into the car, well fed, exercised and happy. The sun had given up its tussles with the clouds and disappeared behind them, the breeze, which had earlier been welcome, now creating a harsh nip to the air. Trish hugged herself as she waited to wave goodbye.

'Remember your manners, Jamie.' Tony reminded, as he belted him in.

'Thank you for having me Aunty Trish.' He obeyed. 'I loved the kite.'

'It was my pleasure, young man. I hope to see you again, soon?' Directing the comment to Jamie somehow removed the pressure, giving Tony an escape route if he wanted one.

'Yes please,' Jamie required no prompting. 'I've had great fun, and you're not grumpy at all.'

Tony coughed loudly to hide his embarrassment.

Trish gave a wry smile. 'Oh, I am sometimes, but you gave me no reason to be. You've been perfect company.' She turned to Tony as he closed the passenger door and moved around the front of the car. 'Don't be a stranger. It's been good to see you.'

'Thanks, you too.' He felt awkward as he climbed into his seat, torn as to whether a polite hug was in order or not, and deciding against. He settled for joining Jamie in an energetic wave as he reversed.

Trish suddenly ran towards the car, waving equally enthusiastically. 'Stop, stop.' Turning and running back into the house, as he paused. 'Just a minute.'

She vanished inside, leaving Tony and Jamie looking at each other in bemusement as they waited for her return. When she did reappear, she was carrying a hefty shoebox, splitting at the seams and tied with bright blue wool. She opened the rear door and slid it into the footwell of the back seat.

'You almost went without the one thing you came for. Your mum's box of tricks. There's all sorts of bits and pieces in there; certificates, letters, payslips and bills and things, not that I've had a good look, but I'm sure something will help you with the family tree. I've slipped a potted history of your mother's on top, but I'm afraid I don't really know anything about your father's past - Robert was always a bit of an enigma. 'A man of mystery' your grandma used to call him.

Hopefully there should be some clues in there though.

Also, there are a few boxes in the garage which really and truly belong to you. Your mother brought them here for safe keeping when they were moving house: things they didn't trust to the removal van, but, of course, the move never actually happened in the end. They've been tucked away here ever since. You can take them anytime you want, or come here and sort through them, whatever suits you.' She closed the door and stepped to a safe distance.

Tony rolled his window down. 'Thanks Trish. I'll have a good rifle through when I get back later; see what I can find out. I'll give you a call about the rest, OK?'

'Yes, do. Bye Jamie.'

He slowly reversed out of the driveway, rolled up the window and started for home, wondering what exactly 'his mother's box of tricks' would reveal about his past.

CHAPTER 5

For the first time in months, when Jamie had been tucked into bed, and Tony found himself alone, he wasn't engulfed by a wave of oppression from the quietness of the house. A muted light filled the lounge, the sun sliding below the tree line at the bottom of the garden, flickering a speckled shadow scene against the wall. He crouched forward in the armchair, a large glass of Merlot perched to one side of his mother's shoebox, on the table in front of him. The blue tie had been cast away earlier, and the envelope from inside, containing his mother's family details absorbed and added to Jamie's homework book. Jamie had gone to bed, freshly bathed and pyjama'd, cheeks newly freckled from the day's excursion, high on the knowledge his great grandfather had competed for the Great British Olympic team in the fifties, and he couldn't wait for morning to come, so he could share the information with his classmates.

Tony was nurturing a new fascination with his past. He had never before considered his father a man of mystery - he was simply Dad, and he was intrigued why others would see him as such.

Lifting the lid felt like opening Pandora's Box. A stale, musty smell tickled his nostrils as he shifted the contents, releasing an aged, long undisturbed sprinkling of dust. The first piece of paper was a faded invoice for car repairs and an MOT, dating almost thirty years in the past, and was swiftly deposited in the upside-down lid as of no interest. This was followed by guarantees and warranty documents, now far out of date and Tony's excitement waned. Next though, he came across a bundle of official looking forms, secured neatly with broad navy ribbon which revealed themselves to be certificates, starting with one for his own birth. He unfolded the sheet, nudging the box away, to make space to lay the form flat. The writing was faded and scrawled, its three decades discernible in the stubborn lines of the folds and bent corners. He reached to activate the task light next to his chair, illuminating an arc around him, plunging the rest of the room into shadow.

There he was, his arrival in the world declared. Antony Viscount, male, his date of birth, the name of his mother, Fiona Anne, and his father, Robert Antony, and the place of his birth - a town in Suffolk. He was surprised; he had assumed he was born on the South coast, where most of his childhood had been spent, in one town or another, but, after consideration, the frequency of their moves through the years and his father's many job changes, it was quite possible they settled temporarily in the east. He refolded the sheet and set it aside.

Next came a medical card and a list of inoculations – nothing of interest there, but clearly viewed as important by his mother, in the same way Vicky had carefully stored Jamie's papers in a special book in the kitchen drawer. A dog-eared green document, when unfolded, revealed itself to be his father's driving licence, a far cry from the neat, photographed plastic cards now. His parents' marriage certificate was the last form in the group, revealing a wedding, a couple of years prior to his birth, at a registry office in the Midlands and revealing his paternal Grandfather's name as Antonio.

A large brown folder contained a handful of photographs of various sizes and quality, showing faces he recognised, alongside others he didn't. Tony settled back in his seat, taking a quick glug of wine and studying each picture in more detail, wallowing in sweet nostalgia. His lovely mum, leaning against a wall, dressed in denim flares and a velvet zip top, so nineteen seventies, a white-flecked ocean visible behind her. Soft blonde curls pooled around her shoulders and heavy blue make up hooded her eyes. She was younger than he remembered her, probably still a teenager, but the wide smile was unmistakably hers and the image tugged at his heart. His parents had been gone for so long their loss hardly affected him anymore or, at least, he had thought not, but seeing her face again brought it back. Until now, he had not owned a family photograph, to remind him, to grieve over. Everything had been wiped out in the fire which killed his mum and dad, but, at the time, the indiscriminate destruction had been insignificant compared to the loss of life and the massive upheaval of his teenage existence. Now, he felt he had recovered something extremely precious.

A dark haired, dark-eyed man, he recognised as his father, stared out of the next photograph, with a smouldering intensity which gave no clues to his mood at the time of its taking. There was no emotion, no personality revealed in the portrait and, if Tony had not had memories to overlay the image, it would have evoked no feelings whatsoever: it was strangely blank. The rest showed family groups and random snaps: him as a toddler with his parents, on a checked blanket in a park somewhere; his mother with a young version of Aunt Trish, their arms linked and heads together as they grinned for the camera; him, prim in a cub scout uniform, complete with cap, with an elderly lady who he knew, rather than remembered, to be his maternal grandmother – the only grandparent he had met. The reverse of the prints were neatly annotated in pencil, with names and dates, and Tony quickly flicked through those he didn't know before filing them back in their folder.

The final photograph was larger, darker, a close up of a mismatched couple gazing lovingly at each other, in shades of black and white. These were complete strangers to him; indeed, the age of the print suggested it dated to before his lifetime, but there was something about the eyes of the young woman, the line of the jaw of the older man, which was familiar somehow, made him give it more attention than the cursory glance he had spared others. Sure enough, the writing on the reverse suggested it was a portrait of his paternal grandparents – names and associations he did not remember ever being mentioned in his hearing, let alone pictures displayed. He wondered at their absence. As a child, he had not given the matter any thought, part of a history he had no time for at that stage in his life. Now, it struck him as odd there had never been any 'Grandpa used to do such and such' or 'Grandma told me something or other'. They had been complete nonentities. Maybe his father's relationship with them had been difficult? Or maybe their deaths had been too recent, too painful to talk about. Tony knew what that was like, but now he wished he had some answers. He would have liked to have known more about this handsome pair.

'Hello Grandma. Hello Grandpa. Fancy seeing you here.' He whispered to the air, amused by the novelty of family history.

As he took in the finer details; their dated clothing; his grandfather's swept back hair, the tring of the telephone intruded. He thought about ignoring it, engrossed by the treasure trove in front of him, but in the interests of keeping Jamie in bed and the maintenance of a peaceful evening, he dropped the photo back in the box and forced himself out of the seat.

'Hello?' He squinted in the brightness of the hallway, after the relative darkness of the lounge.

'Hi Tony. Sarah. You guys ok?'

Tony raised his eyebrows. His sister-in-law never phoned purely for an update on their well-being, and he was immediately suspicious. 'Fine thanks. You?' He leaned back, resting against the dado rail, waiting for her purpose to be revealed.

'Yes. Listen, Tony. Next weekend is the bank holiday and I've promised the kids we'll do something special. I'm guessing you're working over the weekend anyway and I was wondering if Jamie would like to join us. Save you sorting out childcare, and we don't see enough of him these days.'

'Oh!' Tony rarely planned beyond the next few hours, let alone a week away, and his thoughts were jumbled.

'We won't be doing anything mad: cricket on the moor; a treasure hunt at the beach; copious amounts of ice cream, that sort of thing.' She clearly felt he needed persuading.

'That sounds fine. I should check with Jamie tomorrow, I guess.' He didn't want to be rail roaded.

'Well, that's not an issue, I'm sure Jamie will want to come.' Her confidence was solid.

'You're probably right, but I will check and confirm with you tomorrow, if that's ok? When were you thinking exactly?'

'The thing is Tony.' There was a loaded pause. 'Mum and Dad are coming to stay too. They're driving up Saturday morning.' Her speech speeded up, preventing him from interrupting. 'I thought you could drop him here Friday night, so you wouldn't have to see them yourself, and I could bring him back on Monday morning, after they've gone.'

His heart thudded uncomfortably. She was waiting for him to speak, but he could find no words and the gap lengthened.

When she spoke, her tone was softer, slower, pleading. 'They miss him so much Tony. I know you're angry, but it's like they've lost Jamie as well as Vicky. It's very hard for them. You know they would never have done anything to hurt either of them, intentionally, and Vicky – it was just one of those things. Dad really was ill. They couldn't have known she would...'

'Sarah.' Finally, he interrupted her plea. 'What time do you want him?'

'Eight would be good.' Her uncharacteristic meekness quietened his inner turmoil. 'We're planning a barbecue in the barn.'

She was right. He should stop being so angry with her father, it served no purpose except to hurt them both, and Jamie was caught in the crossfire. Vicky would never have approved. Tony hadn't been lucky enough to have a relationship with most of his grandparents. The least he could do was bite down on his wrath and allow Jamie the chance of a relationship with the ones he had. 'All right. We'll see you at about eight.'

The relief when she replied was almost tangible. Her voice was thick. 'Thank you so much, Tony. Thank you.'

He replaced the handset, returned to the lounge and picked up the battered, grey photo from the box where he had dropped it. Looking at the faces there, he pursed his lips. 'This is your fault.' He accused, sighing, and downed the last of his wine.

CHAPTER 6

Rather than wallow at the overwhelming prospect of a child-free weekend, combined with two days free of work, Tony got in touch with Marco. Regular invitations to get together whenever he was at a loose end, made the Rossi's the obvious solution to fill the unforeseen gap, but even so, he dialled with trepidation, anticipating this to be the one occasion they were already otherwise engaged. Within minutes though, his weekend had been organised – watching football at the pub on Saturday afternoon, staying over at the Rossi's to negate the necessity of transport home after copious amounts of alcohol, followed by Sunday lunch to conquer the hangover which, apparently, was a given.

Marco's experience proved accurate and Sunday morning dawned with Tony's head throbbing, his mouth dry and tongue fur lined. He lay motionless in the unfamiliar room, propped up on marshmallow pillows, peering between half closed lids at the furnishings in his line of sight, dark and heavy and old, listening without appreciation to the chirruping of finches on the guttering. An irritating wedge of sunlight cut across the room, skimming the headboard inches above him, putting paid to any ideas he had of going back to sleep.

A waft of something savoury tantalised his nostrils and his stomach gurgled, whether out of hunger or complaint he was unsure. Having rolled off the high mattress, he pulled on clean clothes and made his way, first to the bathroom, then down to the kitchen. Marco was hunched over a range cooker, wielding a fish slice, crisp, spitting bacon dangling precariously from the end.

'There's the man at last. I thought I was going to have to deliver breakfast in bed.' He dropped the bacon onto a large bap, already cut and buttered.

'Oooh!' Tony groaned, waving a hasty hand in denial. 'I'm not sure...'

'Now then! None of that.' He shoved the plate in Tony's direction. 'Doctor's orders.'

Tony watched as Marco poured two rich, cups of black coffee and slapped them down on the table, before turning back to the frying pan, where he chased the remaining rashers around it, manufactured a roll for himself, and joined Tony at the table.

'Which doctor was that then?' Tony pulled the roll apart to examine the contents critically, still undecided how to proceed.

'Doctor Rossi, at your service. Now, get it down you.'

Tony continued to be dubious, eyeing Marco's food with distaste as he applied ketchup to his sandwich. 'You're a doctor in geology. I'm not sure that counts.'

'Of course it counts.' He mumbled through his breakfast, pausing only to swallow heavily, washing any remnants away with a mouthful of scalding coffee. 'Trust me, I know what I'm talking about. Good solid nourishment to settle the stomach, a strong dose of caffeine to boost energy levels and a quick march with young Max around the block and you'll be right as rain. I call it my 'air of the dog' remedy.' Laughter exploded out of him, firstly in appreciation of his own joke, then at Tony's expression as he winced at the noise. 'Come on, grab your jacket. I can see this particular hangover may require fresh air first. Bring the sandwich for when you're a little less avocado around the gills.'

Marco opened the door and called for Max, unhooking a collar and lead from a coat stand in readiness. The dog bounded into the room obediently, lolloping from Marco to Tony and back again, tail wagging with joie de vivre.

'Good lad.' Marco appeared equally pleased to see Max, rubbing his head and patting his flank with vigour. He clipped on the lead, grabbed their jackets from the stand and threw Tony's across to him, before heading out the door, presuming Tony would follow. 'Some people have no stamina Maxi, no stamina whatsoever.'

An hour later, Tony was a reincarnation of himself, wide awake and far more at ease with the day. The kitchen had become a hive of industry in their absence, Ruth flitting from one work surface to another, with pans and dishes, in a cloud of flour. She hustled them out with mugs of coffee and instructions to go watch the motor racing and stay there, out of her way. By the time they were called for lunch, Tony couldn't remember when he had last spent such a self-indulgent morning; no cartoons; no Lego constructions; no listening to whining about when food would be ready, and felt quite renewed by it, with a serving of guilt on the side.

He took his place at the table, surrounded by heaped dishes and glorious smells enriching the air and felt thoroughly spoilt. 'I think you're after a job Ruth. This looks amazing.'

'No, thanks. Sunday lunch is my thing; the rest of the week is takeaways all the way.' She rearranged a dish, to be within everyone's reach. 'Help yourself. It's self-service, apart from the wine, which appears to be absent. Marco, find a nice bottle of white, will you? To go with the pork?'

Marco disappeared into the pantry; a clinking of bottles accompanied his raised voice. 'No such thing. A good bottle of white indeed! Sod the pork, can't we have a Rioja?'

'Philistine!' Ruth announced loudly to the air.

'You'd prefer red, wouldn't you Tony?' Marco's disjointed head appeared around the door.

'Sorry Marco, I'm not taking sides. I'll stick with water. I've got to drive later and I'm working tomorrow. Plus, I'm still feeling the repercussions of yesterday's overindulgence.'

Marco grunted and disappeared again, before reappearing, brandishing a bottle in each hand. 'Here we are. Everybody's happy.'

Ruth accepted a bottle of chardonnay and raised her eyebrows at Tony. 'See what I have to put up with.' She unscrewed the top and poured, before turning to the food and spooning vegetables onto her plate. 'So, where's Jamie? How come you've been relieved of duty?'

Following suit, Tony reached for a dish of crispy potatoes. 'He's staying with Vicky's sister and her family and his grandparents for the weekend. She has a smallholding and children close to Jamie's age, so I expect he'll be running riot, chasing the goat, riding the pig, that sort of thing. There's always something going on there.'

'Oh, how lovely. A far cry from life in the burbs, isn't it? I'd love a farm.' Her face crinkled with pleasure.

'Like hell you would woman! You're complaining after five minutes of weeding the borders, let alone a ten-acre field.' Marco was incensed.

Ruth was unphased by his outburst. 'Mmm, you're right. I just love the idea of a farm, all that space and fresh air. It's great Jamie can spend time with Vicky's family. I bet it's been helpful for him to stay connected. It's so easy for families to drift apart when there's been a bereavement.'

'Excuse my wife's lack of tact.' Marco scowled at her over a tray of parsnips.

Tony smiled weakly, 'No, no. Most people try to avoid the subject all together. Not talking about it doesn't mean it didn't happen.' He turned to Ruth, an unusual wave of candour engulfing him. 'Yes, I think it is good for him to stay connected, but actually, this is the first time he's spent time with his grandparents since. She was on her way to the hospital, because she thought her father'd had a heart attack, when she crashed. It turned out to be a big fuss about nothing and my calculation was, if he hadn't been a drama queen, Vicky wouldn't have been driving like a maniac and would still be alive. I couldn't bear the sight of him for months. Not that I think any better of him now, but I decided I shouldn't punish Jamie by separating him from his grandparents, so when Sarah invited him, I agreed he could go.'

'Good for you!' Ruth patted his hand. 'It's hard to be magnanimous and do the right thing, when it's not necessarily the right thing for you. What changed your mind?'

'The opportunity to spend the weekend down the pub with yours truly, no doubt.' Marco seemed uncomfortable with such a serious conversation and tried to inject some humour.

'No, that was an added bonus.' Tony felt for Marco's discomfort and laughed to lighten the mood. 'Actually, it was discovering some of my own ancestry. You know when we saw you last time, Jamie had to draw his family tree for school? Well, Vicky's family is an open book, but I know virtually nothing about mine. I was brought up by my aunt after my parents died, so I haven't really got a clue where I come from. Anyway,

Aunt Trish dug out a box of old documents and photos and stuff which belonged to Mum and there in the middle was a picture of my dad's parents, and I thought, what a shame I never knew them. It's like I'd missed out on a whole chunk of my past, and I didn't want Jamie to feel the same when he grew up.'

Ruth eyes were alight. 'How fascinating though. A whole history you never knew about. Did you discover anything exciting?'

Max sidled beneath the table and rested his head in Tony's lap, gazing wistfully as the roast pork was forked from plate to mouth. The others seemed oblivious to the dog's arrival and Tony was unsure what was acceptable. He continued to eat, ignoring the soulful eyes. 'Not really. There were a few old certificates and photos I'd never seen, but mostly it only added to the mystery. Dad was some sort of nomad. He never stayed in one place, or one job, for very long and Mum appears to have gone along with it. They were married in the Midlands; I was born on the east coast and the childhood I can remember was spent on the south coast, but I know we moved three or four times even then.'

Marco waved his fork, before stabbing at another potato. 'Sounds to me like a case of wanderlust. Your father was an adventurer.'

'Either that or he was trying to stay one step ahead of the rent man. I would love to know what made him tick. Even more though, I'd like to know where he came from; where my grandparents were from and what sort of people they were. They seemed such an odd couple in the picture.'

'I'm sure there must be clues in there somewhere. If you've got names and a few details its surprising how much information you can find on the internet. I'm signed up with one of those genealogy websites. I could take a look at it for you, if you like?' Ruth appeared as excited as Tony about the prospect.

'Would you? Jamie would be over the moon if you could turn up something interesting, preferably pirates or royalty in the bloodline somewhere. Apparently, the Viscounts are rather boring in comparison with some of his classmates' ancestors. I'm not very popular with him at the moment so it would put me back in his good books.'

'Oh dear. What have you done to upset him? I would have thought he'd be on top form, having a weekend away.'

'Yes, he was all for the weekend on the farm. It's the coming back on Monday morning and sitting in the staff room while I work bit, he's not so keen about. He's fine once he gets there and the staff spoil him rotten, but it's a bit of a come down after building hideouts from hay bales and midnight feasts and whatever else Sarah has planned.'

Having been ignored for some time, Max let out a long-neglected whine, instantly alerting Marco to his presence. 'Dog! Your presence is not required at the dining table and well you know it.' He lurched around to Tony's side and grabbed Max by the collar, escorting him back to his basket in the other room.

Ruth jumped to Tony's rescue in Marco's absence. 'Why don't I take Jamie tomorrow? I'm doing nothing else and there's lots going on because of the bank holiday. Then I could take a look at that paperwork too. See if I can unravel it for you.'

'Oh no. I couldn't ask you ...' He blanched, feeling guilty for mentioning the situation.

'You didn't, I offered.'

Marco returned unencumbered by canine. 'That's ok, isn't it Marco? If we collect Jamie from the restaurant tomorrow, for a few hours of adventure? You know how attached he is to Maxi.'

'Certainly. I can't think of a better plan.'

'There we are then. What time shall we collect him?'

Tony was struck again by their kindness and, before taking his leave, insisted they be his guests for dinner, after their day out with Jamie, as a thank you. He couldn't help but wonder how on earth he would have coped without such good friends.

CHAPTER 7

The restaurant was busy all morning, the bank holiday combining with the dull, grey weather to bring hordes into the town, rather than the beaches and parks they may otherwise have ventured to, and they were all hungry and thirsty and looking for a high point to their day. The staff settled into a steady hum of activity, flitting round the kitchen, keeping one step ahead. The lunchtime rush had subsided, and they were beginning to think they had won that particular battle, when Lewis leaned through the pass and hissed to get Tony's attention.

'Hey, boss! Issue!'

Tony ducked away from his workstation to meet Lewis's gaze, continuing to beat the mixture in his bowl as he spoke. 'What's up?'

'Customer wants to speak to the boss.' He shrugged. 'I offered to help, but no go, has to be you.'

Tony placed a clean tea towel over the top of the bowl and stepped away, wiping his hands on the skirt of his whites as he did so. 'Was there a problem with their meal? Were they kept waiting?'

'Don't think so.'

'Well, did you hear any complaints at their table? Any chatter? What did they eat?' He rarely had to deal with dissatisfied customers, and it was the task he loathed most, but he knew from experience it was best to be prepared.

'They went straight for dessert, oh, and coffee. That

was all. Chocolate truffle cheesecake, I think.'

Tony was bemused. No one found fault with the desserts. They were fresh, decadent and luxurious; everything you would want from a pudding. He opened the fridge and helped himself to a sliver of the dense richness. There was definitely nothing wrong with that. He straightened his jacket, removed his hat and made his way into the seating area.

Lewis had moved to the front door, ready to welcome a group of elderly customers negotiating the front step. He looked up, aware of Tony's low-key entrance amid the hum of the room and pointed with a pen to the table in the far corner, directly in front of the window, where a single female diner sat, her back to the rest of the room. Tony picked his way past the engaged tables, smiling greetings at the occupants, stepping over bags and around highchairs, conscious of maintaining a good impression, whatever the outcome of this encounter.

'Hello. I'm the proprietor here. I understand you wanted to see me? How can I help?'

As the woman's dark eyes rose to meet his, Tony's mouth fell open. It was a face he knew. 'Oh! It's you! Nina!'

Nina's smile was cheeky, her expression quizzical, as she looked up through long black lashes. 'Hello, Tony. The proprietor? I had no idea. I just asked if Tony worked here.' Her tone sunk to a whisper. 'I was checking you out.'

A glance over his shoulder at Lewis's wide grin showed he had known the identity of the diner all along and was now observing their interaction with poorly disguised relish. Tony hovered for a second between embarrassment and gratification, taking in her raised eyebrows, her skimpy vest top, displaying an expanse of perfect, tanned skin, before making a conscious decision to relax and enjoy the experience. He sat in the spare seat opposite hers and pointed at the empty plate between them. 'So, you don't have a complaint about my desserts then?'

'Your desserts? Don't tell me you created this?' She slowly drew her finger across a smear of chocolate, the only remnant left on her dish, and licked it clean.

'Yes.' He coughed to clear his throat as he observed the action. 'I do other things as well, obviously, but desserts are my speciality. Did you enjoy it?'

'Very much. It is a very nice place you have here.' Her accent gave the impression each word was selected with care. 'Good looking, your own business and you cook? Surely, I must be dreaming. Tell me, are you real?'

He was unused to such blatant flirtation and countered it with thoroughly English self-deprecation. 'Real, yes. Perfect, no. I love cooking, but will do anything to avoid the washing up, I watch too much sport on TV and I'm particularly grumpy in the mornings.'

'Really? Grumpy?' She turned her head to one side, viewing him like a bird watching a worm. 'I believe in starting the day with a big smile on my face. Do you not have a girlfriend? A wife, to make you less grumpy?' She glanced at his ring finger.

He automatically reached for the digit, rubbing with his thumb where his ring would normally rest, had it not been removed for work. 'No, no girlfriend. No wife.'

She shrugged. 'Listen Tony. Is there any reason why you could not meet me for a drink sometime? Do you want to?'

Words evaded him as his mouth became desert dry. He was attracted to Nina, but he was not over Vicky, may never be. Was it fair to get involved with someone else, when he still loved his dead wife? Then again, was it fair he was alone?

'I'm sorry. I've embarrassed you. My friends tell me I am too outspoken, but I don't see the benefit of being coy. Surely it gets you nowhere?'

In spite of her directness and the confidence it suggested, he detected a fragment of doubt in the question. He held her gaze, digging for the true roots of her character.

As the silence stretched, her eyes dropped to the table, and she fiddled with a discarded fork.

'I think I'd like to go for a drink with you.'

A slight relaxation of her shoulders as she exhaled, betrayed the fact she had been holding her breath in anticipation, and this nervousness endeared her to him.

'I was just trying to work out in my head how I could shift things round to make it sooner than my next night off.' Not quite true. He didn't work evenings, but when could he organise an evening away from Jamie. He had lost touch with the sitters they used to use, and Vicky had dealt with all that anyway.

'You can't talk the boss into letting you off?' She leaned forward, resting her chin in her hands, bringing her face close to his.

He resisted the urge to move away. 'Not this boss, he can be a tough task master.'

'I bet you can.' She seemed to be studying the contours of his face, reading his expression and he felt strangely exposed.

'Thursday!' He blurted it out. That would give him three days to sort something out for Jamie.

'Sorry?' She sat back, eyebrows raised.

'How about Thursday?' He softened his tone, aware he had sounded demanding, imperious. 'Drinks? Dinner, if you like.'

'Drinks, I think, to begin with.' She drawled, 'Three courses can be a very long time if I decide I don't like you after all.'

Tony laughed aloud at her brutal honesty.

Nina's gaze followed the changes in his face, the laughter lines on his forehead, the crinkling at the corner of his eyes, the curve of his jaw, reading his reactions. The action seemed more intimate than their current location allowed, and he felt heat rise under her observation. 'I think you really are the most honest person I have ever met.'

She shrugged, accepting his comment. 'I don't believe in playing games.' She reached into her handbag, pulled out a card and slid it across the table with one finger. 'This is my number. Call me and let me know where you want to go. I hope to see you on Thursday.'

Tony watched as she walked away, sidling past Lewis, the swing of her hips grabbing the young man's lingering attention as she left the building, but her presence seemed to hover in the atmosphere after her body had gone.

CHAPTER 8

Laughter burst from the door when Tony arrived home, laden with cartons of food, prepared by his colleagues. Jamie and Ruth were on hands and knees in the hall, creating a road network with Lego and printed mats. Tony picked his way through the debris, the food parcels suspended at arm's length, so he could see where he was treading. He stacked the boxes on the table, next to Marco, who sat propped against the wall; feet outstretched on an adjacent stool; a broadsheet spread-eagled in front of him.

'Not part of the road crew, then?'

Marco flung his glasses to one side, ogling the various containers with interest as lids were removed. 'Overseeing, dear boy, overseeing. Every good road crew requires supervision. Now then, this looks like a fine feast.'

'I hope so. I'll bung everything in the oven while I have a quick brush up, and it should be ready in no time. You could have a look at my wine collection for something you fancy, if you want to. It's nothing like your cellar, but there should be a couple of decent bottles.'

Leaving Marco examining labels, Tony hopped over Jamie and Ruth's construction and headed upstairs to change. Shut away in his bedroom in a bubble of calm, he listened to the bang and clatter of playful toing and froing below. It whisked him back to when he would hear Jamie and Vicky getting up to all sorts of antics, while he was busy doing something or other. He wished he'd joined in with the fun while he had the chance. Perhaps, if it was possible for anything positive to come out of Vicky's death, it was the wake-up call he had been given, to treasure every moment.

The meal was a success, with something to suit everyone's tastes and indulgent enough to make them all feel they'd been thoroughly spoilt. After dinner, Ruth whisked Jamie to bed, in fulfilment of an earlier promise to read a particular story, and for once he headed to his room without complaint. Tony and Marco settled in the lounge, shallow measures of brandy reflecting the early summer sun with each swirl of their glasses, as they peered over the garden.

When Ruth returned, she found them in companionable silence. 'Sorry. Should I leave you to your contemplations?'

'Don't be silly. Come on in. Will you join us for a tipple?' Tony offered.

'No, no.' Her voice was hushed, in keeping with the mood. 'Driving duty but thanks. I might help myself to another coffee though, if you don't mind.'

'Let me get it. Was Jamie all right? Not demanding to be tucked in?' She followed him to the kitchen and watched as he fiddled with the cafetiere.

'No, completely tuckered out. Besides, I told him we were going to try and find somebody exciting on his family tree and he couldn't get me out of there quick enough. Competitive, isn't he?'

'I suppose he is.' Tony handed her a steaming mug and they moved back toward the lounge. 'Listen, I appreciate today, but you really don't have to spend your evening rifling through a box of old documents, if you don't feel like it. Much as I'd love to get to the bottom of the mystery, another day would do just as well.'

Marco hooted with laughter. 'Believe me, she finds nothing more gratifying than a box of tattered old documents. Give her a death certificate and a computer and she's in seventh heaven. The only problem will be getting her to call it a day at the end of the evening. You'll be throwing us out come midnight, if she has her way, mark my words.'

'Well, I wouldn't want to stand in your way then, Ruth,' Tony laughed along, 'but what about you, Marco. It's not your cup of tea.'

'Never mind me. Put the boxing on, keep my glass topped up and all my desires are fulfilled. Go on the pair of you, get to it.' Max jumped on the sofa, head resting on Marco's knee, settling in for the night.

The television was switched on, the boxing match located, and the brandy decanter propped within Marco's easy reach. The shoebox was pulled from its corner and, after a quick flick through, Ruth decided the kitchen table would be the best place to organise the papers so she, Tony and the box relocated. Tony pulled everything out and sorted them into piles.

'I think these are the useful bits.' He tapped the collection of certificates. 'Everything else is rubbish really. I can't see a thirty-year-old fridge warranty being of use. I might as well throw it out, but it seems a shame, having only now rediscovered Mum's things.'

Ruth conjured a pair of pink framed glasses from her handbag, preparing for action. 'I know. It's funny what we hang on to, isn't it? But you never know, there could be hidden treasure which you haven't spotted. Fresh eyes and all that. And the certificates will give us a head start. Have you got a computer I can use?'

'Yes, of course. I'll grab the laptop.' Tony devoured

the stairs in a few long strides and quickly collected his computer from the spare room, gathering up the lead and tucking it under his arm. Jamie's room was quiet except for the door, creaking lightly in the breeze from an open window. Tony peeped round the door to check on him. Jamie was fast asleep, the covers thrown back and his cuddly lion caught up in the duvet, only a single paw and an ear protruding from it. Tony freed the toy, straightened the covers and backed into the hallway, propping the door ajar with a pair of rolled up socks, before returning downstairs.

'You've worn that boy out today, he's flat out.'

Ruth was so absorbed she didn't look up. 'I suspect the weekend on the farm may be a contributing factor, if all his stories are to be believed, bless him.' She barely paused. 'You're not wrong about your folks. They did like to keep on the move. Not only are the certificates at different locations, these receipts and warranties are from all over the place.

Tony slid onto the stool next to her, abandoning the laptop, and following her indication.

'An MOT in Shropshire; a receipt for a washing machine purchased in Cambridge and your medical card has a doctor's surgery with what looks to be a Welsh address and, actually, your dad's driving licence shows an address in Wales too.'

'Wales? I didn't know I'd ever been to Wales in my life.' Tony was confused.

'I'm going to sort every piece of paper into date order.' Her hands were already busy with the task, laying pages down and swapping them around like an outsized game of patience. 'And see if I can make any sense of it all, perhaps come up with a route map. If you can set the computer up that would be a help, then you can go and join Marco, leave me to it for a bit.'

Tony jumped to it. He had often wondered how

Ruth managed not to be overpowered by Marco's domineering personality, but he was beginning to see she was more than capable of standing up for herself. She had been part of the pack at college, but her diminutive character had held her in the background of their social group. It was Ruth who had introduced Vicky to him, a tag along at some function or other, and it was only then Ruth had really registered on his radar at all. Months later, she had also introduced Marco, older than them and refreshingly outspoken. His blustering brashness had upset the sensibilities of some, but Tony found the contrast invigorating and they simply seemed to gel. Years and careers had temporarily widened the gap between them, as they forged their futures in differing directions, but it had been a true Godsend when the couple reappeared in his life.

An hour later, Tony returned to the kitchen for snacks and found a scene of organised chaos. Ruth was peering over her glasses at the computer screen.

'I was about to come and get you. This may look a mess, but I think I'm making headway. Come and see.' She ushered him into the room. An A5 pad, covered in scribbled notes, lay next to her and she flipped to a second page, where a timeline was drawn. 'There are no exact dates, but the documents suggest your parents moved every twelve to eighteen months. That's the only pattern I can identify. Otherwise, the locations seem completely erratic – the Midlands, to Suffolk, to Wales, back east to Cambridge and up to Shropshire, then down to the South Coast.' She drew an imaginary line in the air with her pen as each new place was mentioned. 'I can't see any reasoning behind the choice of towns, unless it was because of work. What did your father do?'

'Um, sales I think, but not always with the same company. I only know, because he wore different uniforms from time to time, but he travelled a lot. He lived with us, but often only came back at weekends and, when he was at home, he never talked about work. It never occurred to me then, it was just the way he was, but I don't think he was happy in his work.'

'OK. So internal transfers are unlikely then, but maybe he was changing jobs to better himself, stepping up the ladder or perhaps clinging on to whatever work he could get. The eighties were difficult times, high unemployment, bills to pay, a young family to support…' She left the sentence open.

'So, we come back to my original suspicion about dodging the rent man.' He scanned his memory for evidence, ominous knocks on the door or his mother being stressed when post landed on the mat but drew a blank. He did recall silences though, when he walked into the room and conversation stopped dead. It had upset him as a boy, made him feel excluded. 'There was an air of tension in the house when dad was around. Money was never mentioned as an issue though. Maybe they were struggling, and I didn't realise.'

'Quite possibly.' Ruth chewed the end of her pen. 'OK. As you were. I'll do an internet search. See what I can come up with.'

Tony considered himself dismissed, poured peanuts into a dish and retired back to the lounge, where Marco was flicking through channels, muttering under his breath.

'Hope you don't mind, but I can't abide these never-ending commentaries. The man lost for crying out loud, move on. There's no point dissecting it to death, he will still have lost, won't he, Maxi?' Max snorted an agreement.

'Not at all. Put on what you like. I feel guilty really, Ruth in there poring over my paperwork, while I'm in here with my feet up, and I'm sure you have better things to do at home.'

'There is always something you ought to be doing, but it will still be there tomorrow, so my attitude is, put it off for as long as feasibly possible.' He barked a laugh, causing Max to perk up, before dropping a heavy head back on to Marco's knee. 'As for Ruth, honestly, old boy, this will be the highlight of her weekend.' He cast aside the remote control. 'How about we take Max for a trot around the block? It would be good for him to have a change of scene. Sick of the old haunts, aren't you, Maxi?'

The dog jumped to attention, as if he had been feigning sleep while waiting for the order. Marco stood and stretched dramatically, before clipping a lead on to Max's collar, and they all set out. Tony stuck his head around the door with instructions for Ruth to help herself to anything she wanted, but she waved him briskly away.

The day's cloud had dissipated with the evening sun, leaving the air lighter and smelling crisp and clean. Gravel crunched underfoot, intruding on the quiet, and Tony found himself almost tiptoeing to the end of his driveway. Max led the way, following his nose until he reached a large green, edged on one side with a knee-high stone wall, overgrown by unruly bushes, while the area in front was marked out with well-trod footpaths leading in various directions. They followed one, climbing steeply for a couple of minutes through long grass and scrub, before flattening out, providing a commanding view of the twinkling lights of the surrounding houses.

Arriving at a bench, Marco sat and released Max from the lead, patting him on his flank. 'Not too far, Maxi.

Stay close.'

Max disappeared into the undergrowth, sniffing a treasure trail of his own design. Tony relaxed beside Marco, legs crossed at the ankle at full stretch, his head supported by his hands behind his neck, relishing the view of the parkland foliage fluttering in silhouette, framing and softening the edges of the suburbs beyond. He knew this area, but it was the first time he had seen it quite like this, the neighbourhood glittering magically in the half-light.

'Funny, isn't it?' he mused. 'Even the bypass looks pretty at this time of night.'

Marco growled in agreement. 'Human nature is strange. We fear the dark and yet it hides so much ugliness and, at the same time, emphasises the lights within it.' He paused briefly, then dropped his voice to a dramatic tone. '"Deep into that darkness peering, long I stood there wondering, fearing, doubting, dreaming dreams no mortal ever dared to dream before."'

Should any of Tony's other friends have made such a comment, he would have raised his eyebrows, but Marco quoting poetry seemed the most natural thing in the world. 'Where's that from?'

'Haven't the foggiest, but it clearly seeped into my youthful brain at some point in the past, probably whist having a nap in English Lit. Old Ma Shawcross barely had to open her mouth before we were all snoring.' He chuckled.

Tony breathed deeply. He was aware of a subtle change somewhere within him. He wasn't sure exactly when or how it had happened, but he felt more at peace, more optimistic. The future seemed like a blank page rather than a black one. 'And are you dreaming daring dreams?'

'Only if dreaming of second helpings of that crispy duck you served up earlier is daring. How about you?

Plans of world domination? An Olive Branch in every High Street?'

'Not likely.' Tony kicked at a rough area with his heel, worrying a weed out from a cracked cement seam. 'One restaurant is quite enough. To be honest, I've never been ambitious, it was only ever about making an income to support the family. Now, even the money doesn't bother me much, as long as I can pay the bills. All I want is to enjoy life with Jamie. Luckily, I've got a good team keeping the place running the way I like it. Maybe when Jamie's older, I might go back to it a bit more, but I can't see it happening at the moment.'

'It's early days. You're still getting used to running a household as well as a business.' Marco was pragmatic, 'Ambitious, perhaps not, but as I recall, you always relished a challenge, couldn't be standing still for too long. Back at college, you were always looking one step ahead and once you sank your teeth into something, there was no holding you back. Give it time, you'll be chasing the next project, whatever that may be.'

'Was I?' Tony couldn't remember any pushing of boundaries, but neither did he recall being afraid of anything. His parents hadn't been there to issue warnings against rushing in, and his enthusiasm had always buoyed him along. Fearlessness had, perhaps, allowed him to face challenges others would turn their backs on. He had always considered himself headstrong. Vicky had described it as 'pig-headed', but he had never thought about how others viewed his attitude to life. He wondered how Nina would perceive him, what she would think of his character when she got to know him. If she got to know him.

He cast a sideways glance at Marco. 'Do you think it's too soon for me to see someone? To go on a date?'

'Well now, has a young filly caught your eye?'

The level of excitement in Marco's voice unsettled

Tony, it gave the event too great an importance and he quickly put a damper on it. ‘Not exactly. She asked and I haven’t turned her down, but I’m not sure. I don’t know what the “done” thing is, whether it’s decent for me to be going out with someone yet. I mean, it’s not even been a year. And then there’s Jamie…’

‘Hold your horses.’ Marco halted him mid-flow with a raise of his hand. ‘Are we talking dinner? Or is she moving in?’

Tony drew his legs in and leaned forward, grasping the seat on either side of his knees, awaiting his friend’s verdict. ‘Just drinks actually, not dinner.’

‘Then what the heck are you worried about?’ Marco was all bluster. ‘We’re not talking lifetime commitment here, are we?’

‘No.’ He grasped his chin with his hand, brow furrowed. ‘But what would Vicky’s family think?’

‘I don’t suppose they’re invited, are they? Besides, the more relevant question is, what would Vicky think, and I don’t think she would want you closing yourself off from the world forever.’ He sounded angry with the world. ‘It is a tragedy what happened, but that does not mean your life has to be an ongoing tragedy too. You must go on living. You owe it to yourself and to Jamie.’

Max materialised behind them, front paws on the back of the bench between them, tongue lolling, his breath a rapid pant following his exertions searching the common for some mysterious adversary. Both men jolted in their seats, laughing heartily. Marco christened him with new and colourful names, as he clipped the lead back on and led him to the path. Together, they retraced their steps through the now deeper dark, back down the hill.

‘You think I should go, then?’

Marco shrugged, his mood and tone lighter. ‘That rather depends. What’s she like?’

Tony searched his memory. 'She's about thirty, Mediterranean, possibly Spanish or Italian, petite, dark hair, dark eyes, attractive, funny and a little bit intimidating.'

'Good Lord! If you don't go, I will. What are you waiting for man?' Laughter floated back to Tony on the breeze as Max pulled Marco ahead, arm stretched taut.

Ruth greeted their return, glasses on her forehead; a section of mousey fringe sticking up at right angles behind them. Her pen tapped a steady rhythm on her notepad, eyes focused on a list of scribbled notes. 'If you want coffee, you'll have to put more on. I've polished it off.'

Marco shrugged out of his jacket and patted Max's rump in the direction of the lounge. 'Good grief woman, you'll be bouncing off the walls later.'

'I'll put the kettle on.' Tony rubbed his hands together against the chill from outside, before busying himself at the worktop. 'No noise from upstairs?'

'Not a squeak. Though, I have to admit to being engrossed with my search.' She settled back on her seat, legs crossed, the harsh lighting around the table putting her in the spotlight. 'I must say, it's rather intriguing.'

'You have more patience than I do. If what I'm looking for doesn't pop up in the first five minutes, I get distracted by something else. Any headway?' He reached for a jar from the overhead cupboard.

'Yes.' She paused. 'I don't suppose you've got decaf. Marco's right, I'll be up all night if I have any more caffeine.'

'I'm always right. You know that.' Marco reappeared and perched opposite Ruth.

'Yes, dear.' She dismissed him and carried on. 'I

managed to find a birth for your father. Another Welsh connection actually. We already had his date of birth from the marriage certificate and luckily Viscount is a relatively rare surname, so an online search soon brought it up.'

'I didn't have you down for a Taff, Tony?'

'It's news to me too.' He called over his shoulder. 'Did you want this leftover duck?'

'Rude not to.' Marco patted his stomach.

'Ruth? A bit of supper?'

'Just the coffee, thanks. I'm guessing the Welsh blood is from your grandmother's line. The names on the old photograph of your grandparents were Antonio and Cerys and they're also the names on the birth entry for Robert, so we're definitely on the right lines. Cerys is a Welsh name, but unfortunately, I can't find anything else for her at the moment, because there's no maiden name to work from. Antonio was easier because we already have the surname, so I've managed to narrow down birth entries for him. There are a couple of possibilities, but one seems too recent for him to be Robert's father and the other's a bit early. It's way back in 1909, but could be feasible, as it would make him mid-forties when Robert was born. In the photo he looks older than Cerys, so maybe. Also, I can't seem to find a marriage entry for them, but with no idea about dates or locations, it's a bit of a tall order. To add to the mystery, there's a death entry too, for an Antonio Viscount born in 1909, the death registered the same year Robert was born. It could be coincidence, of course, or a terrible tragedy. It would explain why your dad never talked about his own father.'

'So where do we go from here?'

'The best next step would be to order a couple of certificates. The on-line searches provide limited details, but the certificates have more. A copy of your father's birth certificate is likely to have your grandmother's maiden name on it, which would enable us to pursue Cerys' side further and maybe find her marriage to Antonio. Then, if we can get the marriage certificate, there are all kinds of clues to be had.'

Tony laid cups and plates on the table. 'It's like a jigsaw puzzle, isn't it? Only, with no picture on the box to work from. I want to know all the answers now. How long will it take to get hold of these certificates?'

'Not long, a couple of weeks maybe. I can get them ordered for you. It doesn't cost a great deal, but there's no way of hurrying it up unless you call at each Registry Office in person, and that would mean travelling from one end of the country to the other.'

'Obviously I'll pay, but would you mind ordering them? I don't want to put you to any trouble, but in the meantime, I could go back to Aunt Trish. She said she had more stuff of Mum and Dad's in the garage. There may be useful information tucked away somewhere.'

'I don't mind in the slightest, I can't wait for the next instalment.' She pushed her pad to one side, removed her glasses, then reached for her cup, cradling it with both hands. 'Maybe your aunt could help you further herself, now you know what questions you need answering. You can't beat speaking to someone first hand.'

Tony sipped from his cup, breathing the steam away, his brow creased in concentration, 'You know, I think I'll do that. Take Jamie up there one day this week as they're both on half term. Who knows, perhaps Aunt Trish could have the key to the mystery.'

CHAPTER 9

As he sat by the bar, waiting for Nina, Tony's conscience prickled. The fact he hadn't mentioned Jamie to Nina niggled at him. He hadn't meant for Jamie's existence to be a secret, and, on reflection, there had been no obvious juncture where he should have brought him up, but her words echoed around his head, 'is there any reason why you could not meet me for a drink?', and it felt wrong. It was a situation he intended to rectify at the earliest opportunity, even if it might bring about an early close to their date.

With one eye on the main entrance and the other on the guitar shaped clock, directly above the optics, Tony ordered a glass of red wine. He was no stickler for punctuality, but Nina was late, and part of him doubted she would show up at all. As much as he would be disappointed, it would make for a simpler life. He jangled the keys in his pocket and considered making his way to the car, parked a short walk away behind The Olive Branch, but the idea of leaving now reeked of cowardice, so he stayed put.

The first sip of wine rapidly filtered through his blood stream, settling a dull ache in the nape of his neck. The front door swung open, and two girls tottered in, arms linked, whispering and laughing, then peeled apart as they greeted friends, exchanging a flurry of hugs and a lingering kiss between one of them with what Tony assumed was her partner. She squeezed in next to the young man, his arm thrown around her shoulders in an easy show of affection, her hand resting on his leg as if it belonged there. Sod the simple life, it was time Tony had more to look forward to at the end of the day once in a while and if it meant complications, he could handle it.

He checked his watch against the ticking fender on the wall, only to find they disagreed by several minutes and, if his own timepiece were to be believed, Nina was now a full twenty minutes late. He exhaled sharply, the actual disappointment of her non-appearance far out stinging the feelings he had imagined minutes earlier. What should he do? He reached into his trouser pocket for his phone, to obtain a third opinion of the time. The internet should be accurate, and if it was, then yes, she really was that late. He rested his elbow on the bar top and worried at his top lip as he considered his options. He would give her until half past and then leave.

A brush of his shoulder and a husky 'Hi!' in his ear, informed him of Nina's approach from behind. His head shot up and around to follow her trajectory as she circuited his body to face him. The relief and pleasure he felt in seeing her was instantly apparent, his visage changing from shadow to full sun in a moment, completely removing any possibility of his playing it cool. She rested her hands on his knees, raising her petite body up on to tip toes, until their faces were all but level, and planted a light kiss on his cheek.

She pointed at his glass. 'I see you started without me?'

'Yes, sorry.' He opened and closed his mouth like a beached fish, not sure how to begin, then made a decision. He didn't want to go any further without being completely honest, risk his own status quo by becoming emotionally involved before opening up to her. 'I have a son, Jamie. He's seven and lives with me, and my life revolves around him.'

Her eyebrows shifted up her forehead, slowly resuming their usual position, as she absorbed his words, holding his gaze steadily. Then she helped herself to his glass and sipped from it thoughtfully.

He waited for a response, not wanting to interrupt her thoughts, biding his time for an open reply.

She returned the glass to the bar top and turned back to him, an enigmatic smile behind her eyes. 'I have a cat. She is called Feline and is a complete diva and demands all my attention when I am at home.' She gently prodded him in the shoulder. 'The good news is, my cat is not here right now, so I can do what I like, and she has no say in the matter.'

Slow and softly rounded words, the edges blurred by her accent, added to the impression that each one was chosen with infinite care. She was laughing at his gaucheness, mocking the impetuous blurting out of his life, but in a mindful, benevolent way. His cheeks warmed as he chuckled at his heavy-footed approach, eyes falling down to her manicured fingers, now resting on his knees as she stood directly in front of him.

'Do you know what I would like to do?'

Her voice brought him back to attention. 'No. What?'

She looked up through lowered lids. 'I say we should eat. Maybe not three courses, not yet, but two... definitely two. I think we have enough to talk about, don't you?'

Grinning at her coded acceptance, he stepped down from the stool and clasped her hand in his. 'I know a lovely place, great food, chilled atmosphere... and don't worry, I don't mean The Olive Branch. Shall we?'

She followed his lead, her hand holding his as they weaved through the bar, out into the street.

The venue resembled an old-fashioned pub, with deep padded benches, discreet shadowed alcoves and pale painted woodwork and beams above the bar, dripping with fake vines. They were led to a quiet corner by a young waitress, identifiable by a beige apron over her jeans and t-shirt, sleeves rolled up to the elbow and a notepad sticking out of her back pocket. The large menus she handed them placed a temporary barrier between them. They made small talk to fill the gap until their drinks were delivered, but then, having ordered their meals, the close quarters and quiet surroundings made communication essential. They had exchanged little information on their walk through the streets, and when they were finally left alone it was as if they were strangers. Tony searched for something to say, to get things started.

'So, Nina, tell me about yourself.' He sat back, fiddling with a spoon with both hands, confident he had successfully passed the ball into her court.

Nina smiled and slowly, deliberately sipped from her glass of Prosecco. 'What is this, an interview?'

He was taken aback at immediately finding himself back in the hot seat. 'Sorry. I didn't mean to sound so … Sorry, I just wanted to know more about you.'

'Don't worry, I was joking. Relax. What do you want to know?'

'Sorry, I don't do this much.' He raised his eyebrows in emphasis. 'As you can probably tell, and I'm a bit nervous. I don't know what I want to know. Where are you from? What do you do?'

Nina reached across and rested her hand on top of his, stalling his anxious shuffling of cutlery. 'You don't need to be nervous; I don't bite.' She gradually withdrew her hand as her concentration shifted to answering his queries. 'I don't think there are any straightforward answers to those questions though. Not because I like to keep an air of mystery around me or anything. It's just they are very black and white questions, and I don't have very much black and white in my life. You understand?'

Tony frowned, confused by her response. 'I'm not sure I do.'

'You asked, 'where am I from', and to some people it's easy, 'I'm from here or there', but to me it's not so easy,' she explained. 'I've lived in many places in my life, so now I think I am only from where I am right now. I suppose I could say I am from Spain, because my mother lives there and because I've spent most years there, in one city or another, but I don't think of any one place as home. My home is here in England, for now. Does that make any sense?'

'I think so.' He pursed his lips as he deciphered her comments.

'I don't want to appear too deep, but I think sometimes we use people and places to define ourselves and we shouldn't do that. You know, we like to put things in boxes to keep them nice and tidy, but many things are not neat and tidy. I am me, not my mother, not my father, not the place I was born or the place I grew up. I am... me.' A Gaelic shrug accompanied her final words.

The waitress reappeared with their meals. As the dust settled and the first mouthfuls were tasted, Tony felt he did understand her point.

'I see what you're saying, and I guess I'm the same. I lost my parents a long time ago, so I don't have a family pile to call home, as such. In fact, I've been looking at my history recently, trying to fill in some gaps in the past and you're right. It doesn't matter where I was born or where I grew up, I'm from here now too. Who would have guessed we were from the same neighbourhood?'

She laughed, shaking her head as she filled her fork with creamy pasta. 'You're funny.'

Good wine and growing familiarity loosened them up; the main course developed into dessert and then coffees. They discussed Nina's study in Barcelona; crazy student days in a bohemian city full of character and characters; and her work since, a string of temporary positions across Europe, fulfilling an urgent wanderlust after three years tied to the same university. Now she was acting as nanny to two small children, a stopgap while she decided how to make use of her art history degree. Tony told her all about The Olive Branch, a damp and derelict wreck when he originally found it; how no one else could see beyond the spiders and graffiti; how no one could understand his vision for it or the mentality that drove the mission, when there were far simpler options he could have chosen.

She sympathised with him. 'What would make someone ever choose simple over inspiration and creativity – where is the challenge, the pleasure in that?'

He liked her new slant on his stubbornness.

'So, you refused to be put off? You risked everything and bought it anyway, all on your own? It was very brave.'

He didn't want to talk about Vicky. She didn't belong here, in this conversation, but to deny her role in one of the most important events in their lives was to dishonour her memory and he couldn't do that. 'No, not on my own.' His eyes fell away from hers as he became conscious of the contact, instead staring into the slow swirl of his latte. 'My wife, though we weren't married then, we did it together. And, as far as brave is concerned, she was the brave one, who trusted me and my decisions. I was just… bull-headed.'

Nina held the coffee cup just below her lips, observing him through a gentle stream of steam as she breathed it away. 'I suppose, we've got to go there, don't we?'

'Sorry?' He glanced up.

Her head tilted to one side; brows puckered. 'Your wife? Your son? They are unanswered questions. You are divorced? Separated? Is it complicated? It usually is.'

To his shame, he felt the old well of grief rise within him at having to explain and fought to gain control of it, gulping and grimacing as hot coffee burned his mouth. 'No, not complicated. Vicky died last year. Now it's just me and Jamie. Simple.'

The silence stretched, full of emotion, until Nina picked up his hand from where it lay. 'Oh, Tony.' She whispered. 'You're wrong. Not simple. Not simple at all.'

Before he could respond, the sheepish waitress sidled up to their table and slipped a black plastic tray, topped by their bill, between them, breaking the mood. The rest of the room was empty, apart from staff, waiting for them to leave so they could clean up and go home. Tony swiftly settled the bill, then helped Nina into her jacket and they headed out into the street, now awash with evening revellers.

The abruptness of their exit meant Tony wasn't prepared for whatever came next and they both paused in a doorway. The evening had been a success as far as he could ascertain, but he was unsure what his next move should be.

'It's been a lovely evening, but it's still early.' He shrugged. 'Another drink? Or can I walk you home? Share a taxi?'

Nina turned to face him, a sad expression leaching the light from her face. 'Thank you, but no.'

His heart ducked into his stomach. 'Oh, ok, but can we do this again? Or something else? Whatever you like.'

Cupping his cheek with one hand, she met his eyes, unblinking for a few seconds, and stood on tip toe to place a kiss on his cheek before turning away. 'You're a nice guy, Tony. I'll call you maybe. Ok? Take care.'

Dim light rushed in to conceal her body as she walked away. Her non-committal answer was a poor disguise for the refusal he took it to be, and his chest tightened. He had failed. He wasn't sure why or how, but he had failed, and he felt sure he wouldn't hear from her again.

He thrust his hands deep into his pockets, shrugged his shoulders against the chill of the night and headed for the taxi rank, kicking at the edge of the pavement as he went.

CHAPTER 10

The loft above Trish's garage was surprisingly spacious, despite the heap of sagging boxes stacked along one wall. The air was tinged with damp and the musty odour of mildew, and the thick cardboard bent and gave easily beneath his fingers. He had climbed through the hatch raring to go, armed with heavy duty scissors and a roll of bin bags, ready to sift through his parents' belongings. Snapping on the single light bulb, swaying from a wire in the centre of the ceiling, he had been taken aback by the array of unmarked containers and his enthusiasm had dipped at the enormity of the task ahead.

He started with a box, sitting apart from the rest, and ripped back the parcel tape along its centre. As he folded back the leaves at the top, a pile of newspaper wrapped objects were revealed and he frowned at the crumpled sea of black and white print. He snatched one out at random and unwound the newspaper pages until a tubular lava lamp appeared. A second package contained a large porcelain vase and a third, a matching but smaller version of the same. Tony huffed and laid the items to one side. This appeared to be a road to nowhere, but he didn't want to miss anything important, so he dived an arm into the box up to his shoulder and swirled it around to see if he could detect anything worth a second look. Nothing, so he repackaged the items, laid them back in the box and reached for an alternative.

The weight of the second case immediately suggested it contained something other than paperwork, so he cast it aside, instead tugging out a heavier, more solid one. The side collapsed under his efforts, ripping from top to bottom, displaying a pile of gaudy fabric - old curtains or bedding, he guessed, but of no interest. He sat back on his haunches, surveying the remaining wall of cardboard, disillusioned. If not for his eagerness to find answers he would have given up, but a phone message from Ruth the evening before had piqued his interest. At first, he had been disappointed to hear her voice when he picked up the recording, the flashing red light having ignited the hope of wished for, but unexpected contact from Nina, but a surprising connection between his grandfather and a village in the north of Scotland had left him both confused and intrigued, and now he was dying to find further clues.

Another half hour bore no fruit, except for a selection of toys, once firm favourites, but discarded or outgrown long before his parents had died, possibly retained by his mother for sentimental reasons. They had spent many hours together, while his father worked away, toiling over Meccano constructions or gluing Air fix models. When his father returned, her attention was engaged elsewhere and Tony sometimes felt he almost ceased to exist to her, but the minute the front door closed behind her husband, she would be back at the kitchen table, wielding a miniature spanner or tiny pots of paint, ready to be second mate to his captain.

'Any luck?'

A call from below disturbed his reverie and he shuffled to the hatchway, peering down at Trish. 'Nothing much. Some old stuff of mine Jamie may enjoy, but no clues about the old folks yet.'

'Kettle's on, if you fancy a break, and we've made buns.'

He swung his legs through the hatch and lowered himself down the ladder, bringing a selection of games tucked under one arm. Back on solid ground he rubbed his eyes and nose and patted his trousers free of cobwebby residue. 'Fresh air wouldn't be a bad idea.'

Jamie was in the kitchen dabbing chocolate buttons on the top of little cakes, his cheeks daubed with icing, his forehead creased with the precision of his work.

'My, you've been busy.' Tony washed his hands at the sink.

'You can have one, if you like. They're delicious.' He glowed with pride.

Trish handed Jamie a plate. 'Pop a few on there, young man, and we'll take them to the garden. I'll bring drinks.'

He swiftly followed orders, almost sending the cakes flying in his haste to jump down from the stool.

'Careful as you go. Dad'll get the door. I'm right behind you.'

The garden was bright after the gloom of the loft and Tony enjoyed the warmth of the sun on his face as he settled at the picnic table, legs stretched out, making the most of the space after the morning's confinement. Within minutes the plate of cakes was depleted, and his cup drained. He nursed the china, as an excuse to delay resumption of his hunt. Jamie, much taken up with his father's toys, took up residence in the sunroom with a box of Lego.

'I suppose I ought to get back to it.'

Trish tidied things onto a high sided tray. 'Find anything interesting?'

He chuckled. 'Depends what you call interesting. Anyone with a penchant for seventies and eighties décor would have a field day. What do they call it now?

Vintage? Nothing helpful as far as my past is concerned though. Plenty of reminders from my youth, not that I wanted to be reminded of that particularly.'

Trish pushed the tray away and sat opposite him, looking over the lawn and the still, low bushes to the hills beyond. 'Your childhood was happy enough, wasn't it?'

'Yes.' His answer was flippant, throwaway. A standard answer to what, in most circumstances, would be a superficial question. He drew his legs in and met her gaze. 'Yes, it was happy enough. A lot happier than many others, I'm sure, but, you know, I can't remember the happy times without thinking about the sad ones too. They're all interconnected.'

An intrepid white butterfly gripped the attention of both as it fluttered between them, bobbing and diving.

'Did I do the wrong thing? Should we have gone through this stuff before? The boxes were there, in the loft, I just couldn't bring myself… I missed your mother so much and it was somehow easier to ignore her things.' The words erupted from her in a rush, as if they had been waiting to be spoken for a long time. She paused for a moment to compose herself. 'Would it have helped? You were so… so angry, I didn't know what to do for the best.'

The fissure in Trish's composure hit Tony. She was always so together, to see her unsure, in need of reassurance, smacked him hard and fast and he grabbed her hand with both of his. 'You did do the best. You did everything you could, taking me in, giving me a home. And nothing would have helped. I *was* angry; angry they died; angry I didn't; angry they sent me away before it happened.' He smoothed the beginnings of her barnacle knuckle absent-mindedly with his thumb. 'I couldn't understand why they did that. It's not like I was a little kid. I was a teenager. I wouldn't have been in the way. Why *did* they send me here?'

Trish's shoulders briefly flexed beneath her blouse. 'I suppose it was simply easier that way, one less person to worry about with everything going on. You usually came to me for a few days in the summer anyway and, knowing your father, things probably weren't entirely organised at the other end. Every time they moved, it was always on the spur of a moment and things never ran exactly smoothly. There was always a gap, staying in digs and belongings stored somewhere, until things were sorted out.' She raised one cynical eyebrow. 'That sort of life would never have suited me, but your mother seemed to thrive on it.'

Tony sat back, releasing Trish from his grasp as the conversation shifted. 'So, why did they keep moving around? Was it for work, or what?'

Trish shook her head, rubbing a finger round the rim of a glass on the table. 'Your guess is as good as mine. As far as I could tell, he would come back from wherever he was working, without any warning, and announce it was time to move on. That would be it, bags packed, in the car and off they would go. A couple of weeks would go by and your mother would be on the phone, telling me which town they were in and where they were staying. She thought it was such a lark, but to me it was like living life on the run; flitting around; never putting down roots; making friends, but then, perhaps I'm boring.'

Tony's eyes narrowed as he studied her distant expression. 'You didn't like him, did you?'

'Is it obvious?' Her rueful smile barely affected the rest of her face. 'I tried to, for your mother's sake, but it's difficult to like someone you don't understand, and he was a very closed book. Plus, to all intents and purposes he took my sister away from me and I never forgave him for that.'

'We used to see you though, me and mum. I remember visiting.'

'Yes, but we had been best friends, not just sisters, until she met him. It was a shock to the system. She went on a girls' weekend at the seaside with friends from work and never came back, at least not in the same way. She wasn't the open, candid Fi I had always known and loved. I suppose I felt excluded.' She brushed imaginary crumbs from the spotless knees of her trousers, her tone becoming matter of fact as she did so, as if she were brushing those old feelings into the grass. 'He worked some sort of spell on her. If it was love, I've never felt anything like it, to make me throw everything else in my life away. It didn't feel right to me.'

'In retrospect, she did live an isolated existence, but you don't realise when you're growing up in that environment, do you? But there were never any friends popping in for a chat or anything. It must have been lonely for her.'

Tony changed direction. 'Where was he from originally? Some of the documents suggest somewhere in Wales, but I never heard him talk about the place or remember going there. Was it just another place he travelled through?'

'There was definitely a Welsh connection. He had an accent sometimes, not all the time, but it would creep in here and there. You can't hide your roots completely, can you? No matter how hard you try?'

'Do you think he wanted to? Hide his roots?' Tony frowned, deep in thought. 'I wonder why he would want to do that. What about Scotland? Do you know anything about any links up north?'

'Scotland? No, nothing. I'm afraid there's still plenty of mystery about your dad. I'll be interested to hear what you find out. It'll be as much news to me as it is to you. Who knows, perhaps you're a distant relative of Robert the Bruce? Wouldn't it be fun to find out you have royal blood?'

'I don't know about that; royalty tend to have an awful lot of skeletons in their cupboards. Jamie would love it, of course.' He glanced at the little boy, head down, crouched over his growing creation. 'I'd be happy to find out who my great grandparents were.' He rose to his feet, stretching to the sky. 'Right, I'm going to get back to it. There's got to be something tucked away up there that'll help.'

The renewed vigour with which Tony returned to his investigation diminished the moment another cardboard box collapsed, but he was cheered by the discovery of a carton of vinyl records. Their dust covers were a colourful array of sixties and seventies graphics, their bent corners and torn edges testament to much use and how well loved they had been in their day. Certain titles stood out as favourites of his mother. Images filled his mind of her dancing as she ran a duster between ornaments on the mantel, or standing at the sink, absent-mindedly drying the dishes, humming softly to something or someone far beyond the window, and he smiled at the bittersweet memories. She had seemed so grown up to him then, a wise old woman with answers to all the world's mysteries, but now he realised how young she had really been then, and when her life had ended, far too young.

A couple of document wallets sat at the back of the box, and he dragged them out. The first held recipes, roughly torn from magazines, or meticulously copied in his mother's hand. Perhaps his love of cooking came from her after all. The second held a variety of documents; articles about gardening; growing vegetables in containers, and he remembered one summer and their unsuccessful attempts to grow carrots in a window box.

From among the papers, he pulled out a scrap book and it fell open naturally at the centre, the early pages splaying with the weight of their pasted in contents, the end of the book yet to be filled. There were photographs of him and his parents; report cards from school; a shiny swimming certificate from when he was six, but the earliest entries dated to before he was born. He turned to them with growing attention, sitting back on his haunches, the bare bulb washing the pages. There were greetings cards; congratulating his parents on their wedding; anniversary cards from his father, brief in words but heavy in sentiment; and newspaper clippings, not yet stuck in, bunched together inside the front cover. One article stood out, partly due to its tatty appearance and dark staining and partly due to the headline, "Fatal Fall at Railway Bridge". It seemed a peculiar bed mate for amusing ditties about the blessings of having children and positive anecdotes about dancing in the rain.

Tony repositioned himself directly beneath the lamp, straining to read the smaller print through the dust motes. It spoke of the death of a postman, after falling from a railway bridge, into the path of an oncoming train. A local boy had arrived at the scene shortly afterward but had not seen the fall. Realising there was no time to raise the alarm, he had tried to remove the injured victim from the path of the train but had been unable to shift him and witnessed the man's horrific demise. Tony winced at the imagery, wondering what would have possessed his mother to keep the cutting. With the last sentence, it made more sense – the victim had been identified as a man from a nearby town, Antonio Viscount, forty-six.

Tony inhaled sharply as the facts tallied up, 'Good grief Grandpa. What a way to go!'

He reread the report with renewed interest, studying the photograph of the bridge, taking in the rough stonework, the height, the distance his grandfather would have fallen. Somehow, knowing he was related to the poor man, made the story even more gruesome. He could picture the man, gazing so lovingly at his young wife in the photograph in the shoebox at home, lying in agony on the rails, a speeding train approaching. He could imagine the terror his grandfather must have felt when he realised there was no possibility of escape.

The thought of his grandmother having to cope with such dreadful news, having just given birth, tugged at his heart, but there was something niggling at the back of his brain, something which didn't quite add up. Then the penny dropped. Antonio Viscount, according to Tony's timeline, had died long before his mother had been born, so, if it was the Antonio that formed part of his history, how did she come to have the cutting? He glanced to the top of the page and flattened out the crumpled and crumbling edge to find the date - fifteenth March nineteen fifty-six. His mother had not snipped the story from the paper. It must have come from his father or elsewhere, as his father was only a baby himself at that time. His grandmother, Cerys. She must have been the one, the one to consider the story of such importance as to place the flimsy scrap to one side, somewhere safe, to show her baby son when he came of an age to know. Tony pursed his lips in distaste. Grown up son or not, he felt some of the graphic details in the report need not have been shared. Enough to know his father had died tragically, surely?

Tony slipped the papers back into the wallet, placing

the article at the front, to refer back to later. The story had taken the wind out of his sails and the desire to continue the search guttered for that day. He had new information to be going on with, a new lead, and he couldn't wait to report back to Ruth, to get her take on the events of six decades ago.

For the remainder of the afternoon Tony was distracted by the news of the shocking circumstances in which his grandfather had died. Jamie's chatter floated over Tony's head in the car, as Tony compared his own situation with that of his grandmother; both widowed young; left alone to cope with small children. He wondered what had become of her, the sad, young and lonely woman of his imagination, whether she had married again, begun a new life, or perhaps she had not coped at all and that was why his father never mentioned her.

The close of the day found him with more questions than it had started with. At least he had uncovered something. Now he needed those certificates to arrive, in particular his father's birth certificate, so he could finally put a full name to his grandmother and find out more about her. The elusive documents could even take him back another generation, hopefully a more fortunate generation than those he had encountered so far. He planned to get Jamie to bed as quickly as could be managed, then to phone Ruth and bring her up to date.

When they arrived home, Jamie manhandled a heap of toys through the front door, some old favourites, others he had acquired thanks to Tony's explorations. Tony followed, pushing the door wide to allow easy access for the boy and his burden. He bent down to retrieve a selection of letters and circulars already on the mat, Jamie's footprints now scudded across their fronts.

'Find somewhere in your room for those, mate, and then straight into your jim-jams, ok? You'll have time to play with it all tomorrow.' He headed into the kitchen.

Jamie hollered down the stairs, 'I just want to finish a bit...'

'No chance!' Tony shut the arguments down. 'The extra half hour at Aunt Trish's was on the understanding it would be straight to bed when we got back. Don't make me stop trusting you.' He heard Jamie huff as he battered his way into the bedroom, but walked away, shaking his head at the muffled muttering which followed.

The phone rang and Tony headed to the kitchen to find the handset, dropping his mother's document files and the newly delivered letters on the worktop, as he snatched it up.

'Tony, it's Marco. All well with you? How did the journey back in time pan out?'

'Yes, interesting. We've literally just got in the door.' He idly sifted through the correspondence as he continued the conversation. 'I was going to ring you once Jamie was settled.'

'All good, all good, but as it happens, we had to come up to your neck of the woods on an errand this evening and thought we might pop in for an update. Is it too late for a night cap?'

Tony smiled. 'Not at all. It would be good to see you. I've got a story and a half about my grandfather. What we need now is for those certificates to turn up and we'll be forging ahead.' He tugged a letter from the pile which looked more official than the rest. 'Actually, this could be one here now. Hold on and I'll open it.'

He gripped the phone between chin and chest, using both hands to rip the top from the envelope and pull out the contents. He scanned the text, eager for information, but as he located the heading and digested the words printed there, everything seemed to stop, except for the banging of his heart in his chest, the undulations inside his head creating a strange, floating sensation. He exhaled abruptly, the bolus of breath hitting the roof of his mouth like something solid, forcing a groan from his body. It wasn't the long-anticipated birth certificate, it was notification of the coroner's inquest into Vicky's death.

She had been gone for nine months. He had survived without her all this time, almost got used to the way things were, and yet the permanence of her absence hit him again, as if he had not truly known it before. Everything else faded away and he couldn't remember why he had the phone to his ear.

'Tony? Tony?'

The words were distant, disconnected and when he tried to reply his tongue refused to follow orders, his lips numb and thick. For most people, there was a funeral to mark the end, a turning point at which the view of those left behind shifted from the past to the future, but for Tony, the funeral had been only a pause. The inquest had always been there on the horizon, looming, excusing him from moving on. He felt adrift.

'Tony, is everything all right?' There was a frantic air to Marco's tone.

'The inquest. I've got a date for the inquest.' His breath was coming short and shallow.

'We'll be there in ten minutes.'

The phone went dead, and Tony sat down hard on the stool, staring at the handset cradled in his hand.

CHAPTER 11

Tony trawled through the next few days like a robot, automatic, disengaged. He booked Jamie into every after-school club going and worked extra shifts, although the restaurant was fully staffed, scrubbing already clean cupboards rather than have unoccupied time. He needed to shut himself off from everything until the inquest was over, until he could handle his emotions, unlike those he had corked up inside him right now. His friends recognised the bubble he created from the way he had been immediately after Vicky's death and allowed him to maintain the security blanket of safe distance, ready to step in when or if circumstances required.

When Monday did inevitably arrive, Marco and Ruth turned up early, helping Jamie to breakfast and bundling him off to school. He was oblivious to his father's struggles, enjoying people fussing around him, chatting and giggling like every other day. Tony would have been pleased, if he had even been aware of it.

The morning passed in strangely disjointed chunks, leaving Tony bemused by how he had jumped from one event to another. One moment he was viewing his image in the long mirror in his bedroom, straightening an already linear tie; then in the rear of Marco's car, knees bouncing beneath his fists as the wheels negotiated the cobbled entrance to the courtroom car park. He was briefly aware of being in a small, quiet room with pale blue walls and a window overlooking an enclosed concrete yard; shaking the hand of the coroner's officer, who smelt like coffee, and explained the order of proceedings in a monotone, but may as well have been speaking Russian. He heard Marco's voice, replying in lieu of his own and felt Ruth's hand at his elbow, a light, reassuring pressure. Then he was in the courtroom, Ruth and Marco on either side, whether in support or to prevent him from running away he was unsure, but he was glad they were there, in any event.

Sarah, demure in a crisp navy suit, so unlike her usual jeans and jumper, shuffled into their row of seats, introducing herself to Ruth and shaking hands as she leaned past to speak to him. Her ordinarily jolly face struck him with its peculiarly wan and serious expression. He noticed the harsh contrast of her lipstick and tiny wrinkles around her eyes which he had never seen before.

'Hi Tony.' She dropped a dry peck on his cheek and gripped his hand, 'Listen, Mum and Dad are here. At least, they're outside. They don't want to upset you but, you know, they had to come... felt they had to... their daughter...'

There was a drawn out pause as everyone waited and he realised he was supposed to respond. His thoughts jumbled together: Vicky's mum and dad; the strange hush of the room; Matt Bridgeman, below them in the gallery, bending and talking to someone with a typewriter, patting their shoulder then turning to find a seat; Jamie bouncing in the doorway before he left for school that morning; had he given him any lunch money?

'Tony?' Ruth's voice entered his mind and he looked at her.

'Yes.' He coughed to make his voice louder. 'Yes, of course, they must come in.'

Sarah squeezed his hand and retreated. Moments

later he saw her return, parents in tow, and take up seats in the row behind. In his peripheral vision he could see his mother-in-law, passing a crumpled tissue from one hand to another. He could smell her perfume, sweet and cloying, wafting every time she shuffled in her seat.

A door at the front of the room opened to afford entry to a middle-aged man in a dark suit. Tony found himself rising to his feet along with the rest of the room, assisted by arms on either side of him, before resuming his seat, an expectant hush replacing the buzz of before.

The man's voice was low, but commanding, demanding the attention of those present with its quiet authority, and began to recite a well-versed passage about the nature of an inquest; it's limitations and aims; the expectations of those attending and the behaviour which would be accepted.

'I will invite questions at the close of each witness statement and I would ask you to refrain from interrupting until such time. You do not have to agree with what is being said, but I would ask you show respect to each witness and allow them to offer their version of events, in the knowledge an opportunity to demur will follow.' He shuffled his papers, checking details and setting them straight in front of him. 'That being said, we have a lot to get through, so let's begin. Can we hear the first statement please?'

The coroner's officer referred to a loaded clipboard. 'The antecedent statement will be presented by Mrs Sarah Turner on behalf of the family of Victoria Viscount. Mrs Turner?'

Tony steeled himself as Sarah passed to the front of the room. Matt Bridgeman had approached her to present the family's statement, knowing Tony would struggle, and she had willingly agreed, eager, if not happy, to do something useful. As she straightened in the witness box, he could see the sheet of paper, crammed with notes, clutched in her hand, shaking violently. She appeared conscious of it too and rested it on the front of the lectern, restricting the tremors. He had to strain to hear as she spoke, a low, broken voice, describing her relationship with Vicky and Vicky's movements on the day of the accident. When she reached the part about her father being admitted to hospital, Tony became aware of the man himself sobbing quietly, the only outward sign stuttered breathing through his nose, as he tried to contain it. His wife clung to him, whether in support or seeking consolation, it was unclear. Tony couldn't deal with their grief as well and forced his mind away, shutting out everything about the courtroom.

As various speakers delivered their reports, Tony devised new menus for The Olive Branch; planned daytrips with Jamie, out to the country; he wondered about Nina, where she was, what she was doing, but a guilty conscience about being disloyal to Vicky sent him crashing back to the inquest, so he quickly moved on.

He remembered his grandfather and the shocking way he had died and wondered if his grandmother had to endure a similar ordeal, listening as strangers described in detail his injuries. Had she been strong enough? Or had she turned her back and concentrated on her baby boy? He wished he knew what kind of woman she was or, indeed, anything about her. When this was over, he intended to get some answers. He should find out her name any day now, where she came from. He wondered if she had been able to rebuild her life, where she died. He should show his respects in some way. Go and put flowers on her grave, perhaps? Yes, he would take Jamie to Wales, assuming she ended her days in the place she had lived, and they would lay a wreath, show the world she was not forgotten.

An increase in shuffling brought Tony back to the room and he glanced around to see what was happening. Ruth was fiddling with her handbag, but Marco was watching him.

'A quick cup of tea is in order. Half an hour to stretch our legs.' Marco leaned in. 'It's almost over. You're doing a fine job.'

Was he? He got to his feet and sidled out, following Ruth. Trish was waiting at the aisle, smart as ever in a tweed skirt suit, her face neutral.

'Trish? What are you doing here? I didn't expect you…' He hadn't spoken to her since his visit. In fact, he felt slightly ashamed she hadn't crossed his mind since then and didn't realise she was even aware of the inquest.

She hugged, the awkwardness of recent meetings history. 'Nonsense. When Ruth called me, I couldn't possibly be anywhere else.' She leaned past him to acknowledge his companions, shaking hands with them. 'I'm sorry I was a little late, but I had to hand over to a cover teacher, but, hey ho, better late than never and I knew you were in good hands. Come on then, strong, sweet tea and a sticky bun. That'll see us through until lunchtime.' She took his arm and led him away.

Tony hadn't known he was hungry until he started to eat, and the warmth of the tea revived him a little, like liquid energy. Conversation swirled around his head, but he listened as his companions exchanged notes about the morning's proceedings. The general consensus was that another hour would see a close to the inquest. He felt relieved. The worst was over. The family statement, the post-mortem report, the police report and the harrowing detail they contained, all done and dusted. As they headed back toward the courtroom, he steeled himself for the final session. With only minutes to go, he side-stepped into the men's bathroom, while the others conferred in the corridor outside.

Washing his hands, he studied the haggard face in the mirror, pale in its dark-haired frame. He would cope. Soon this would be over. He would be able to move on, keeping the memories of Vicky he wanted to keep and discarding the rest.

The door swung in, wafting soap scented air toward him, and he glanced over his shoulder at the person who had entered. His father-in-law. As their eyes met, the older man stopped, a look of fear washing over an already tired and strained face and Tony could almost read the calculations behind the man's eyes as he tried to decide what to do. Tony had hated this man with a vehemence which made his brain ache. He had blamed him, but, inquest or no inquest, in his heart he knew it was not his fault in reality. It had simply been a kneejerk reaction, being angry an escape from pure unbearable sadness.

'Tony. Sorry... I...'

Tony stepped towards him, meeting the man's gaze. 'Neil. It's good to see you.'

Neil's entire body crumpled in on itself. 'Is it?

'I'm sorry about how I've been with you.' Tony felt tension seep away as he finally let his anger go. 'You didn't deserve it and I'm sorry.'

Neil allowed a single high-pitched sob to escape, his hangdog expression intensifying rather than fading. 'But I did deserve it, didn't I. You were only saying what everyone else was thinking.'

Tony pulled him in to his shoulder, patting his back curtly before releasing him and meeting his eyes once more. 'It was not your fault,' he emphasised each word.

'I needed a scapegoat, but it was nobody's fault. It was an accident. An awful, tragic accident and the coroner's going to prove that before the morning's out.'

Neil shrugged and wiped the heel of his hand across his cheek.

'It's time we put it behind us. Jamie needs a grandad. Agreed?'

The door swung in behind Neil, nudging the pair of them back, and Marco's concerned head appeared around it. 'Everything all right?'

Tony nodded, then turned back to Neil. 'Agreed?'

Neil bobbed his head brusquely and Tony skirted past, following Marco out. Two small huddles stood outside, all wearing furrowed brows, as they realised the two men had come face to face. Tony managed a watery smile. He gently squeezed Diana's arm as he passed, many words conveyed with a single gesture. Falling in beside Trish, he made his way back to the courtroom.

Tony faced the remainder of the inquest with renewed optimism. This was a good thing. An underscoring of the past. A steppingstone to the future, a different future for him and his family, if he had anything to do with it. He tuned in and out to the final statements as he felt able, including that of the witness to the crash. He had expected to dislike the guy, but realised it wasn't this man's fault either. Besides, everything he said added up and when he finished speaking Tony had no questions. It was clear.

When everyone had spoken, there was a lull as the coroner checked notes, ticking things off and crossing lines through other sections. He raised a couple of quick questions with the coroner's officer and documents were located and handed to him. He re-read them, lips pursed, his brows reaching for his cheeks. Then he pushed the paperwork to one side and faced his audience.

'Right.' The word echoed around the space, silencing the buzz which had begun. 'It is my duty to declare a verdict and give a title, if not a reason, for the death of Victoria Viscount.' He paused. 'There are a number of possible outcomes in this instance, and it is right and good for me to explain why I have decided upon this one in particular. The verdicts available to me are that of Accidental Death, Death by Misadventure, Unlawful Killing or, if there is not enough evidence to return any of these, then an open verdict may be declared.'

Tony felt his head become light, his vision swimming, and realised he was holding his breath. In minutes it would be over. He clenched and unclenched his hands, repeating in his head, 'accidental death, accidental death'. Those were the words which would relieve both himself and Neil of blame. It would be recorded in black and white – a horrific, heart wrenching accident, and then they could go home and start over.

'So, to begin with, the verdict of Accidental Death. This would suggest Victoria's death was strictly due to accident, that no other party was involved, no hazardous behaviour had been undertaken and no blame could be apportioned. I do not believe this to be the case and therefore the verdict of Accidental Death is discarded.'

A murmur ran around the courtroom. Tony felt the floor shift beneath him, and he leaned forward, grabbing at the ledge in front for support. He felt Marco edge forward and grasp his arm.

'The verdict of Death by Misadventure would relate to a deliberate act by Victoria, resulting in her own death. Please understand this is very different from a verdict of Suicide, where the deceased sets out with the intention of taking their own life. I consider the reported speed at which Victoria was travelling did play a part and find it highly unlikely, had she been travelling within speed limits appertaining, the collision would have occurred or, if it had, the impact may have been far less catastrophic. However, Misadventure would suggest no blame should be apportioned elsewhere and once again, I do not feel this to be the case and therefore this verdict is also discarded.'

For one petrifying moment Tony imagined the coroner pointing his finger directly at him, accusing him, he should never have allowed her behind the wheel.

'To bring forth a verdict of Unlawful Killing there would have to be sufficient evidence to prove a third party had been the predominant cause of the collision and can only be declared when beyond all reasonable doubt. The evidence we have heard, though persuasive, is not substantial enough. In my mind, the balance of probabilities, suggests the third-party driver of whom we have heard mention, bore some, if not all, of the blame, but at this point I am prohibited from declaring such in legal terms. I therefore have no option but to bring an Open verdict.'

He looked at the faces observing him and smiled a tight smile. 'To the family, I appreciate this is not the verdict you would have been looking for and I would very much like to give you closure today.' He caught Tony's eye briefly. 'Unfortunately, however, what you or I would like does not influence the facts and I hope you will understand the limitations within which I operate. Thank you for the graceful way in which you have conducted yourselves today and I trust as many questions as could be answered, have been answered.'

He rose to his feet, headed to the back of the room and left the same way he had entered. The Coroner's

Officer rose also and announced the conclusion of proceedings, and everyone prepared themselves to leave.

As Tony stared out over the courtroom, replaying the coroner's words in his mind, Matt Bridgeman stood below, searching through the faces in the elevated area behind him until their eyes met. He slowly shook his head and mouthed the word, 'Sorry,' his shoulders shrugging as he spoke.

Tony turned to Marco. 'An Open verdict? I don't get it! It was an accident, wasn't it?'

Marco breathed slowly and deeply. 'Of course it was, just some fandangled legal mumbo jumbo way of saying so, that's all. Come on. Let's get you home.'

He was bundled out of the courtroom and into the car, no less subdued than he had begun the day.

CHAPTER 12

Back in Tony's lounge, the friends discussed and debated the connotations of the open verdict. They each took their own view on what it actually meant, but there was no absolute conclusion to be reached and the topic moved in circles, heat rising, threatening to build into a crusade. Marco intervened. He tapped shot glasses on to the table and filled each with a measure of brandy, from a caddy retrieved from his breast pocket. When he was done, he waited for them to fall silent, his own glass held aloft.

'Let's be honest.' He looked at each in turn, 'We all know the truth of the matter, and today's result was complete and utter crap!

No one denied Marco's bluntness, silently wondering where he was going with it.

'And we could sit here debating the whys and wherefores 'til the cows come home but getting angry will achieve nothing but heartache. Today should not be about all that paper pushing nonsense. It's about a very, very special lady, who we all knew and loved and will remain in our memories and our hearts for evermore. Let's drink to Vicky and then do what she would have wanted us to do – get on with life. To Vicky.'

He downed his brandy with a flourish, challenging them to follow suit, with his eyes. They slammed their glasses down in turn, coughing and spluttering, eyes moistened with the fire of the alcohol in their blood now, rather than emotion.

Aunt Trish blinked and threw a hand to her neatly suited chest, her voice gravelly. 'Good lord. It's the Christmas party all over again.'

They all exploded with laughter at the image of this prim, white-haired lady cavorting at a drunken bash and the mood altered, the mantle of despondency cast off.

Ruth turned to Tony. 'What next then, Tony? What happens now?'

He shrugged. 'I don't know. More of the same, I guess.' He rolled his empty glass between his fingertips. 'In some respects, it feels like Jamie and I have been on our own forever. We've established a routine between us. Not that everything always gets done on time or completely successfully, but we do all right.'

A general murmur of reassurance circulated the table.

'In other respects, it all seems like it only happened yesterday. Is that normal?'

Marco set about refilling the glasses. 'Is there such a thing as "normal"? All I know is, if it was me sitting here, in the same situation, if something had happened to my Ruth...' He shook his head, unable to contemplate the idea. 'I don't think I would have coped half as well. You've been a tower of strength for that young man, a tower of strength.'

The tender glance which passed between Marco and Ruth sent a shiver of jealousy down Tony's spine. He missed that closeness with another; that special connection of emotions shared without words. His mind turned to Nina and the possibilities he had briefly dared to imagine, but he quickly pushed her away. This was not the right time.

'I might take a bit of time off over the summer,' He spoke the words aloud before the thought had fully formed. 'I think it would be good for me and Jamie to have a few adventures. In fact, I thought about a road trip to Wales, tracking down my old grandmother's roots, find the town my dad actually came from. As soon as his birth certificate arrives and I have a last name for her, I'm going to start searching.'

Ruth grabbed at her handbag, scrabbling through the pockets. 'I almost forgot. Sorry, Tony. I have it here. I ordered it to my address, and it arrived at the weekend, but I thought it would be the last thing on your mind right then, so I left it to bring with me today.' She slid an envelope across to him.

He ripped it open and unfolded the contents, a single sheet of paper. As he took in the content a dubious smile crossed his face. 'Something tells me this might not be a great deal of help. She was called Cerys Williams. Only one of the most common surnames in Wales, but we have a town of birth. The power of the internet will come up with something, I'm sure.' He glanced at the others. 'Would it be rude to get my laptop out and have a quick look?'

Marco laughed. 'Sounds like just the ticket. I'll walk down to school to meet little man. They were expecting me or Ruth to collect him today anyway. Max is with a neighbour for the day, so I'm missing my fresh air and exercise. Trish, do you fancy a trot? Leave the historians to it?'

The pair made off, leaving Tony and Ruth to continue their investigations.

Heads bent close to the screen; Tony entered search details to a genealogy website. 'Cerys… Williams…No middle initials.' He spoke aloud as he typed. 'Year of birth? What do you think?'

Ruth tipped her head. 'It's hard to say. A good bit younger than Antonio, by the photo. Try a broad margin, maybe nineteen thirty-five to forty?'

Tony glanced back at her sharply. 'Good grief. That would make Antonio a bit of cradle snatcher, if she was mid-twenties when he died and he was forty-six. I wonder what her parents thought of that.'

He entered the information and waited as the computer processed his request.

'Nothing wrong with an age gap.' Ruth smiled. 'Although, there's only eight years between Marco and I, not the twenty-odd between them. I suppose it may have raised eyebrows, but maybe people were less judgemental in those days.'

'That's me told.' Tony grinned back.

'No. I just mean the war wasn't long over. People had to make adjustments to the way they thought and lived. Besides, there was a time when parents were happy if they thought their daughters would be well looked after. The fact the husband was a bit of a father figure was irrelevant. Though, from the photo, it does look like a love match rather than one of convenience.' She retrieved the photograph from a pile of papers to one side. 'Look at them, totally loved up.'

A list of names appeared on the screen and their attention flicked back, sifting through the data.

'There's a lot of them, aren't there?' Tony's eyes slipped from one entry to another. 'How do we work out which one it is?'

Ruth edged forward, nudging him out of the way with her elbow. 'The hard way, I'm afraid. Look at each one in turn and see if there's any way of ruling it in or out.'

As she turned toward him, meeting his eye, Tony smelt the flowery aroma of her perfume. He felt her breath on his face and became aware of how near their faces were, bodies pressed together, shoulder against shoulder. Part of him wanted to pull away, but at the same time enjoying the contact in a way he had never considered Ruth before.

'Tony.'

'Yes?' He realised his breath was caught in his chest.

'Put the kettle on and let me get on with this, will you? I'd love a coffee.'

Retreating to the kitchen area, he hoped she hadn't detected the direction of his thoughts. He had known her for a long time, since college days, but she had hardly registered until she turned up with a stunning acquaintance in tow. From that moment on he had made it his business to get closer to her, so he could get close to Vicky, but he had never seen Ruth as anything other than one of the boys. He chastised himself; she was a friend; the wife of another friend; a kind, intelligent and attractive one, but that was it. He needed to pull himself together and stop imagining chemistry which didn't exist.

Tony placed a mug in front of her and she glanced up from her jotter. 'Thanks.' She sipped and grimaced at the heat. 'You know what? Life would be much simpler if everyone had middle names.'

He slipped back into his seat next to her but edging it away. 'No luck?'

'Well, I've narrowed it down, by restricting the registration area search and discounting those with additional names. Three Cerys Williams had births registered in our specific area of Wales at about the right time and one of those was also registered as deceased the same year, leaving two. Both were born within twenty miles of each other, so it could be either. If we knew what her parents were called, of course, the mystery could be solved, or it could throw up a whole other can of worms, if it turns out to be neither of them.'

'So, what do we do?' The lack of progress frustrated

him.

She rubbed her chin with her fingertips. 'If only we could find a marriage registration for Cerys and Antonio. They usually have parents' names on them as well, which would be ideal. I can't really understand why nothing's coming up. Viscount is such an unusual name, and I would have expected to find it quite quickly, even without an exact location.'

'Have you tried other spellings? I read somewhere, lots of searches hit a dead end because people mis-spelt their own names.'

'True.' She mused, 'It's worth a shot. Let's get creative.'

He sat back, cupping his mug in his hands, watching as she beavered away, transposing letters, spelling phonetically and trying every possible version of his name. His mind wandered, so he began to flick through the paperwork he had, feigning a search for clues, feeling guilty Ruth was doing all the work, but wanting to allow her space. His attention was caught again by the newspaper clipping describing his grandfather's death. To anyone else it would be no more than a grisly story, but it sent shivers down his spine as he looked beyond the blood and gore to the lives blown apart in the background.

He studied the blurred black and white photograph which accompanied the text. It showed a view of the bridge from which his grandfather had fallen, presumably taken from the train tracks below. He could make out the top of an old police car above the wall edging the bridge, and a number of uniformed men leaning over and pointing.

'How the heck would you accidentally fall over a wall that high?'

'Hmm? What?' Ruth dragged her eyes from the screen.

'Look!' He thrust the paper under her nose. 'The bridge where he fell. The wall is so high it comes up to the chest of the policemen. How on earth could he have tripped and fallen?'

Ruth took the article, repositioned her glasses and peered at it. 'I don't know. Perhaps he had been sitting on it or climbing up to get something off the ledge.'

'Seriously? Out in the middle of nowhere, first thing in the morning, you climb up onto a dirty old wall for a sit down and accidentally fall off? That doesn't ring true.' He paused as he considered the options. 'Do you think he jumped?'

Ruth's head jerked around to face him. 'No. There's nothing to suggest it, but then, all we have to go on is the story. I would expect the death certificate to arrive any day now, which will give a definitive cause of death. If it's suicide, it will say so. I think the headline would have been worded differently though, you know, not "Fatal Fall" but "Man Jumps" instead. The media were as guilty of sensationalism in the fifties as they are now.'

Tony felt surprisingly upset by the possibility his grandfather's death was intentional, angry on behalf of his grandmother. 'I sincerely hope so.'

Ruth rubbed her hand down his arm reassuringly, the warmth from her hand filtering through the thin fabric to his skin. 'It's all history, Tony. Don't let it get to you.'

He met her concerned gaze, conscious of the heat where her hand rested on his elbow. Their eyes held for a moment too long, creating an undercurrent Tony didn't know how to handle. He should have looked away, changed the subject, ignored the sensations rushing through him, but he didn't want to. Neither could he respond to those feelings; it wouldn't be right.

The front door banged against the wall as Jamie burst into the hallway, Trish and Marco a few steps behind.

'Steady on, young man!' Marco's voice cut through the atmosphere like magic.

Jamie hollered through the door, before charging up the stairs. 'Dad, I'm getting changed so I can go to the park with Aunty Trish.'

Trish poked her head around the door. 'What he means is, "Dad, is it ok if I go to the park with Aunt Trish". Is that ok?' A small frown formed as she took in the frozen scene.

Tony stepped away from the desk and from Ruth, gathering his composure. 'Of course. We have no plans.'

'Great. I won't bother taking my shoes off, then. See you in half an hour or so.' Trish sidestepped past Marco back into the hallway.

Marco blustered in and flung himself onto a stool opposite his wife, elbows on the worktop, sleeves rolled up his forearm. 'Well, Miss Marple? Have you solved the mystery?'

'Not so as you'd notice. In fact, I've come to a dead end for today, so we could head off if you're ready.'

Tony guessed her sudden desire to leave was a response to the tension they had shared. Clearly his behaviour had made her uncomfortable, and yet, she had felt something, he was sure.

Marco was confused by her attitude. 'It's not like you to give up so easily, you're usually annoyingly tenacious. What's got you beaten?'

Ruth jumped to her own defence. 'Nothing has beaten me. It's merely a pause in the investigation. As soon as Antonio's death certificate arrives, I'll be right back on it, or his birth certificate. That's an interesting branch of the history, a step into bonnie Scotland.' She turned to Tony. 'You see, Tony? Even if you can't get any further with your grandmother's line, there's a lot more to find out, a lot of other branches you could follow.'

'I know. It's just, it's such close history. I wanted to know who she was. There may be relatives, cousins, I never knew existed. Besides, now I want to know why Antonio died. There's something not right about it all.'

Marco frowned. 'What's this?'

Ruth pushed the newspaper cutting towards him and explained the conundrum. Marco read the piece thoroughly, chin in hand, then cleared his throat.

'So, you can't find your lady, Cerys?'

'No.' Tony was despondent. 'I had thought I might go to Wales, see where dad was born, where she came from, but I guess that can't happen if we can't track her down.'

'Nonsense. There is a multitude of ways to skin a cat. If you can't find her birth, try a new tack. Forget the paper trail. Go more hands on. Find your grandfather's grave. Who knows, she may have been buried with him later, assuming she didn't remarry, but either way such small towns, you're likely to come up with new leads. Everyone knows everyone in a place like that. And what about young...' He glanced at the article again, 'Young Tomasz, here? Tomasz Kowalski, who found your grandfather. It doesn't strike me as your common or garden Welsh name, and yet he's described as a local lad. He would be... what...in his seventies now? But there's a possibility he's still around, and far easier to track down than a Williams, I would imagine. He could tell you the whole story first hand. Why don't you leave Jamie with us for a weekend and take off? Have some "you" time.'

Tony was caught up by Marco's vigour. 'I guess I could.'

'Course you could. Give it some thought.' Marco got to his feet and stretched, turning to Ruth. 'Anyway, my sweetness, if we make a move now, we can beat the rush hour.'

They gathered their belongings and headed out, with a promise to be in touch as soon as anything new cropped up. Tony sat in the quiet warmth of the kitchen after they had gone, unsure which direction he should allow his mind to wander: the inquest verdict; his ancestors and the perplexing tales he was uncovering, or his friends and the confusing emotions they were promoting within him.

He cleared the table, preferring action over contemplation. One glass of brandy remained untouched, the hazel liquid glinting as it swirled at the base. He swiftly swallowed it, swept the remainder of the dishes into the sink and headed to the park, to catch up with Jamie and Trish.

CHAPTER 13

Tony stepped out of The Olive Branch days later, not only his kitchen duties complete for the day, but also another loose end tidied away. He had gone in early and nabbed Ian before he became too involved with work. Ian had confirmed, in his gruff Glaswegian way, he would be happy to take over the running of the restaurant on a semi-permanent basis, allowing Tony space to decide what he wanted to do with his life. He felt unshackled.

Jamie's school sports event was due to start late morning and Tony left the car in town, to walk and enjoy the fresh air. Aromas and snippets of music billowed out of shop doorways, teasing his senses and he absorbed them with a new joyful awareness, as if he had previously been numb.

Things seemed to be slotting into place. Only last night, Ruth had phoned. He had been agitated, waiting for her to make contact, worried he had blown their friendship. Then she called, out of the blue, and launched into conversation as if nothing had happened. She told him his grandfather's death certificate had arrived and the cause was given as 'vehicular trauma'. There was no mention of suicide. He was relieved, but still sceptical. Equally interesting, the certificate had given his address at the time of death, a short distance from the railway bridge, and Tony had decided it would be a good place to pursue his enquiries. The excitement had buoyed him along and ranged for Jamie to stay with the Rossi's for the ekend, so he could head west to play detective. The elief his relationship with Ruth, and Marco for that matter, was to continue untarnished, was enormous and he vowed to ensure boundaries were strictly maintained in future.

The crowds dwindled outside the town centre, reducing to a trickle as he approached the school grounds. He slowed to a stroll, taking in the greenery peeking over low garden fences and borders bright with vivid colour, previous rain having caused nature to explode with radiant life. A couple merged with him as they turned through the gates and exchanged small talk as they crossed the car park to the playing fields.

It was Tony's first sports day. Vicky had attended the previous year, and he was pleased to follow their lead. A young female teacher greeted them on the path, clipboard in hand and searched through a list of names to direct them to where their particular children would be. Tony was sent to the far end of the grounds and picked his way through the hordes already gathered, some standing in groups, others laying out rugs and deckchairs like it was some kind of holiday. The layout of the field bemused him, small rectangles of grass marked with white paint, tall flags at the corners, surrounded by excited parents. In his day, sports day had consisted of one large area across which all races were run one at a time. A hand on his sleeve drew his attention and he turned to see Charlie's mum, Adrienne, leaning out from a huddle of giggling, pink cheeked women.

'Hi Tony. Ready for the off?'

Although he'd done his best to avoid the woman in the past, and the gossip factory to which she belonged, he was glad to see a friendly face amongst the throng. 'I think so. I'm at area seven apparently.'

'Ah, the obstacle run. A great way to kick off. Should be fun.'

He moved closer to allow another parent to pass behind him, drawing the interested glances of the nearby women. 'How does this all work? Is there not a racetrack?'

Laughing at his naivety, she shook her head, looking up at him through lowered lashes, feeding her avid audience with flirtatious behaviour. 'Clearly a sports day virgin. It's non-competitive sports these days. The kids follow the circuit, so they get to take part in all the events. You follow your child so you can see it all.' She leaned into him and pointed out the direction the children would travel. He followed the arc of her finger, from one end of the playing field to the other, until his eyes encountered a familiar profile in the distance and his attention switched off. 'There's no winners or losers. They're all awarded points for their house group. Then there's an award ceremony, where the house groups receive either gold, silver or bronze. Everyone gets a medal...'

'Thanks. I'll see you later.' He interrupted her mid-flow, concentration focused on the figure in the distance, and strode away.

She turned to her friends, affronted by the rudeness of his dismissal.

Tony, ignorant of the chagrin he had caused, was desperately trying to keep sight of the face in the crowd. He couldn't be sure from this distance, but it looked like... He stepped around a cluster of chatting bystanders. Yes, it definitely was Nina. What was she doing here? She was talking to an older woman as they walked, her hands gesticulating in accompaniment to her speech, in her usual way. He leaned one way, then another to try and catch her eye, but to no avail.

As he drew closer, he remembered how their

last meeting had ended, and held back. After all, presumably she hadn't called him for reason. If she'd decided not to see him again, he should just accept that. He bit his lip as he considered the options. Nina stopped by area six, but her friend continued on, leaving her alone. He had to pass her. Perhaps it would be better if he kept his head down and carried on. He huffed. No, you got one chance at life and if she told him to sling his hook so be it, but if there was even the slightest odds she would give him the time of day, he had to take it. He stepped out of the flow of traffic and tapped her shoulder.

The look of pleasure which flooded her face when she saw him, filled him with a warm glow. Whatever the reason she had for not calling, it clearly wasn't that she disliked him. He could work on anything else.

'Tony. I didn't expect to see you here.' She welcomed him with a hug and the warmth radiated to his toes.

'My son, Jamie, comes here. How about you?' She had released him, but he stayed put, enjoying the closeness.

'The family I work for, my eldest charge, is at school here too. The parents are away on business, so I am representing them. Who would believe such coincidences, eh?'

'It's a small world.' He shrugged, unsure what to say. He wanted to stay with her all day, even if it was mere small talk, but what was the point if they parted later, and he was no further on. He decided straight talk was the best way forward. 'You didn't call me. I thought we had a really good time.'

He was surprised to see a blush come to her cheeks. 'Yes, I did have a good time. I enjoyed our evening ...'

'I sense a "but" coming. Go on, tell it to me straight. I can take it.' He was making a joke of it but, in reality, he wasn't sure he was ready for her answer.

She avoided his eye. 'No, there is no "but". I enjoyed

spending time with you.'

A cheer went up as the children marched, sporting shorts and t-shirts and coloured sashes. Tony spied Jamie on the edge of a group, his neck craned in search of his father, and Tony's heart melted. This was the reason he was here today. Facing Nina, he smiled. 'Saved by the bell. My self-esteem survives another day. Good to see you. Perhaps we'll catch up sometime.'

Walking away, his heart dropped, but the excitement on Jamie's face as he spotted his father among the throng lifted him. Nina could have brought a great richness to his life, but Jamie was the single most important thing in the universe to him and nothing could take that away.

Each event was a frantic mess of small bodies, laughter and cheering, followed by a mass migration from one area to another, whenever the bell rang. He laughed and applauded as Jamie bounced, ran and rolled his way through the course. Every now and then he caught Nina's eye, and she seemed equally caught up with the events, a small blonde girl clinging to her as each activity drew to a close. He suspected she hadn't given him another thought since he'd walked away.

Area three was given over to refreshments and the adults and children mingled during the hiatus, collecting juice and fruit from a table manned by a couple of assistants. He ruffled Jamie's hair.

'Did you see me throw the bean bags dad? I got seven in the bin. Did you see?' His breath was rapid as he briefly hugged his father's legs.

'I did. You were fantastic.'

'I know.'

Tony smiled at his son's lack of humility,

'I'm going to sit with Maddox cos he's on my team.' He walked backwards toward the huddle of excited children. 'If you watch, we might get a medal at the end.

Maddox says we'll definitely get a medal. See you later.'

'See you later.' Pride filled his chest, beaming from his face. He didn't care about medals or winning or any of that, but his son was a happy, vibrant child, full of fun, and that meant everything. He sipped his juice and scanned the horizon to see what was going on elsewhere, only to catch Nina watching him. She smiled fleetingly and turned away. He chuckled into his paper cup. Perhaps she had spared him some thought after all. As the bell rang to move on, a vibration in his pocket alerted him to a phone message and he retrieved it. An unknown number had texted him and he quickly read the content.

'I didn't not call you.' It read. 'I just didn't call you yet. Coffee after this? Nina x'

He swung his head to catch her eye, but she was leaning down, talking to the child skipping beside her. He grinned to himself and followed Jamie. Yes! Sports day was getting better and better.

Before the applause at the award ceremony could die away, Nina sidled up beside Tony. He stood waving, as the children marched back inside, for a celebratory party.

Nina waited for Tony's attention to turn toward her. 'You're not busy, I hope? I figured it wasn't worth going home now and coming back to collect the children later.'

'No, I'm not busy. Where did you want to go?' They joined the slow flow of parents trickling toward the exit.

'There is a cabin in the park here. They do surprisingly good latte, if you don't mind plastic cups. You're not a coffee snob, I hope?' Her tone was playful.

'I'm not any kind of snob. Chips out of the wrapper,

coffee out of plastic. As long as it tastes good.'

She cast him a sidelong glance. 'You see, I learn something new about you every time we meet.'

They were forced to pause on the pavement, as someone backed out of a car. As the body straightened up, Tony saw it was Adrienne and inwardly groaned. The rumour mill would soon be in full action. She apologised, without looking, and pushed the door closed, leaning against it to allow them by. For a moment he thought she might not notice him, but at the last second, she realised who it was and called after him.

'Oh, Tony. A few of us are going for a quick glass of something naughty to kill an hour. Fancy tagging along? You would be very welcome.' Her tone was unmistakeably flirtatious.

He turned to respond, but continued to back slowly away, trying to cut conversation short. 'It's a bit early in the day for me, but thanks for the invitation.'

'You know what they say, the sun is always over the yardarm somewhere in the world.' She raised her voice to bridge the growing distance between them.

He was reticent to offend, as their mutual child-minding arrangement was far too valuable to jeopardise, 'Next time, maybe.'

'Oh, that's a shame. Are you sure?' She wasn't going to be easily put off.

Nina pointedly grasped Tony's hand and pulled him away, proclaiming over her shoulder. 'Sorry, we have plans.'

He trotted to keep up with her suddenly increased pace, amused by the territorial show of strength, pleased to note her warm, soft hand remained holding his as they rounded the corner. 'I need to be polite. She babysits for me.'

Nina was adamant. 'Take it from me, she is a

predator. Her type do not do anything for nothing. She has, what is the saying, "her eye on you"? You need to be clear, or she will be trouble in the future.'

They slipped through black wrought iron gates into an expanse of green, punctuated by trees and shrubbery borders, providing an instant feeling of privacy from others sharing the web of pathways.

'Trouble? What kind of trouble?'

He was mocking her, and she knew it and, although she softened her voice, allowing a self-deprecating chuckle into the flow as she viewed him askance, the words were still deadly serious. 'The worst kind of trouble.'

Tony laughed aloud, taking the opportunity to soften the blow of his amusement by pulling her towards him, letting go of her hand and slipping his arm around her waist. 'Would you be jealous?'

At first, she accepted his embrace, but then put her hand to his chest and pushed him away. 'Jealous? I do not do jealous.'

He didn't want to let her go and renewed the hold of her hand so she would at least remain close.

'If you have reason to be jealous, you walk away. That is what I believe. If you don't feel you are the most important thing, if you are not confident of someone's affection, then the relationship is bad, so what's the point of staying?'

He raised his eyebrows at her philosophy. 'Harsh, but probably true.'

A blue-stained wood cabin, with open white shutters, appeared as the path hooked to the left. Bench tables spread haphazardly about the grass around it, mostly unoccupied, sparrows pecking at their bases. A radio played quietly from inside, soft jazz bleeding into the air, and the smell of coffee surrounded the kiosk like an aromatic cloud. They purchased their beverages and Nina led him past the benches and off the path to a felled tree, providing rough seating, but an uninterrupted view of a broad and, at first glance, still pond. On further inspection, the water teemed with wildlife, insects flitting about the lily pads; birds greedily watching the insects at work.

They sat quietly for a while, then Nina broke the silence. 'I did not learn much from my mother, and what I did learn was from her mistakes rather than her wisdom. Lesson number one, in relationships, do not accept second best and do not be anyone's second choice.' She looked straight at him. 'That's why I didn't call you.'

Tony frowned, confused. 'I don't…'

'Your wife.' She shrugged. 'I didn't want to risk starting something with you, if I would be second best after your wife. If you were divorced then there is anger, resentment maybe, but because she is dead, I can't compete with that. Am I selfish?'

'No.' The frown remained as he stared at his hands in his lap. 'I don't think it's selfish, but maybe a bit… unfair. You're judging me before I even have a chance to prove otherwise. I'm not going to lie. I loved Vicky. She wasn't perfect, our relationship wasn't perfect, but I did love her. She will always be a part of my life, if only because of Jamie, but I've had a long time to think about my future over the last few months and that's where my priority lies, with the future, not the past. Vicky is the past.' He met her gaze. 'Maybe we could be part each other's future?'

Her eyes narrowed as she studied him. 'If I am fair to you, maybe I am not fair to me. I don't know. When I met you, I thought "yea, he seems like a nice guy, we could have some fun", but then I met you again and it was different.'

'Different?'

'Yea. You know.' She was suddenly coy, looking away, across the pond, then back. 'I realised it was not just about fun, I was imagining you in my life. That makes it different. Also, it is not only we who could get hurt if we mess up. You have a child. Suddenly I am not thinking only of my own happiness. I have a responsibility to him too. It makes things complicated. Makes things risky, and I don't like risky.'

'Look, I don't like risky either. Nobody likes risky, do they? But sometimes you have to take the risk to achieve something really worthwhile or life would be stale. Wouldn't it?' He could see she was torn. She had been open with him, but something was still holding her back.

He ran his hand down from her shoulder to her elbow, drawing her closer. 'Look. We don't have to jump into anything feet first. We don't need to involve Jamie in anything yet. I'm happy to take one day at a time and see what happens.' He reassured. 'If losing Vicky taught me anything, it's that we only get one go at life and I would hate to miss out on having you in it, simply because I was afraid.'

Nina bit her lip as she considered his words.

He thought perhaps he was gaining ground. 'I won't ever intentionally do anything to hurt you. Besides, I don't see how you could ever be second best to anyone.'

Whether it was the boost to her ego, or the suggestion of being afraid, he didn't know, but her gaze suddenly moved from his eyes to his lips and back again and she leaned in to press hers to his. The kiss was slow and gentle, but the heat generated as skin caressed skin left him breathless with the desire for more. Her face was flushed, her expression shocked and unsure at the emotions swirling within. He brushed a loose strand of hair away from her eyes, tempted by the idea of another kiss, but he held himself in check.

'If that's taking things slow, I can live with it.' He smiled and she blushed like a schoolgirl. This was a new side of her he was seeing, a vulnerable side, but he liked it.

'I guess we should be getting back for the children. It's nearly time.'

He took her hand as she dismounted the tree trunk, helping her back onto the main track. 'Listen, I'm going to Wales at the weekend, but maybe we could get together one evening next week. Another three courses, if you can put up with me for that long?'

She tolerated his mockery and threw it back on him. 'I don't know, maybe just another coffee to be safe.'

He squeezed her hand, accepting her teasing.

'No, three courses would be good. What's in Wales? Business? Or pleasure? I've never been, is it beautiful?'

He shrugged. 'I've never been either, and it's neither business or pleasure really. Do you remember I said I was investigating my family tree? I've found a lead for my grandparents and I'm following it up, that's all. Jamie's staying with friends so I can search local church records and stuff without him getting bored. That probably sounds really dull, doesn't it, but I just want to know more about where my father came from, what made him tick.'

'If I could work out what made my father tick, I would be right there. I never could understand him. I think Wales sounds interesting. I hope you find what you're looking for.'

As they stepped back onto the main thoroughfare, Nina dropped his hand, he guessed conscious of onlookers. He was grateful for her thoughtfulness but missed the warmth of her skin touching his. Tony made a snap decision and spoke before he could change his mind. 'You could come if you like. It'll take most of the day, and it would be good to have company in the car.' He paused, afraid he had overstepped the mark. 'I'm sorry, I expect you're busy.'

'No. I'm not busy at all, and actually I would love to come.' She smiled.

'That's settled then.'

His trip to Wales suddenly felt like a whole different kind of adventure.

CHAPTER 14

As soon as Nina appeared at the gate of the tall Edwardian house where she lived, Tony jumped out to open the passenger door for her, then climbed back into the driver's seat and leant across the gap for a brief kiss.

'Are you ready?'

She smiled. 'Yes. Let's go.'

They travelled quietly until they joined the motorway, heading west, the chatter and music of the radio station filling the car.

'So, what exactly do you have planned for today?'

Tony changed gear and settled into the middle lane. 'I want to go to the graveyards local to my grandfather's last address, to see if I can find his grave and, hopefully, my grandmother's too. I can't seem to track her down. It's like she disappeared off the planet the same time he did.'

He moved into the slow lane, flicked the car to cruise control and shuffled to make himself more comfortable. 'I don't know how it works in Spain, but here, family members often have plots near each other, so I may be able to glean information to help with my search.'

'I think it's universal that families wish to be close together, even after death.'

'I suppose. I've always thought once someone's gone, they're gone. Perhaps it's because I lost my parents so early, but I have little sense of continued existence after death. It's a nice idea though, isn't it, reunion at some point in the future?'

'What happened to your parents? Do you mind talking about it?' Her voice was gently probing.

'No, I don't mind. They died in a house fire when I was thirteen. I was staying at my aunt's, because we were about to move, and they wanted to go on ahead and get the place ready. Dad travelled for work a lot and we upped sticks and followed him every few months. I was distraught when the fire happened, as you can imagine, but it feels like a lifetime ago now.' He felt no emotion as he relayed the story, as if it was someone else's history.

'It must have been terrible. I lived away from my father from a young age and that was tough enough, but to lose both your parents...' She shook her head at the thought.

'Aunt Trish was amazing. I gave her a hard time, but she took care of everything. You don't realise as a kid though, do you? I saw her as a sort of wicked godmother, telling me what I should and shouldn't do, when all I wanted was to run wild. I left the minute I could and went away to college. We've reconnected recently though, now I'm mature enough to see what a hero she was. She's like a surrogate grandmother to Jamie, which is nice, and she's filled me in about my mother's side of the family, so it's only dad's side that's blank.'

'Did he never talk to you about his family? His childhood?'

'No. He was so often away, and when he was at home, he was always busy. He wasn't the most communicative guy in the world.' Tony became thoughtful. 'I wish I'd thought to ask him, but... you know, hindsight.'

Nina rested her hand over his on the gearstick. 'I hope you find what you're looking for.'

He became conscious they had talked only of him. 'What about you? Do you know your own history, where your parents stem from?'

She laughed aloud, 'Trust me, I know enough. I don't want to look any further, there may be more skeletons in closets than I wish to find out about.'

As they approached the border, Tony pulled into a service station for a comfort break and programmed the scant details he had into his satellite navigation system. The hours had flown past. It was the longest time they had spent together uninterrupted, but he had been far from bored, sharing stories of teenage years and college escapades, the close quarters and straight roads conducive to easy communication. She returned from the station with cups of steaming coffee, a bag dangling from her wrist.

'Provisions.' She stated, shuffling in next to him. 'To keep us going if we're going to do detective work. Croissant? Or something else?' She ripped open the bag of sweet pastries.

He watched as she examined the choices, a frown of concentration playing across her forehead. The breeze had ruffled the hair around her face, leaving a stray lock across her cheek. 'Something else.' He smiled.

She glanced up at his tone and their eyes met, the frown sliding away instantly. 'Oh, yes?'

'Definitely.' He cupped her face in his hand, wiping the curl away with his thumb, and leaned in for a long, slow kiss.

As he pulled away, she grabbed an almond pastry and thrust it into his mouth. 'Here you are,' she teased. 'Something else. Now drive. We won't get to Wales sat in a car park.'

Extricating the slice from his mouth, he held his hands up, a fake browbeaten air to his voice. 'Ok. Ok,

I'm going.'

He pulled back onto the motorway. 'We leave at the next junction. Half an hour and we'll be there or thereabouts. You never quite know with country roads.'

'You want to try the mountain roads in Spain. It's like riding on a roller coaster.' She continued to eat, taking in the changing scenery.

Tony left at the next exit, onto roads swiftly more constricted than those they had left.

'Tell me what you know about this place, and your grandfather.' She sounded genuinely interested.

'As far as the place is concerned, only what I could find on the internet, so I guess we'll see when we get there. My grandfather was born in Scotland but died in Wales and I have no information in between, so goodness knows how he came to be down south.' Tony spotted a signpost with names he recognised from his research and prepared to turn off again. 'He was working as a postman when he died. Not the sort of career you move hundreds of miles for. He was married to Cerys, a local girl, quite a bit younger than him, and my dad was a baby then. It was nineteen fifty-six.'

'That's sad. What happened to him?'

'It was sad.' He confirmed, 'He was hit by a train after falling onto tracks. I found a news report in my parents' belongings recently.' He glanced at her as he manoeuvred around a corner, attempting to read her reaction. 'Perhaps it sounds gruesome, but I'd like to go there, to the place where he died.'

She frowned at his words. 'I guess it would be good to mark it in some way. Flowers, maybe? To remember him?'

'Yes, but really, it's because I need to see it to set my mind straight. Ever since I read the story, it didn't quite add up. I can't see how it could have happened and been an accident. His death certificate doesn't suggest otherwise, but I need to clarify it in my own head. My friends, Ruth and Marco, who have been helping me with the research, think I should speak to the young man who was there on the day, if he's still alive and I can find him, to hear what he has to say.'

'You think he was murdered?' She stared at him.

'No, that never crossed my mind.' It hadn't occurred to him a third party could have been involved. 'I think perhaps he jumped. Suicide. I mean, why would anyone want to kill a country postman, a family man? He wasn't exactly a high roller.'

'Suicide? That's horrible.' She breathed deeply. 'But does it matter? I mean, does it make a difference to anything?'

'I suppose the only difference it makes is to the type of man it makes him. It helps me paint a picture. What sort of man kills himself, with a beautiful young wife and a new-born baby at home?'

'A man who is very troubled, I suppose.'

Tony pulled up at a small cross way. The roads were clear in every direction. The voice on the navigation system had instructed them to take a left, but a cracked wooden signpost displayed several destinations and one in particular stood out. 'That's it. If we take a right here, that's where he died. Should we go there first?'

'It seems to me, it's where you need to go, to get the most important answers.'

Considering he was looking into a tale from years earlier, which had no bearing on his life now, this suddenly felt extremely important, and his heart thudded in his chest.

Nina squeezed his knee, waiting for a response. 'Come on. Let's go and see, together.'

He looked at her, smiling and frowning at once, confused by the emotions battling within him. 'Yes. Let's go.'

They followed the road as it narrowed almost to single track, field gateways the only means of passing any vehicles they encountered. Tony focused on looking for signage as they headed into deeper countryside. Tall oaks leaned over the road, away from a common wind route, casting sufficient shadow to make it seem evening had arrived early. The road swept into a wide bend as they emerged, and the ground either side fell away, suddenly allowing sweeping views to the left and right, obstructed only by a cob stone wall.

Tony slammed on the brakes. 'This is it!'

Nina grasped the dashboard at the abrupt stop. 'What? Here?'

'Yes, here! I recognise it from the photo.' He released the seatbelt, threw the door open and slid out. Three short steps took him to the wall, and he leaned against it, to take in the scene and the distance from the bridge to the ground below. His stomach clenched as the drop became clear. The rail tracks were no longer there, only a tarmacked path marking where they had once been, but otherwise he guessed the scene had changed little in sixty years. The rounded coping stones pressed against his chest as he stretched to see the ground and, as he became aware of the contact, he ran his hands along them to either side, studying their contour.

Nina strolled up and stood to one side, placing a supportive hand on his shoulder.

'You see?' He turned, holding her shoulder with one hand and indicating the wall with a swing of his other arm. 'How could a person accidentally fall over a barrier this high? It's not possible.'

He marched across the hump of the bridge and paused at the crest. 'To land on the tracks he would have had to go over here! That's madness!'

Nina followed his lead. 'It does seem unlikely now,

but perhaps the wall was not always so high. Many things may have changed in such a long time.'

He considered the logic, crouched down and examined the brick work, brushing his fingers over the dusty pointing. 'No, I don't think so. It all looks old and worn. If a level had been added we would be able to see the join, surely? In the type of stone? Or the colour of the mortar?'

She stood back, observing the construction. 'I don't see any markings, but it is an old wall. It may have been completely rebuilt since your grandfather's time and we would know nothing about this. It's impossible to know these things, isn't it?'

He looked around, rubbing the top of his hair with the flat of his hand, as if, if he studied it long enough all would become clear. 'There must be some way…'

A black Labrador emerged from the woods behind their car, snuffling at the ground close to the back tyres, pulling a middle-aged man, struggling to hold on to its lead. The man was muttering, shoulders hunched, heaving the dog away from the vehicle. He spotted the couple on the bridge and his demeanour immediately brightened.

'Morning!' He made to pass them, carrying on toward a small terrace of houses, nestled to one side beyond the bridge.

Tony saw his opportunity. 'Excuse me! Are you local to the area?'

'I am that. Have you lost your way, squire?' He seemed eager to be of service, back tracking a few steps and the Labrador doubled back, sniffing Tony's feet.

Tony bent down to fuss the dog, rubbing its ears. 'No, no. We know where we are. I was wondering about the bridge. How long has it been here, do you know? Has it been rebuilt at all?'

The man removed his flat cap, rubbing the wrist

of the same hand across his forehead. 'It's been here donkey's years, as far as I know, but as to building works, I can't help, I'm afraid. The railway line fell foul of old Beeching in the sixties, so I understand, but although I'm local now, I've only been here a couple of years, since I retired. If you want to know the history of the place you could pop down to The Lamb.' He hitched his thumb over his shoulder, in the direction he was walking.

'The Lamb?'

'Yes, old Mike, who runs it, is born and bred to the place. He knows everything there is to know that's happened around here, in the last fifty years, anyway.' He edged away, the dog pulling towards home.

'Thanks.' Tony turned back to face the wall and the broad gap in the forest, where the old railway had been cut through, absorbing the feel of the place. Nina was only a short way away, gazing into the distance and he reached for her hand. 'It's lovely, isn't it? Peaceful. Or at least, it would be, if I could get the image of my grandad lying dead down there out of my head.'

She released his hand and slipped her arm around him. 'You should not think about it in that way. It was a long time ago. It's not good to hold on to the past if it is painful.'

'I know.' He shook his head, as if to rid it of the images.

'Do you want to speak to the man in the village? You think it might help?'

'It can't hurt, can it? Come on.' He patted her on the back and headed back to the car. 'Jump in. I shouldn't leave the car like this, blocking the road.'

The pub was a stubby, thatched affair, crouched at the edge of the road, down a lane. A hand-painted parking sign indicated a hidden entrance just beyond it, curling around to the rear of the property. It was currently empty. They parked and made their way through the back entrance to a low ceilinged, cosy interior, resembling a homely cottage with a bar in the back corner.

Despite the absence of other customers, the barman, almost as squat and rectangular as the building he presided over, stood behind the bar, polishing glasses. He nodded in acknowledgement of their arrival and paused in his endeavours, waiting for one of them to speak.

'Hi. Are you Mike? A guy down the road said a Mike worked here, would know the history of the place?'

'Did he now?' The man's eyebrows raised a level at this piece of information, before settling back in their usual resting place, low on his brow. 'What can I get you?'

Clearly a purchase was required before any exchange of knowledge. Tony turned to Nina, hovering behind him. 'Drink? Fruit juice or something?'

She nodded and slotted into a bench seat, close to the bar, leaning against a neat little round table littered with beermats. Tony ordered and, while the barman was about his business, returned to the topic at hand. 'Have you lived here long?'

'Man and boy, in this very place. This was my father's pub before me, so it was.' An air of pride marked his words.

'It's lovely.' Tony accepted his change and passed Nina her drink, before returning for his own.

'You're not Welsh yourself, are you? What brings you down this way?'

Tony picked up the glass and leant against the bar. 'My grandparents were Welsh.' He guessed the fact may buy him brownie points. 'From not far from here actually. I'm rediscovering my roots, so to speak.'

The publican flicked his tea towel to rest over his shoulder and winked, settling in for a long conversation. 'You can take the man out of Wales, but you can't take Wales out of the man.' He reached across and patted Tony hard on the arm. 'It's in your blood man.'

'So I'm starting to discover. Listen, I was looking at the bridge across the rail track down the way. How long has it stood there? It looks very old.'

'Old? I would say so. The first bridge was built there in the dark ages. Been replaced many times since then, of course, stronger and broader to fit modern times.'

'Really? When was it last worked on? Recently?'

'Not so as I can remember.' He rubbed his chin, searching his memory. 'There was some strengthening carried out some years back, underneath that was, to the pillars. Some pillock tried to drive a juggernaut across it. You know the type, latest sat nav, but no brain cells to rub together. Proper palaver that was. Had to get cranes in and all sorts. As if you need sat nav to tell you a bridge that size wasn't up to the job. I ask you, what's the world coming to? Common sense has gone out the window.'

Picking up a glass, he resumed polishing, rhythmically rubbing the exterior then holding it up to the meagre light, checking for smears. After a few moments he stopped abruptly and stared at Tony. 'Here. You're not one of those "no win, no fee" merchants, are you? Tripped over a loose stone or suchlike? We don't take kindly to that kind of thing round here.'

'No, no, nothing like that.' Tony was quick to reassure, keen to keep such a valuable source of local knowledge on side. 'There was an accident here, about sixty years ago, that's all. My grandfather fell from the bridge.'

'Did he now?' He slotted the spotless glass onto a shelf above the optics.

'Apparently. I found a newspaper report, but it was a bit vague. I hoped if I came here, I might be able to find out what happened.'

The barman nodded, his only response a gruff grunt.

Tony sat next to Nina, sipping his drink, concerned what had appeared to be a promising lead had dried up prematurely. Perhaps he should have used a different approach. He met Nina's eye and she smiled, and he couldn't help wondering what he was doing, sitting there fretting about something that happened two generations ago. He had almost decided upon leaving when the barman broke the silence.

'Sixty years ago, you say?

Tony quickly confirmed the fact. 'Yes, nineteen fifty-six.'

The barman shook his head, smiling. 'I was only a nipper back then, of course, but I have heard it talked of since. Quite a big story in a place like this, as you can imagine. One of my old regulars was there when it happened, so he was. Used to harp on about it every time he had one too many, which was most Friday nights. Got quite agitated if I let him go on. Many's the time I had to pack him off home early with a flea in his ear. Put everyone off their ale if I didn't keep an eye on him, he would.'

Tony slammed his glass down on the table in excitement, small drops of lemonade spraying out onto his hand and the surrounding table. 'Really?'

'Yes. Old Tommy Poland, we called him. No idea what his proper name was, mind.'

Tony's heart sank at the past tense. 'Tomasz Kowalski, I'll bet. He was mentioned in the article as a witness. Has he passed away?'

'Old Tommy? No. He moved into town, living with his niece there, so I understand. Getting on a bit, you know. Needed a bit of support, but still alive and kicking.'

'Town?' He had visions of trying to trace the man in a massive, cosmopolitan city.

'About five miles up the road. He pops back once in a while to catch up with the local news, you know, but I've not seen him for a month or two. I'm sure I would have heard if anything had happened to him though. He's got old friends around here.'

'Do you have an address for him? A contact number?' Tony grasped Nina's hand and squeezed it tight.

'No, but he shouldn't be too difficult to track down. His local's the White Hart now, up by the playing field. If you can't find him in the phone book, you could nip in there.' He checked over his shoulder and through a door to the rear, to ensure no one was listening and lowered his voice. 'Have a word with Maggie behind the bar. Old friend of mine, she is. Tell her Mike said hello, will you?'

Tony thanked him, downed his drink and replaced both empty glasses on the bar before rushing out to the car, Nina following in his wake. As soon as they reached the drive he pulled her into his arms, hugging her so tight her feet left the floor.

She laughed at his exuberance. 'This is good news, yes?'

'This is really good news.' He confirmed. 'I've got a feeling we could be getting somewhere. Let's go and find Tommy.'

CHAPTER 15

In town, they headed into a café to purchase coffees and borrow a local telephone directory. Within a short time, they had narrowed their search to two possible numbers and one call was sufficient to locate their man. With little questioning, Tommy's niece confirmed the address, and agreed a meeting in the afternoon, when he would have returned from watching cricket. She had no doubt he would be happy to discuss the events of years gone by, assuring them he often talked of it. The incident had made quite an impact on him.

With time to spare before the meeting, Tony obtained directions to the two local cemeteries and drove straight to the nearest one. A stile barred the side entrance to the churchyard, and Tony climbed over, before lending a hand to Nina. They strolled along the cracked stone path to the main area of the graveyard, the banks either side of them teeming with fragrant meadow flowers. Buoyed on by recent success, Tony almost expected his grandfather's grave to be obvious the moment he entered the grounds, but as they drew level with the first row of headstones, the extent of the yard became apparent, and he realised there was a lot of work to be done. Undeterred, they passed along the regimental channels between the stones, checking the engraving on each one. It was a laborious task, the writing on many of the tablets reduced to fragments through the passage of time, and what remained was barely legible under the lichen and staining. Ten minutes into the task, they split their efforts, to cover ground more quickly.

Tony read each message carefully. The brief, but often poignant words, were powerful reminders that an actual person rested beneath, and it felt like he owed them the respect of reading their last imprints on the world. Nina made lighter work of it, checking only the names before moving on. His attention remained on the sad notations in front of him, a dull ache in his heart. He finished the text and raised his eyes to run over the entire yard. So much loss.

Tony spotted Nina, almost at the end of her row, nearly back to the path which led to the giant doors into the church. She had stopped and was talking to an older man. The man gripped a briefcase under one arm, while pointing with the other, sweeping it across great swathes of the churchyard. As he straightened up, took his leave of Nina and carried on his way, Tony could see the man had a clerical collar topping off his blue, short-sleeved shirt. Nina waved, beckoning Tony over, half turning toward the other side of the church building. As he approached, she shouted and began walking slowly backwards in the direction the Vicar had pointed.

'We need to look at the back of the church. This part is too old and newer graves here are only part of family groups. The reverend said there is a section at the back which dates to the nineteen fifties.'

He caught up with her. 'Did he know of my grandfather? Is the grave definitely there?'

They rounded the corner together. A broad expanse of tombs and monuments revealed themselves as they did so, and Tony wondered where to begin.

'No. He has only been here a few years, but he said if we could not find it we should go and see him inside.

There is a book where such things are registered, and he may be able to find an entry. Here.' She selected a junction in the path and turned away from the building. 'He said we should start from this edge and up to the fence. They should all be from the right period.'

She reeled off dates as they passed each tomb, her head ticking from side to side as she strode forward. 'Forty-six. Forty-eight. Fifty-one. Here! Tony, this is where we need to look.' She backtracked and indicated either side. 'The fifties start along here. You go that way. I'll go this way and see where we find nineteen fifty-six.'

They covered the entire section, locating a small huddle of graves dating to the correct year, but Tony's grandfather was not among them. They checked and double checked, but Antonio Viscount did not appear anywhere.

Tony rasped his hand through his hair. 'It's not here. After all this, I bet it's at the other cemetery.'

Nina stood akimbo, hands on hips. 'You're probably right, but let's check with the reverend before we go. Who knows, perhaps he is with family here somewhere. There may be relations you never knew about hidden away. Come.'

He followed her back to the church entrance, chuckling under his breath. When Nina was on a mission, she was a force to be reckoned with.

The vicar sat at a desk at the rear of the church, books and pens spread in a halo around him. The late morning sun spilled through a stained-glass window, creating a kaleidoscope of light on the slate paving and the adjacent wall, and he was staring up at it, as if conjuring images from the flickering specks. He glanced around as the door creaked and pushed himself away from the desk.

'Did you find what you were looking for?' His

sonorous voice resonated through the atmosphere of the empty church.

Nina replied. 'No, I'm afraid not. I wondered if you would check your register.' She looked at the pile of paperwork he had abandoned on the table. 'If you are not too busy?'

'Not at all.' He waved for them to follow him down the aisle toward the pulpit. 'Just working on the sermon for tomorrow, but currently find myself between ideas. A short distraction is exactly what is required. I'll go back to the drawing board in a few minutes and find inspiration, no doubt. Sometimes you can't see things for looking. Is it your grandfather you're looking for, did you say?'

'Not mine.' Nina patted Tony on the shoulder. 'My friend here, it is his grandfather.'

The vicar bypassed the pulpit and stepped around to a stumpy door leading into a small storage area, lined with boxes and filing cabinets.

'Aah, right! Fifties you said, didn't you?' He heaved open a drawer, flicked through the contents and closed it again, moving to the drawer below. Finally, he pulled out a box file and rested it in a gap on a shelf, so he could open it without fully bearing the weight. He retrieved a hard-backed tome from the box, checked the rest of the contents and closed the lid. 'Only one register for the fifties. We're very good at keeping records you know, churches. Provided nothing intervenes, bombs dropping, that sort of thing, we usually have documents going back hundreds of years. Fantastic historical resource often overlooked. What year exactly was he interred; do you know?'

They relayed the information, and he turned the pages, first in large chunks then, a few pages at a time. 'Of course, we don't have the same quantity of events these days. Weddings and burials, and christenings for that matter, are not as common as they used to be. Still a few traditionalists out there, but we've lost a lot of trade to the registry office and crematorium in recent times. All very well, if that's what you like, but there's something about the grandeur of a proper old church which makes for a memorable ceremony, don't you agree?' He didn't seem to expect a reply. 'What was grandpa's name?'

Tony was straining not to grab the book and look for himself, such was his impatience. 'Antonio Viscount.'

The vicar ran his finger down the copperplate entries, muttering names under his breath as he did so. 'Viscount. Hmm. Not a name I've come across in these parts. Certainly no parishioners of that name now, though numbers have dropped since those days. Viscount. Viscount. He may have been buried at the chapel cemetery, of course. The Welsh do love a chapel. No, no. Here he is. Antonio Viscount.'

Both Tony and Nina surged forward to read the entry, and the vicar edged away to make room. He rubbed his finger along the line, highlighting the text.

'Yes, he was buried here. The service paid for by Mr Reginald Williams.' He looked up at Tony for signs of recognition but saw none. 'He wasn't placed in a family plot though, he's on the far right, at the back, by the gate to the old vicarage orchard.'

Tony clicked his fingers as the information pieced together in his head. 'Cerys was a Williams. I wonder if Reginald was her father. It would make sense, young couple, possibly struggling financially. She may have had to turn to her father to pay for the burial.'

'And Cerys was...?' The cleric left the question hanging.

'His wife. My grandmother. My father was only born a matter of weeks before his father died.'

'Aah! So, if I look back a page or two, I might find

a christening entry for him. Although I don't recall seeing any other mention of Viscounts anywhere.' He was already working backward from the burial notation. 'Here you are. Ah, that explains it.'

'What?'

'Cerys Williams christened a little boy here. Robert was his name. Does that tally?'

'Yes. My father was Robert Viscount.'

'There you are then.' He paused for Tony to put two and two together, then filled in the gaps. 'They weren't married. Rarer in those days, I'll grant you, but it did happen.'

'They weren't married?' Tony's mind tingled with the new data. 'That's why we can't find a marriage certificate, or a death certificate for Cerys Viscount. It's just, the newspaper article referred to him as married, and the photos of them together, it probably sounds silly, but they looked married. That's what assumptions do for you, lead you up the garden path.'

'Happens to us all. I hope it's helpful anyway, set your search straight.'

'Yes, it does, thank you. I've got some rethinking to do, but at least we have a solid base to work from.' He turned back to the vicar. 'Could you point me in the right direction for the grave? I would like to pay my respects while I'm here.'

The vicar looked taken aback. 'Oh, I'm sorry. I should have said. There is no grave as such. He was buried in the paupers' area. Mr Williams paid only a nominal amount for a funeral service, so Antonio was interred on land purchased by a benefactor many years previously for the purpose of providing burial grounds for the poor. There are no headstones or markings, as coffins were placed close together to maximise the usage of the plot. I can show you where the plot is if that's of any help?'

Tony felt the excitement of discovering his grandfather's whereabouts seeping away, replaced by sadness that the man's existence was so little marked in the world. 'Yes. Yes, please. I suppose there doesn't have to be a marked grave. I can still pay my respects.'

'Of course you can.' The reverend placed a solid hand on Tony's shoulder and guided him from the storage room and the church, into the fresh air. 'I think our dry spell may be coming to an end. There's a moisture to the air which wasn't here earlier.' He made small talk as they picked their way through rough ground.

When they stopped, it was the vicar's turn to appear uncertain. He waved an embarrassed hand over a patch of brambles, overgrowing from the hedge, creeping towards the closest marble slab, some feet away. 'This is it.' He shrugged. 'I should have a quiet word with the gardener when he comes next, tidy the place up a bit.'

Tony couldn't speak, so Nina stepped to the fore. 'Thank you. You have been very helpful.' She shook his hand and he tiptoed away.

Tony studied the ground, trying to detect some sign of someone lying below, his face set in a grim frown. 'It's sad, isn't it? To end up here, like this, with nothing to show for your time in the world but a bump in the ground.'

She stepped toward him and hooked her arm into the crook of his, without speaking.

'It doesn't make any sense. The photos. They looked like such a happy couple. I can't believe he ended up here, like this. Abandoned.'

'It does not mean she did not love him.' She reassured. 'Perhaps there was not the money to do it properly. What choice did she have? You cannot tell now, maybe then, she visited, brought flowers, but it was such a long time ago, we could never know.'

Tony released her hand from his elbow and clasped

it between both of his, drawing her towards him until he looked straight into her eyes. She gazed back uncertainly. He leaned in and kissed her slowly and gently on the lips. 'I'm glad you came with me.' He kissed her again, then rested his forehead lightly against hers. 'Thank you.'

Stepping back, he backed away from the wasteland and led her to the path. 'Come on.' He muttered. 'Let's get some lunch.'

CHAPTER 16

True to the reverend's prediction, the afternoon closed shrouded in a heavy drizzle. Tony and Nina had a late lunch in a pretty pub with picture windows at the back, overlooking a bank of lace cap hydrangeas, until it was time to make their way to Tomasz's address.

The house was a tiny red brick affair, mid-terrace, with a handkerchief yard, hemmed by a short block wall and bordered by back-to-back parked cars. By the time Tony had inched his car into a tiny space, they were late. They urgently identified the correct gate and strode toward the front door, where a wizened face appeared through half-closed vertical blinds and the door was thrown open before they had time to ring the bell.

The old man was short, partly thanks to the stoop of his shoulders, and he rested on a wooden cane with one hand as he ushered them inside with the other. His head was almost completely bald except for a few dark strands curving from behind one ear, across the dome to the other ear. A middle-aged woman in lycra, who proved to be the voice on the phone earlier, carried in a tray laid with cups and saucers, biscuits and an old-fashioned tea pot, complete with red knitted cosy. She kissed her elderly uncle on the head before heading out for a run, so the group could talk. In the pause after the front door banged shut, the man looked at the pair and shook his head, as if in disbelief.

'So, you're Cerys's grandson, are you? As if I couldn't

tell. You've such a look of her, about the nose, though the rest of you is all your grandfather, there's no doubt.' His accent at first appeared thoroughbred Welsh, but a tell-tale inflection suggested another influence.

Tony was taken aback at the familiarity suggested by the speech. It was peculiar for a stranger to recognise him in faces of people he himself had not known existed until a few weeks ago. 'You knew them then?'

'Of course I knew them. I grew up with Cerys. We went to the same school, though she had a few years on me, but I always had one eye on her, as did most of the lads in these parts. A beauty, she was. Your grandfather was a lucky man, I'll say that for him.' Tomasz was staring into the mid-distance as he reminisced, a happy sigh punctuating the end of his speech.

Tony was loathe to drag the man away from happy memories, but in the interests of obtaining answers, edged him towards the event which had brought them together. 'He wasn't always lucky though, was he? Not at the end, anyway.'

The senior's eyes quickly snapped back from far away, the happy glint replaced by something sharper. 'No. Many's the time I wished I could be him, but not that day, that's for sure.' He looked out the window for a time and Tony wondered if he was using the hiatus to pull himself together. 'I suppose you and your young lady want to hear the story?'

Nina leaned towards him, but on his perch, in an upright armchair, directly in front of the window, he was beyond her reach. 'Only if you are happy to tell us. We would not wish to upset you. You were such a young man. It must have been a terrible thing for you.'

Tomasz studied her for a few seconds then turned to Tony and winked. 'You're a lucky duck yourself.' He thrust his hand between the seat cushions, rummaged around and, pulling out a miniature bottle of rum, threw it to Nina. 'Put a drop of that in the brew. It'll oil the wheels along, you understand.'

Nina looked to Tony for guidance, and he shrugged, entertained by the man's eccentricities. She poured them all a cup of tea, adding a slug from the bottle to each, before handing them out.

Tomasz took a long vibrating sip and settled back, resting the cup and saucer on his rounded belly, eyeing them over the rim. 'I didn't know your grandfather very well. He didn't mix with us of course, because we were just kids. Nobody could work out what Cerys saw in him really. He was so old you see, at least he was to us young'uns, and she was so popular. She could have had anyone, but when love comes knocking, there's no arguing, so I'm told.' He winked at Nina again.

'How did they meet? Do you know?' Tony urged him on.

'I always assumed they bumped into each other when he was doing his round or something, but I'm only surmising, you understand. I used to see him sometimes. He'd be doing the post, when I was delivering the papers, so our paths would cross now and then. That's how I came to be down in the village the morning it happened. It wasn't my usual round, a bit of a trek on the pushbike, but I'd stand in now and again for a bit of extra cash when old Owen needed me to, if one of the other boys was off sick or whatnot.' He paused for another sip and smacked his lips appreciatively.

'The post van was parked on the village side of the bridge, and I'd passed your grandpa on the footpath down to the old railway cottages on the far side. Whistling like a good one, he was. I remember thinking he'd got plenty enough to be happy about and I'd be whistling too, in his shoes. Anyway, I delivered the papers to the cottages. Can't have been more than a few minutes 'cause there's only half a dozen down there, though I stopped for a quick natter with Nancy Evans, I admit. She was admiring my new bike, I remember, and I didn't mind showing it off, as you can imagine. Beautiful it was. My pride and joy.'

He slipped into the past, smiling to himself, and shaking his head at the memory, then snapped back to the present. 'Anyway, where was I? Oh yes. I thought I heard shouting when I came back up the footpath. Not an argument, you understand, just a raised voice, calling out, but I couldn't work out where it was coming from. Then, when I got to the bridge, I saw his bag in the middle of the road, letters all over the path, like he'd turned it upside down and shook it, and I realised the yelling was coming from down below. So, I looked over the wall, and there he was, laid out on the tracks, all broken and bleeding.' Tomasz' voice dropped to a croak and his body shuddered at the image, setting his cup rattling in the saucer.

Nina scrambled to her feet, reached out with the pot, and poured him more tea, patting his forearm in comfort. Tomasz glanced purposefully at the rum bottle, on the edge of the tray, and nudged his cup as encouragement. She poured him a generous serving and returned to her seat.

Tony desperately wanted to hear what happened next, but not at the expense of tormenting the old man. 'I'm sorry. If you would rather not go over it again...'

'Between you and me,' his voice was a hoarse whisper. 'I go over it every night in my sleep, so I can't see as how saying it out loud can be any worse.' He downed the contents of his cup and set it to one side. 'I was fourteen years old. Fourteen! I didn't know what to do, as you can imagine. I thought about running to the pub for help, but there was no early opening in those days, so no one would have been around except the Landlord, and I knew from experience he would more likely still be drunk from the night before. I thought about running away too, if truth be told, but then I remembered the seven fifty from Cardiff would be along soon, and I had no choice but climb down and see what could be done.'

He pinched the skin on the end of his chin between finger and thumb hard, as he called up the pictures from the past. 'His legs were broke. I didn't need a doctor to tell me that. They were sticking out at angles, completely unnatural, and the ground around him was wet with the blood he'd lost, from a gash on the side of his head, more than likely. By the time I managed to get down the slope, he'd stopped shouting. Didn't have it in him anymore, I suppose. But he could still manage a few words.' Tomasz glanced up and met Tony's eye. 'He knew my name. I didn't know he knew me. I was just one of the lads, you know, but he knew my name and that made it personal somehow. "Help me, Tommy", he said. He was crying and groaning with the pain, but he saw me, and he knew me, and he said it twice, "Help me, Tommy", but I couldn't help. I tried, but I couldn't do it.' His voice trailed off.

Tony levered himself up from the low sofa and crouched in front of the old man, holding him by the shoulder. 'You did everything you could. It was a tragic accident, that's all.'

'That's what the police said, but then they said a lot of things.' There was an air of bitterness about the comment. 'I tried to move him. I saw the train round the corner at the bottom of the valley, and I tried to get him out the way, but he was too heavy and the pain… He screamed every time I pulled at him, and in the end, I couldn't stomach it. All the time the train was coming closer, and I just didn't know what to do. Then he passed out and I thought, "I can drag him out now and he won't be any the wiser", but I grabbed his shoulder, and he came to. His head went back, and he looked right at me.' The momentum of Tomasz's speech had increased with every word, but paused abruptly as he took a ragged breath, returning as a slow hoarse whisper. 'He looked right at me, and the pain was gone. His face was as calm as if he was just relaxing in the sun and he said, "He found me, Tommy. He found me". If my ear hadn't been right up against his mouth, I wouldn't have known what he said, but it was, and I did. Then the train was on us. I'll never forget the rush of the wind as it passed, the smell of oil, the screech of brakes. I fell back and he was gone.'

They fell into silence as the story ended and the words were absorbed by all.

Tony was the first to break the silence. 'He found me? What did he mean?'

'Your guess is as good as mine. I didn't see anybody else there. The police said I made a mistake, that he said "Tommy, you found me", that he was confused, or I was confused, but I swear to you, I wasn't. He said it clear as day, "**he** found me". Maybe they were right about him, though. Goodness knows he'd been through enough for his thoughts to be muddled, but he was so calm and clear about it. I don't know. The police wouldn't have it, anyway. They put it down as an accident, so an accident it was.'

'There was no investigation? No inquiry?' Tony sat back in his seat, shocked by the revelation.

'Not so far as I know. I didn't let it go, not at first anyway, but the local bobby came to see me and my mother at home some months later, told me to keep quiet. I was upsetting the family apparently, with my "gossip", they called it. So, I shut up - I wouldn't have upset Cerys for the world. Time moved on, but I never rested easy on the matter. How could I? I see his face again every time the sun goes down.'

Nina's face was pale. 'It was a terrible thing, but the past is the past. There was nothing more you could have done. You must be satisfied you did all you could.'

The man shrugged.

Tony felt for the elderly man, this one horrific event had clearly left an imprint which had stayed with him forever. 'I didn't know my grandfather, and it was a shock to find out what happened, but I'm glad to know you were with him at the end. I don't suppose anything short of a professional medical team could have done more for him and even then, I doubt it. Thank you for trying.'

An atmosphere had settled over the room, everyone subdued by the retelling. Tony felt a need to get away, to clear his head. Sensing Tomasz could also use space with his thoughts, they made to leave. He accompanied them to the door, leaning even more heavily on his stick than before. Tony thanked him again, patting his shoulder, before passing into the yard, internally analysing the afternoon's revelations.

'Remember me to Cerys when you see her, won't you?' Tomasz called after them, his voice chirpier.

Tony stopped in his tracks at his grandmother's name, the sole of his shoe slipping on the gravel with the suddenness of his manoeuvre. He had been concentrating so much on Antonio, he had forgotten to ask about his grandmother. 'Cerys?'

'Yes. Well, I'm guessing you'll be calling to see her while you're here, won't you? You wouldn't be coming all this way and not.'

'She's still alive?'

'Of course. Is that not where you got my name from?' At Tony's look of bewilderment, Tomasz continued. 'She's in The Warren now, the residential home next to the secondary school. I've not seen her in a good while, my legs being how they are, but my neighbour visits her every now and again. She's got nobody else local, you understand, not since your father left.'

Tony reached for the man's hand and pumped it gratefully. 'Thank you, Tommy. I didn't know. Thank you.'

He walked down the path to where Nina was waiting on the pavement, her face alight with excitement at this new discovery, and they joined hands as they retraced their steps to the car.

He couldn't quite believe it. 'Did you hear that? My granny is still alive!'

Nina giggled at his enthusiasm. 'I know.' She hugged his hand to her chest. 'What a day, huh? Let's go and find her.'

CHAPTER 17

They traced the nursing home where Cerys was living easily, but staff informed them she had already been given her medication, and settled for the night, and was unable to see visitors until the next day. Tony was torn. He had planned to return home the same night, but now he knew she was alive, he didn't want to leave without seeing her. Jamie was catered for until Sunday lunchtime, but Nina had expected only a day trip. She had been listening to his side of the conversation with the home from the passenger seat and, when it ended, he wondered how to address the issue.

As the silence lengthened, she prompted. 'Well?'

'She's already been put to bed.' He huffed. 'We can't see her until tomorrow.'

'But that's ok. Isn't it? You've found a grandmother you didn't know you had, and it's only one more day.'

'I know, but I said I'd get you home tonight. I don't want you to think I planned this, I mean, that's assuming you're even able to stay. I can still take you back if you need to go.' He had made the offer, but his heart wasn't in it.

Nina shook her head. 'This is not a big problem. I don't need to be back until late tomorrow. I'm sure we can find a hotel. They have hotels in Wales, yes?'

'Yes, of course, but it wasn't my intention, to get you alone in a hotel somewhere.'

'Tony. I know this.' Her tone was light. 'Anyway, just because we stay, it doesn't mean we must share a room.

No problem.'

Tony felt like a fool, blowing the issue out of proportion. 'Of course. Two rooms.' He put the car into gear, a small frown settling over his brows. 'There was a hotel off the roundabout by the industrial estate. I'll drive down and see what they've got.'

The hotel had plenty of space. They checked in, booked a table at the restaurant for later in the evening and took a lift to the second floor. Mounted signs pointed them to adjacent rooms at the far end of a long corridor. Tony felt a little awkward as they arrived at their prospective rooms, but Nina gave him a quick wave, hoisted her rucksack through the door and announced she would meet him later in the bar.

Tony let himself into his own room, hung his jacket on a plastic hanger in an open wardrobe by the entrance and sat on the bed, wondering what to do for the next two hours. The room was pleasant enough, with a double bed, a pine desk, doubling as a dressing table, and a flat screen television, mounted on the wall opposite the bed. He found the remote control and switched it on, flicking through the channels. Nothing appealed to him, so he turned it off, reaching for his phone instead.

A brief call to Jamie, via Marco, reassured him all was well at home, and he took the opportunity to update Ruth with the day's events, carefully omitting details relating to Nina. Ruth promised she would get onto the search for his great grandparents, and the Scottish connection to his ancestry, now they were sure they were following the right leads. He finished the call with renewed excitement and headed for a shower, washing away the strains of the day. Redressing in the same clothes and flattening his hair with his fingers, he settled on the bed, and viewed Gaelic television, over the top of his crossed feet, waiting for the clock to tick round to the agreed meeting time with Nina.

Tony woke to a loud Welsh female voice, repeatedly shouting a phrase on the television, which his fuddled brain could neither decipher nor ignore. He opened his eyes and the digital numbers at the bottom of the screen broke through the haze. He was fifteen minutes late for dinner. Jumping off the bed in a state of panic, he turned off the TV and checked his appearance in the mirror, before exiting. Nina's door was closed, and he rapped on it as he passed, in case she too was running late, but with no response from within, he jogged to the lift.

The lobby was busy with huddles of people and luggage, waiting for the reception desk, but there was no sign of Nina. He bypassed them and continued through double doors into a wide l-shaped bar area. The counter jutted round the corner from where he had entered, with upright pillars of pale brickwork restricting the view. Tony wandered the length of the hostelry, checking alcoves and tables, and back again, eventually concluding Nina had already moved through to the restaurant. He hated being late and it wasn't the impression he wanted her to have of him.

A wooden podium instructed diners to wait to be seated and he shuffled from foot to foot as he waited for the Maitre'd to appear, leaning to try and spot Nina inside. After a couple of minutes, with only the distant view of a waitress buzzing between customers, his impatience got the better of him and Tony rounded the lectern and paced down the central aisle. In the back corner, the absence of both the restaurant manager and Nina was explained.

She was resting back in her seat at a small table there, smiling and chatting over a large glass of red wine to a young, handsome uniformed man, leaning on the back of the chair opposite. Their interaction was animated, drawing the smiling attention of other diners and irritated Tony immensely. He strode forward, deposited a territorial peck on Nina's cheek and slid in front of the other man to claim his seat.

'Ah, the wanderer appears.' The waiter's accent matched Nina's and Tony realised he had not made out their conversation as he approached as they had both been speaking Spanish.

'Yes, sorry I'm late. I would have been here sooner if I hadn't been waiting out front to be seated.' Tony's dry remark was aimed with a steady gaze at the other man.

The man seemed to remember his position and stepped away, the heels of his shoes snapping together as he whipped a notebook from his back pocket. 'Can I get the gentleman a drink?'

Tony ordered a glass of wine, with a straight face, only producing a smile when he faced Nina, after the man had walked away. Her eyebrows almost nestled in her hairline at his behaviour, but she said nothing, and Tony felt obliged to fill the quiet. 'They won't win any prizes for customer service in this place.'

'Actually, he was very helpful and friendly. He grew up not far from me, so he brought me a complimentary drink.' She raised her glass to demonstrate the point.

'I bet he did.'.

She carefully replaced the glass on the drinks mat. 'Tony, the green-eyed monster is not agreeable. I was just talking to him. I like talking to people. I'm a friendly person.'

'Why didn't you knock for me? I would have come down with you.' His tone was petulant.

'I believe we agreed to meet in the bar. I am not your mother, to be making sure you arrive on time.' She sipped her drink. 'Anyway, what's your problem? Why are you in such a bad mood? It's you who are late, not me.'

Tony took a deep breath and exhaled tension from his body. He had been abrupt and rude, and it wasn't Nina's fault. 'Sorry. I hate being late.' He shrugged. 'I woke up mid-way through an episode of some soap or other and realised the time. I thought you'd be fuming down here, waiting for me. And then I saw matey leering over you and ... Sorry.'

Glowering over the rim of her glass, she studied his expression, then broke into a smile. 'I'm glad you're sorry. I shall think of some way you can make it up to me.' She snatched the menu from a Perspex holder to one side of the table, unfolded it and pushed it in front of him. 'Now, choose some food before I have to eat my own arm.'

He scanned the menu, but his mind was on other things. Once again, he was vividly aware of the differences between Nina and Vicky. Nina had a fiery temper, the sparks in her eyes ready to fire out at any moment when she was annoyed, but then, just like that, they were gone. Vicky used to simmer. He knew if he upset her, the toxic atmosphere could hang around for days. It was one thing he didn't miss.

A uniformed girl appeared at their table with the promised drink, introduced herself as their waitress for the evening and flipped out a notepad to take their order.

When she left, Tony sipped his drink. 'What a day, huh? I certainly didn't expect it to go the way it did.'

'Many unexpected turns.' She frowned slightly as she perused him. 'How do you feel about it all? I know you were worried about how your grandfather died. What do you think, now?'

He took some time to think about it. 'I just don't know how to process it all. I came here pretty convinced Antonio committed suicide, but desperately hoping otherwise. When I saw the bridge, the height of the wall, I couldn't imagine there was any other possibility, but then, Tommy...I suppose it could have been foul play, but why? What could be the motive? Theft?'

She pursed her lips in concentration. 'From the post bag, do you mean? No, I think not. Tommy said the post was all over the road. If someone was going to commit such a crime to steal, they would have taken the whole bag, surely?'

'But what other motive is there? To shut him up perhaps, if he witnessed something dodgy. Or someone with a grudge?' He shook his head. 'I don't know.'

'I can't help thinking, in all these cases, something would have been revealed since. In so many years, secrets don't stay secrets, do they?'

'Perhaps it was an accident.' He was grasping at straws. 'Maybe he didn't jump but wasn't pushed either. What if a car came across the bridge and hit him? It's conceivable he could have been thrown over. The driver could have panicked and driven off. It happens.'

'I don't know. There would have been signs on the bridge, I think, blood, tyre marks, or something. Also, his words, "He found me". What did that mean?'

Tony rested his chin on his hands. 'I don't suppose we'll ever know. Maybe Cerys will have answers tomorrow.'

'Yes, your grandmother.' She rested forward, towards him and caressed his cheek with one hand. 'This is exciting, no? To have a grandmother you never knew about. It's amazing, really.'

The touch of her palm against his skin brought heat to both his face and his heart. She seemed to truly understand what the news meant to him, he, who was otherwise almost devoid of family connections. 'Thank you.'

Her forehead creased in bemusement, her hand moving as she played with his earlobe. 'What for?'

Nina's unoccupied hand rested on the table between them, and he reached for it, but instead of taking it in his own, he rubbed the centre knuckle gently with his middle finger, travelling a little further up her hand and wrist with every slow circle. 'For being with me in all this. For sharing it with me. Somehow, it means more.'

The atmosphere shifted. Her eyes dropped to the action of his hand, following the concentric shapes he traced up her forearm, approaching the point where the crook of her elbow pressed tightly against her chest, her breathing becoming shallower with each breath. 'It's my pleasure.'

The restaurant clatter withdrew into the background as he observed her face. He saw the pink flash of her tongue appear as she took the corner of her bottom lip between her teeth, as the circuit of his finger came ever closer to the curve of her breast.

A small cough from the waitress sent them springing apart. Nina reached hurriedly into her handbag for a tissue, hiding the blush of her cheeks, as plates of hot food were placed between them. Tony was amused by her girlishness, raising a quizzical eyebrow as he waited for the girl to leave them alone again.

Nina blushed further beneath his scrutiny, picked up a fork and prodded his hand with it. 'Eat your food.' She said, throwing him a sideways glance.

He let out a guttural chuckle and reached for his own fork. 'Ok, ok, I'm eating.'

The meal was completed with minimal conversation, superficial questions receiving perfunctory answers, more communication taking place via glances and subtle strokes of the hand. They both declined desserts and Tony settled the bill and together they whisked through the bar and past the lobby. An elderly gentleman held the lift door for them, and they ascended to their floor in silence, but for his monotone humming of an unrecognisable tune. He trailed them, a few feet behind, as they walked hand in hand down the corridor and Tony began to think he would have no chance to speak to her privately before they reached her door, but the man stopped a few doors prior to their own, rattling his electronic card in numerous failed attempts to gain entry. As they arrived at her door, Tony heard the tell-tale beep of the man's lock releasing and, as Nina turned towards him, leaning back against the frame, he saw the man disappear inside. They were alone.

She made no move to find her own key, her back arched against the wood and Tony stepped forward, his body close, but not quite touching, the hairs on his arms standing up, reaching for her. Nina ran one warm palm up over the contours of his chest and he leaned in, never breaking eye contact, so close her breath tickled the skin of his nose and mouth. Pausing, he waited for her to make a move, to indicate how she wanted the evening to end. He was taking nothing for granted.

Every second felt like an age, and in the chasm of time, he allowed his eyes to drop to her lips, as they swooped up to claim his. Their bodies melted together in the intensity of the kiss, taking his breath away. He pulled away, his mind swimming, giving her space to back off if things were moving too fast, but she scrabbled for her key card, unlocked the door and, taking his hand, pulled him inside.

CHAPTER 18

Tony woke to a room flooded with early sunlight after only a few hours of sleep. Nina slept on, oblivious to the intrusive rays, and he lay still next to her, enjoying the presence of a body close to his. Eventually, he slipped out of bed quietly and crept into the bathroom, retrieving the untidy heap of clothes from the floor where he had discarded them, on the way.

He was slightly, but pleasantly, shell shocked as he viewed his weary face in the mirror, his hair an unruly tangle. As much as he had hoped his relationship with Nina would develop during their trip to Wales, the actuality had blown all expectation out of the water. A hot shower washed the cobwebs away and he dried and dressed, before going back to the bedroom. Nina showed no sign of stirring, despite the fact breakfast was about to be closed, her face a blank canvas in slumber. He dived on to the bed, sending her body bouncing, nuzzling her ear to get a reaction.

She promptly rolled away from him. 'Go away.'

He was amused by her temper. 'Come on. They stop serving breakfast in ten minutes.'

She rolled back and opened one eye. 'What time is it?'

He dropped a quick kiss on her pouting lips. 'Ten to ten. We're supposed to be at the nursing home by eleven, sleepyhead.'

'I tell you what.' She shuffled up against the headboard, pulling the duvet up to her chest and tucking it under her arms, tight. 'You get breakfast while I soak in the bath. I'm exhausted.'

'I'm not surprised.' He slipped one hand under the duvet. 'I could join you in the bath.'

'Uh uh!' Scrabbling away from him, her head waggled a definite negative. 'Not if we're going to be there by eleven. Besides, you can bring me back a croissant.'

He backed away, the rumble in his stomach the need which demanded urgent satisfaction and retrieved his wallet from the desktop. 'If you're sure.'

'Yes. Go on, go. Go!' She shooed him away, then called after him. 'Make that two croissants. I'm starving.'

He chuckled as he closed the door behind him. He couldn't remember when he had last been this happy.

The nursing home was an imposing Victorian building, with irregular extensions, jarring in their lack of keeping with the original, but surrounded by well-kept, colourful gardens, intersected by level paths. Tony pulled up in the small car park out front, in the shade of a tall, narrow shed. A couple of elderly folk roamed in the sunshine among the plants, the air filled with low level jazz, emanating from the open shed door. Tony wondered if the grey-haired lady, tending a patch of rose bushes, could be his grandmother. He had only seen one photograph of her, when she was still young, and he doubted he would know her if he saw her, but he studied the woman's features nonetheless for signs of familiarity. There were none. His stomach fluttered in anticipation of what he would find within, and he was glad of Nina's hand holding his as they approached the entrance.

Inside was warm and the air was tinged with a malodourous mix of cooking, cleaning fluids and other aromas. They followed instructions to sign in and waited for someone to appear to direct them, trying not to listen to a telephone conversation escaping from an office a little way down the corridor. When the call ended a head and shoulders appeared around the doorframe.

'Can I help you?' The woman was neat in appearance, her hair in a bun, with glasses balanced on the tip of her nose, so she could look over the top of them.

'Oh, hi!' Tony stepped forward, 'I spoke to someone last night. I believe my grandmother, Cerys Williams, is here. They said, if I came in this morning, I could see her.'

The woman turned her head to one side. 'Cerys? I wasn't aware she had family.'

'My father was her son. He died a long time ago and I didn't know about her. I've been tracing my history and found out she's still alive. I had no idea until yesterday, but now I know, I'd love to meet her. Is that ok?' He began to doubt he would be allowed access.

'I see. What's your name? I'll go see Cerys. See what she has to say on the matter.'

Tony gave her his details and the woman jotted them down, before instructing him to wait for her return. She was gone several minutes, leaving Tony drumming his fingers on the table as he waited. When she returned there was little explanation, merely a curt instruction to follow her. Both he and Nina hastily fell in behind her, almost trotting to keep up, as she turned down corridors, up a weathered staircase and through doorways, the distance and complexity of the trek justifying her lengthy absence. Finally, they were shown into a small room, containing only a bed, a small wardrobe and an armchair.

The white-haired old lady crumpled between pillows in the chair bore no resemblance whatsoever to the photo Tony had used for reference. A nurse fussed around, plumping the pillows and straightening Cerys's nightdress, talking loudly.

'Someone to see you, Cerys. That's nice, isn't it? Your grandson.' Turning to Tony and Nina, she lowered her voice a notch. 'Her memory's not fantastic and you'll have to speak up. To be honest with you, she may or may not understand. Sometimes she's in our world and sometimes she's not. Catch her on a good day and she's as lucid as you like, but others... well, you know. I'll grab a couple of chairs from down the hall.' She turned back to Cerys and returned her volume to the higher level. 'I'm going to get some chairs.'

As the nurse disappeared, Tony examined the old woman's face. She was peering at him through half open slits. He crouched to her level and took her papery hand in his, bringing his face closer so she could see.

'Granny?' She smiled but made no response.

He tried again. 'Cerys? It's Tony, Antony, your grandson. Do you know me?'

Her eyes suddenly focused, the translucent lids elevating slightly. She lifted one shaky hand to his cheek, leaving the other in his grasp. The nurse bustled back into the room with two bright orange plastic chairs and Cerys turned to her without releasing Tony from her grip, a broad grin transforming her face.

'Bobby!' She whispered loudly. 'My Bobby!'

Tony turned to the carer for clarification. 'Bobby?'

'She talks of Bobby a lot. Her son, I believe.' She deposited the chairs and stepped back into the hall.

'Of course, my dad. He was always Robert in our house. No, Cerys, it's not Bobby, it's his son, Tony.'

A frown puckered her face as she tried to understand, then she tapped his cheek with her hand, before allowing it to drop into her lap, shaking her head. 'Poor Bobby. I told him not to come, but he wouldn't listen.'

Tony glanced at Nina, eyebrows raised in question, unsure whether Cerys was in the real world or not, whether he should humour her or not. 'You told Bobby not to come?'

'Of course I did.' She seemed quite put out by the question. 'I loved him, didn't I?'

'You told Bobby not to come, because you loved him?' Tony was confused.

'Yes. They got his father, and they'd get him too, so he had to go.' A tear dripped onto her cheek, but she was either unaware or ignored it, allowing it to sit, a perfect globule glistening against her skin. 'Dolores from the post office told me they were looking, you see, so we couldn't wait. I couldn't lose him too.'

'I don't understand. Lose him? Who were looking?'

Her face straightened, as she looked him right in the eye. 'You're not my Bobby.' She accused.

'No Cerys. I told you, I'm Tony, your grandson.' He was finding it difficult to follow her train of thought.

'Don't be ridiculous, Tony was from Glasgow. You don't come from Glasgow.' She squirmed in her seat, backing away. 'I don't know you. I don't know who you are.'

'I know.' He tried to recapture her hand. 'I know. I'm not Tony from Glasgow.'

Before he was able to elaborate, she slapped his hand away. 'Of course you're not. Tony's been dead for years.'

'No, I'm a different Tony. I'm Tony your grandson. Bobby's boy.'

Her face was a picture of bewilderment and she thrashed around, looking for something or somebody. Tony felt panic rise within him, and he turned to Nina. 'What do I do?'

Nina slipped forward out of her seat and crouched next to him, holding Cerys's hand and hushing her, soothing her. Cerys calmed, scrutinising Nina's smiling face, her own mouth forming a matching arc.

'It's all right, Cerys. There's nothing to worry about.'

As soon as Nina spoke, a look of fear took over Cerys's countenance and she began to shout. 'Brenda! Brenda! They're here! Brenda!'

The nurse's footsteps pounded down the corridor and she charged through the door. 'Whatever's the matter, Cerys? What's the matter, dear?'

Nina sat back to make room. 'I don't know what I said to upset her. She was fine then started shouting.'

Cerys grabbed the carer, hugging her tight and sobbing. 'They've come for me, Brenda. Make them go away.'

'There, there, dear. No one's going to hurt you.' She soothed, turning her head to the concerned pair, still holding the old lady to her chest. 'Perhaps you'd better go. She gets so confused, bless her. It's the dementia, you know. Turns things inside out for the loves.'

Tony didn't want to leave with things as they were. He had only just found his grandmother and it felt wrong leaving her in such a state. 'Is there anything I can do?'

'Time and space. And a bit of patience. Go now. Come back another day and, no doubt, she'll be completely different.'

'If you think that's for the best.'

'I do, pet, at least for now. I'm here most days. I'll talk to her about you, get her used to the idea of you, and then we can try again.' She turned back to give Cerys her full attention, rocking her gently.

Tony backed away, shrugged to Nina and held his hand out to her. They retraced their steps to the foyer and outside. As soon as the doors closed and they were alone in the car, Nina embraced him tightly. The disappointment had rocked him, the excitement at finding out Cerys existed, now wiped away by her rejection.

Nina was distraught. 'I'm sorry I spoiled it. I don't know what I said to upset her.'

'Don't be silly, it wasn't you. Goodness knows what was going on inside her head. Dementia's a horrible thing.' Tony reassured. 'I don't know what I expected. Some sort of joyous reunion, I suppose. I'm just glad you were there. I didn't know what to do, what to say.'

'Don't give up. You must go and see her again. You heard the nurse. Give her time.'

'No, of course not. She's still my granny, dementia or no dementia.' He flipped open the case of his phone to check the time. 'I suppose we ought to head back. It'll be mid-afternoon by the time we get home.'

A swathe of messages flashed on his screen, and he frowned as he ran through them. 'I've had eight missed calls from Marco. What the heck?' He continued to scroll.

'What is it? Is everything ok?'

His face paled. 'No.' He hastily started the engine. 'It's Jamie. He's fallen on the cliffs. They're at the hospital. I need to get there, now.'

Finding first gear, he put his foot to the floor, and the car shot out of the gate and onto the main road.

CHAPTER 19

The journey back was in stark contrast to the trip the day before. Tony drove, as heavy footed as he dared, dictating frantic messages for Nina to text to Marco, to establish Jamie's condition. Marco's responses were short and to the point: Jamie was fine, but they were going into X-ray, or the trauma room, or some such observation, but Tony needed details. He wouldn't relax until he saw him safe, with his own eyes. Images of Vicky, laid out on the slab, flickered in his memory. That was the last time he had visited a hospital.

They pulled into the car park and Tony jumped out, suddenly aware of Nina's predicament. She had been adamant about not moving too fast with their relationship, but here she was, being thrust into the midst of Tony's crisis or having to find her own way home. He was torn between concern for his son and his responsibility to her.

'Sorry. I should have dropped you home first.'

She slammed the door and tripped towards the entrance to the hospital. 'Don't be silly. I'm not going to leave you at a time like this.'

He followed her lead, racing to the main doors, attracting glances from other visitors, meandering down the path. Signs led directly to the hectic Accident and Emergency Department; their progress halted as they joined a queue for Reception. Tony hopped from foot to foot, searching the crowds for his friends or his son in the waiting room or beyond double doors, leading to the clinical area, as they opened and closed with the passage of staff.

When they reached the front of the queue, the prim receptionist was straight-faced and to the point. They were to wait until someone fetched them and she had no further information. In exasperation he found a vacant seat, Nina alongside, her hand gripping his forearm, while he drummed agitated fingers on the arm of the chair. At last Marco appeared and Tony sprang to his feet, hands wringing, Nina only a fraction behind.

'Sorry to worry you, old man. Nothing too major occurred, but we felt obliged to let you know.' His keen eye fell upon Nina.

Tony still needed answers. 'What's happened? How's Jamie?'

Marco chuckled, oblivious to the level of Tony's anxiety. 'Little tyke. Can't take your eyes off him for a second. I thought Max was sneaky enough, but combined, they have the upper hand on me, I don't mind telling you. Between them, they masterminded a jaunt over the side of the cliff down by Sandy Beach, you know, where we walked the other Sunday. One minute they're safe as houses, marching along the top, next minute they run headlong over the edge. Goodness knows what got into them. Gave us quite a fright, as you can imagine.'

A groan escaped Tony's throat and his knees momentarily buckled. Nina's arm shot around his waist to prevent him from falling and he held tight as he regained his composure.

Marco's face paled and he patted Tony's shoulder. 'Sorry. Sounds worse than it is, honestly. Jamie's fine, apart from a sore wrist and a twisted ankle. They've done X-rays to be certain and we're just waiting for confirmation of the results so we can take him home. He's happy as Larry, being fussed about by the nurses, the little lothario, plying him with stickers and suchlike. He'll be happier still to see you, of course.'

'He's really alright?' Tony's voice was hoarse with concern.

'Yes, yes. Come on, let me show you where they're keeping him, and you can see for yourself.' Marco held the door open, eying Nina as she passed through. 'Aren't you going to introduce me to this young lady?'

'Sorry, yes. This is Nina. Nina, this is my friend Marco.'

Marco held out his hand to shake hers, before continuing down the corridor. 'Pleased to meet you.'

'Pleased to meet you too.'

One eyebrow shot up at her accent. 'Ahh! The Iberian beauty. Yes, I've heard all about you. Only good things, of course. Come along this way.' He strode to a curtained area and put his face close to a gap in the drapes before walking through. 'Knock, knock. Look who I found loitering.'

Jamie was propped up in bed in an outsized hospital gown, bandaged limbs protruding from beneath. The smile on his face denied any discomfort or melancholy.

'Daddy. Look at my leg.' Jamie wasted no time on greetings but moved swiftly to the main event. 'And I've got a Superman sticker because I'm a hero. Kelly, my nurse, said so.'

Tony found himself smiling along. 'You were a brave boy, were you?'

'Yes. Well, most of the time. Kelly says if I have a plaster cast my friends can write messages on it. I hope I have to have one. It would be so cool.'

Ruth sat the other side of the bed, her expression strained. 'He has been a very brave boy, but everything's ok, now. Sorry, Tony. I don't know how it happened, I really don't. One minute he was right in front of me and the next...' She threw her arms up in an elaborate shrug.

'I told you; I was chasing Max and...'

Tony interrupted. 'How is Max? Is he ok?'

'Yes, yes.' Marco patted him on the back and moved around to join his wife. 'Feeling a bit sorry for himself, but otherwise fit as a fiddle. I'll not be letting him off the leash for a day or two though, that's for sure.'

As Marco moved forward, Nina became visible to the rest of the cubicle and Ruth's glance from her to Tony and back again was pointed. Marco stepped in. 'Ruth, this is Nina, Tony's...' He paused as he considered how best to describe her. 'Friend. This is my wife, Ruth.'

The women nodded awkwardly at each other, but Jamie came to the rescue. 'And I'm Jamie.' He clearly did not want to be left out.

Nina reached forward, shaking the boy's hand 'Pleased to meet you, Jamie. I'm sorry you have had such a troubled day.'

'I like your voice.' Jamie was straight to the point. 'If I have a plaster cast, you can write on it if you want to.'

She smiled at the gift so readily bestowed. 'Thank you. I would love to.'

Tony met and held her gaze. Only days ago, he had been reticent to introduce Jamie to anyone new in his life, until he was sure they were a long-term addition, but those reservations had melted away. In a few short hours, he and Nina had faced numerous emotional challenges together and it felt right. As far as he was concerned, she was here to stay.

The hours crawled by. A crack in Jamie's wrist was found to warrant a cast and he celebrated with a fist pump in the air with the other arm, not caring it meant more waiting. His ankle injury was merely a sprain, requiring rest. Marco and Ruth left, to transfer Jamie's belongings from their home to his, and the others eventually got away late in the afternoon. Nina was delivered to her lodgings, Tony walking her to the door so they could share a more intimate goodbye than the car, with its young witness, would allow. When Tony carried Jamie into their home, they were met with the mouth-watering aroma of Ruth's cooking and the eager barking of Max. It felt like weeks since they had left, and it was good to be back.

Jamie was whisked to bed early, completely exhausted after the day's exertions. Marco wandered out to enjoy the cool of the evening with Max. Ruth insisted on clearing away, while Tony relayed the revelations he had discovered in Wales. When he finished, she faced him across the table, their coffee cups between them.

'Where does Nina fit into all this?' Her question was cool and concise.

'What do you mean?'

She leaned back on the stool away from him, drawing in her mug, giving it her attention. 'Nina. I've never heard mention of her before, but she clearly went with you. Is she your girlfriend?'

Tony was taken aback. Ruth's tone was more than inquisitive. She was annoyed. He remembered the heated moment which had passed between them and wondered if it had been less one sided than he had thought. 'It was spur of the moment, really. We've been friends for a while.'

Ruth did not comment but raised her eyebrows in challenge.

'We've been out a couple of times and I thought it was just going to be a day trip. She offered to keep me company.' He felt like he was facing an interrogation. 'I guess you could say she's my girlfriend. I don't know.

It's early days.'

'Not too early to introduce her to Jamie though.'

Her attitude irritated him. As if he would risk Jamie's happiness! However, he bit back his annoyance, conscious he may have already unintentionally injured Ruth's feelings. 'Don't worry. Jamie spends time with all my friends, and he doesn't need to know she's any more than that. He will always be my priority.'

Her tone changed, as if she realised, she had overstepped the mark. 'I'm sure you know best.'

She leaned down to retrieve a notepad from her handbag, pulled a pen from the spiral binding and placed it on the table. A long pause, as she sipped her drink, marked an end to that particular line of conversation and the launch of another. 'I should bring my notes up to date, make sure we're both following the right lines.' Her glance was nonchalant, but Tony suspected it held more import than she allowed to show. 'Assuming you still need my help, of course?'

'Definitely!' He had hurt her feelings. He was sure of it now. 'I couldn't do this without you. You know that.'

She shrugged and concentrated on the page of notes. 'Finding out Cerys and Antonio weren't married is an enormous step forward. What do you want to do with that now? Do you want to follow the Williams' line any further?'

Tony rested his chin on his hand, giving it consideration. 'I don't think so. Maybe I'll come back to that later, but for now, it's the Viscount side which intrigues me. It's so diverse. There's no pattern. You know, no location I can say the family comes from; no work or trade handed down father to son; almost invisible ties between one generation and the next. It's odd, isn't it? So far, the only thing any of them have in common is dying in tragic circumstances. Not a great legacy, is it?'

'It's early days. You've only looked at a couple of generations. There's probably more congruity the further back you go. You'll make sense of it in the end, I'm sure.' She scribbled notes in the margin. 'It looks like the Scotland link with Antonio is correct, doesn't it? I expected to receive the birth certificate before now, but I suppose it has a long way to come.'

The door rattled as Marco returned from his stroll.

'If we take that connection as read, we can do some more on-line work, look a little deeper into your great grandfather.'

'I suppose. I don't feel like I've finished with Antonio yet, though. I mean, he's such a mysterious character. What made him move from Scotland to Wales?'

Marco flounced onto a stool. 'Good Lord! Are you pair at it again already? I thought you'd be taking a break after today's excitement.'

'No, not really. I'm only filling in the gaps with Tony's discoveries.' Ruth looked at her husband's weary face. 'You look like you need a pick me up. Why don't you pour a couple of brandies for you boys? I'll drive.'

Marco pulled himself to his feet with the aid of the tabletop. 'I don't need telling twice. You don't mind me playing fast and loose with your liquor, Tony?'

'Knock yourself out.'

'We'll make no reference to bodily injuries after a day like today, thank you very much.' Marco guffawed as he headed for the drinks' cabinet in the lounge, as always, the most entertained by his own joke.

'There is one interesting thing the internet threw up.' Ruth checked her log. 'There was a newspaper article reference to an Antonio Viscount in the late nineteen forties. It listed him with a number of interpreters operating during World War II, who were recommended for a medal or something like that. I suppose it could be your grandfather. He would have been the right age for service about then. I didn't pay much attention, but it might be worth trying to find it again.'

'An interpreter? Interpreting what?'

'No idea. Marco?' She called to her husband, and he promptly appeared, two glasses in hand. 'Howard knows his way around military history, doesn't he?'

He slid a glass to Tony. 'Howard Shoreland? Yes. A bit of a whizz at it, all considered. Needing assistance?'

'Possibly. I'll take another look first, but if you're happy to have another pair of eyes on it, Howard's your man.' She closed the notebook and slid the pen into place.

'Fine by me. I'm going to be stuck at home for the next few days with that young man, so I'll spend some time on it too.' He rested his hand on Ruth's. He didn't want her to feel displaced because of his relationship with Nina. He still valued her and Marco's friendship above others. 'Thank you for your help. I do appreciate it.'

Her face momentarily appeared pained, before a brief smile flashed across it. 'It's ok. I like to help.'

Only minutes later, Marco and Ruth drove away, leaving Tony alone with his thoughts and the remnants of his brandy. He watched their car as it disappeared from his driveway, then downed the fiery liquid in one swallow and headed up to bed.

CHAPTER 20

After two days stuck at home, Tony and Jamie were stir crazy. They had some visitors: Charlie and Adrienne delivering comics; a couple of other school friends with their parents, all wanting to be able to report back on Jamie's progress, as well as leave their marks on his cast. By Wednesday Jamie's ankle was bearing weight, though still painful, and Tony struggled to keep the boy's energy safely contained.

Nina had telephoned and offered to call around in the afternoon, to play board games and Tony was as pleased at the prospect as Jamie, until Ruth phoned to announce she had new information and would also be calling in. Tony was nervous about the women coming together again so soon, but on the spur of the moment could think of no suitable excuse to put Ruth off and couldn't bear the thought of deferring Nina. Indeed, Nina's visit was a boon. She had Jamie giggling in minutes and Tony observed their play, one ear enjoying the banter, while the other strained for the sound of Ruth's car tyres on the drive, but confrontation was narrowly avoided, with Nina leaving minutes before Ruth arrived.

Ruth blustered through the door, efficient looking in her office attire, and greeted Jamie with a bear hug. 'I am so glad to see you up and about again.'

Jamie was happy to receive her attentions, proudly demonstrating his improvement by hobbling up and down the hallway and was rewarded with a bag of jelly babies. He hopped, back to his computer game, as soon as conversation turned elsewhere, leaving Ruth and Tony to catch up. They followed him into the lounge, raising their voices above the roaring of engines from Jamie's racing game on the television, and settled down to study the documents Ruth had brought.

'I spoke to Howard yesterday and he suggested a few military websites to check out, but I haven't come up with anything much yet. He took what information we had so far and promised to give it the once over. It'll be a day or two before he comes back, but he's the sort you can trust to do something if he says he will.'

She pulled out a printed article. 'I did find the newspaper story I mentioned, but it doesn't give much away. It's mainly a list of interpreter personnel who were honoured retrospectively for services to International Intelligence. It doesn't explain what they were interpreting or for whom, but it does say they were transferred from the Isle of Man in the forties to bases throughout England. It all sounds very cloak and dagger. I'm guessing it's something to do with the code breaking, you know, Enigma and all that, which would explain the scant detail.'

Tony scanned his eyes over the article as she spoke, bemused by the vagueness of it. 'Fancy that, some sort of logic genius. Bit of a come down though, isn't it? High tech code breaker to postman. And the Isle of Man? We've got a birth record in the back of beyond in north Scotland; Cerys's comments suggested a link to Glasgow and now the Isle of Man? Perhaps that's where my father got his wandering genes.'

'Yes. It's odd, isn't it? The upside is, because of the different addresses, I broadened the search on the genealogy website. I haven't managed to find anything else for Antonio, but I searched the names of who we think were his parents and came up trumps.' Ruth indicated a hand drawn family tree with the blunt end of her pencil, dragging the end from Antonio's name to a pair of names scribbled above. 'Leonard and Donata.'

'Donata? Is that a traditional Scottish name?' Tony was intrigued.

'No idea. They would have been born last century remember, so we wouldn't expect Darrens or Tracys, would we? Anyway, I haven't found their marriage, which means I could only search for his birth, because we don't have her maiden name and unfortunately, I haven't been able to find his entry yet either.'

'Please tell me there's a "but".'

She prodded him, amused by his enthusiasm. 'There is a "but"! Firstly, I found his registration of death, which dates to nineteen fourteen, at which point he is noted as being thirty years old. So, we know he was born round about eighteen eighty-four.'

Tony groaned. 'Does nobody in my family make it to middle age? How did he die?'

'Bayonet wound to the chest, apparently.' Ruth read from her notes.

'Bayonet wound? That sounds like... Hang on, nineteen fourteen. World war one. Was he a soldier?'

'That would certainly make sense. There's no mention of a title, like private or sergeant, but it sounds like death in action to me. I assume you'd like me to order a copy of the death certificate? There may be more info on the actual paperwork. Also, I'll get Marco to pass the extra details to Howard, so he can add it to his investigation.'

'Brilliant. Thank you.' He was humbled by the effort she was putting in on his behalf. 'I don't know what I'd do without you.'

Ruth seemed embarrassed by his gratitude. Her gaze dropped and she fumbled with the paperwork self-consciously. 'I'm sure you'd manage very well.'

Jamie's noisy computer game drowned out what could otherwise have become an awkward silence.

'Have you been on that thing all day, young man? You'll have square eyes if you're not careful.' Her admonishment was playful.

Without turning from the screen, Jamie shook his head. 'No, Daddy won't let me play for more than an hour. I was playing Frustration with Nina before you came. She won once and I won twice. Daddy was the loser.'

Tony's stomach tensed at the mention of Nina's name.

The smile froze on Ruth's face, and she picked up her handbag. 'I don't suppose Daddy minded losing to you, or Nina. Right, I'd better be off.'

Tony tried to pull things back. 'Really? I haven't offered you a cup of tea or anything?'

'No, it was only ever going to be a flying visit.' She avoided his gaze. 'We've got friends round for dinner later. Lots to do.' She marched to the hall. 'Bye, Jamie.'

Tony followed her, but she was halfway to her car in moments. 'Thanks again.' He called, but she held her hand up in a wave without turning round.

He frowned as the vehicle disappeared into the distance, the sun glinting off the silver trim as it rounded the corner. He had the distinct impression her feelings had once again taken a battering, but he was at a loss how to handle it. He didn't want to lose his friends, but there was no way he was giving Nina up.

'Dad, I'm bored!' Jamie slouched against the door frame; exaggerated pain plastered across his face.

'I know, buddy. It's not that exciting having broken bones, is it?' An idea sprung into his mind, a possible answer to both his and Jamie's problems. 'Perhaps we could call and visit Aunt Trish when she's finished school tomorrow. She always knows what to do.'

'Yes!' Jamie's face lit up, optimism refuelled by hope for tomorrow, and he hopped back to the console.

One quick phone call had been sufficient to secure an invitation to Trish's. Jamie's chatter was filled with kite flying and adventures he expected Trish to have planned, but Tony doubted they would transpire, partly due to Jamie's injuries, but also thanks to the heavy drizzle spattering the windscreen. As before, she appeared before they had climbed from the car, hands clasped in anticipation, and Tony was surprised to find he was equally eager to see her again. Jamie hobbled towards her as quickly as he could but was swiftly admonished.

'Slow down, young man! One arm in a cast is quite enough, don't you think?' She leant to his level to accept him into her open embrace.

When he had extricated himself, he held the bandaged arm aloft. 'Do you want to read the messages on my plaster? Some are very funny. Charlie drew a monster.'

'Come inside and I'll take a look. Mind where you're going.' She turned to Tony, who was bringing up the rear. 'That boy's a walking time bomb. No wonder you look tired.'

'Do I?' He glanced at his image in the gilt hall mirror, as he passed.

She reached up on to tip toes to slide an arm around his shoulder, planting a light kiss on his cheek. 'Don't fret. It's only because I know you so well. You're still as handsome as ever.' She released him and he settled into the largest sofa in the lounge, while she paused in the doorway to the kitchen. 'You're just missing your usual sparkle. Working too hard?'

'No, not at all, actually. I'm taking an extended break.

I have to cover the odd shift, but the restaurant pretty much runs itself, so I'm having the summer with Jamie. Then, we'll see.'

Yes, we'll see. I can't see you sticking it for long, but a break will do you good. Remind you what makes you tick. You'll go back with renewed enthusiasm, when you're ready.' She was clearly dubious about his withdrawal.

'You think so?'

'I do, but as you say, we'll see. You're keeping your options open. Coffee?'

'Please.'

Listening as she rummaged in the kitchen, cupboard doors opening and closing, he contemplated her comments. Funny how she knew him so well, even after all these years. He wondered if she was right about his zest for work. It was a while since he'd felt any genuine motivation.

Trish wandered through with a glass of milk and a plate of biscuits for Jamie, who had already found art supplies, laid out on the low table in the conservatory. She set the tray down a safe distance away from where he was gluing. Tony heard her saying something about milk being good for bones and smiled at Jamie's eager compliance, instantly laying down tools to take up the glass.

'You've got him right under your thumb.' Tony chortled, as she returned through the lounge.

'You've either got it or you haven't.' She laughed, stepping out of the room and returning with their own beverages. 'There was a time you looked up to me like that. More's the pity we all have to grow up.'

He picked up his cup and held it in his lap, watching the steam curl upward. 'Life's certainly simpler at that age, isn't it? I sometimes wish I could be back there again.'

Trish patted his knee. 'You've had a tough time. You'll get through it.'

Tony was embarrassed, she had automatically assumed he was referring to losing Vicky. He glanced at her sideways to gauge her response. 'I've been seeing someone.'

She appeared amused by his sheepish remark. 'What are we talking here? A new love interest? Or a therapist?'

'A girl. I mean, a woman. Nina, and she really is quite lovely. You'd like her, I think. She's Spanish.' The words fell from his mouth.

'Ah, I see. Well, good for you.' As she reached for a biscuit, he couldn't read her expression.

'You don't think it's too soon, do you? Some people seem to.'

'Some people!' She pooh-poohed, throwing the biscuit into her mouth and chewing with passion. 'Like it's anyone else's business. Listen Tony, life is short and what's right for one person isn't necessarily right for another. All we can do is try to be happy. As long as it's not at someone else's expense, of course.'

He picked at invisible specks on his trouser leg, too self-conscious to meet her gaze. He felt like a teenager again. 'The thing is, I think it may be at someone else's expense. Trish, I think I may have got myself into a bit of a situation.'

She watched him squirming and set her cup down firmly on the table. 'Come on then. No beating around the bush. What's it all about?'

He took a deep breath. 'It's Ruth.'

'Ruth?'

'Yes. For some reason, she seems very anti Nina.' He glanced at the conservatory door to ensure Jamie wasn't listening. 'I don't know if she thinks it's too soon, she implied as much, or whether she just doesn't like Nina. They met on Sunday, at the hospital. I hadn't intended introducing her to my friends yet because it is early days, but with one thing and another, the decision was out of my hands, but, if looks could kill.'

'She's jealous.' The statement was matter of fact.

'I don't think so. Ruth and I have been friends a long time, never anything more.' He pushed the idea away, although in his heart he suspected there may be some truth in it.

'I wasn't asking, I was telling. She is jealous.' Trish shook her head. 'I don't know what sort of games you've been playing, but I saw the way you were together after the inquest. There was definitely… something. Besides, it goes back further than that.'

'Honestly. There's never been anything. She's been a great friend since Vicky, and I suppose I've been lonely, so I was glad to have her around, but that's it.' He felt obliged to clear his name. 'She's married to Marco. I couldn't… I wouldn't.'

'I'm pleased to hear it but believe me it goes way back. Look. I don't want to speak out of turn, but Ruth - how can I say this?' Her frown deepened and she studied her thumbs, twiddling in her lap. 'That woman has an agenda. She always has had.'

'What?' He was astonished by what he was hearing.

'I wasn't going to say anything, but I already knew about Nina. Ruth phoned me, suggesting I might want to have a quiet word with you.'

He opened his mouth to speak, but Trish continued.

'" Vulnerable" is, I think, the word she used to describe you. Didn't want to see you taken advantage of while you're still recovering.' She tutted loudly. 'But let's be honest, she was thinking of herself, not you. You've never been able to see it, but she's been in love with you since you were teenagers, following you around, turning up at every party you went to. Don't you remember?'

'No. I don't. She was always around, but we were just in the same group, that's all. I'm sure she never...'

'Believe me, she had the air of stalker about her. I was concerned about it at one time, but then Vicky came along, and she backed off. Don't get me wrong, she was nice as pie on the phone, but in my heart of hearts I thought, she's been playing the long game. She's been waiting, because while Vicky was around, she never stood a chance, but now she's spotted an opportunity.'

Tony didn't want to believe it. 'She loves Marco.'

'Does she?' She paused, then nodded abruptly. 'Yes, I think she does, but that doesn't mean she's ready to see someone else step into the space Vicky so recently vacated.' Her hand sprung to her mouth. 'Sorry, that was harsh. I didn't mean it to come out like that.'

He shook his head sadly. 'It's ok.'

They sat in silence for a time.

'Can I give you some advice?' Trish's voice was calm and low.

'Please do.'

'If you can give Ruth a wide berth, I think you should, for a while. If you have to see her, make sure Marco is in close proximity. Give her a chance to remember what the basis of your relationship actually is.' She observed him through narrow slits. 'Do you have to see her?'

He shrugged. 'It would look odd if I didn't. She's done so much work on my family tree recently. It's all starting to come together, and I couldn't have done it without her. It would seem ungrateful if I suddenly backed away.'

Jamie marched into the room; a picture held up like a banner. Trish made one last comment to Tony. 'Think about it. See if there's a way you can step back.' Then she turned to Jamie. 'Goodness. Look at this masterpiece.

Spread it out on the table and let me have a good look.'

Tony followed her example, admiring Jamie's work, saying all the right things, but his mind was a whirl of conflicted ideas.

As Tony tucked Jamie into bed that night, he listened to his tales with a distracted smile. He left him with a small lamp on so the little boy could spend five minutes more looking at a book Trish had loaned him and retired to the lounge.

A photograph of himself and Vicky, on a shelf in an alcove, caught his eye and he picked it up to study it. It had been taken years earlier, before Jamie was born, at a festival in the pouring rain. Their hair was plastered to their faces, but regardless of the weather, their faces were alight with joy. They had been happy then.

He tried to recall the day it was taken. Fragments came back, mere moments of an exhilarating weekend, dancing into the early hours and sleeping into the day. They had been part of a sizeable party, tents huddled around a shared campfire. Ruth had been there, but not Marco. It was before he came onto the scene. She had come with another girl instead but spent much of the time tagging along with Tony and Vicky, when the other girl hooked up with one of the single guys. In fact, it was Ruth who had taken the photo. He placed it back on the shelf. In the pit of his stomach, Trish's words rang true. Ruth had always been on the periphery of his and Vicky's relationship, more perhaps than was natural.

He stepped into the hall and collected the telephone, dialling from memory. The call was answered almost instantly.

'Hi Lewis. Can Ian get away from the kitchen for a minute?'

'Boss!' He responded like a long-lost friend. 'Good to hear from you. Hold on a sec.'

There was a rustle and the low hum of restaurant clatter as the phone was placed to one side on the bar. Then Ian's gruff Scottish brogue grunted a greeting.

'Tony? What can I do for you?'

'Would I be in the way if I came in for a few hours this week?'

'You bored already?' Ian laughed. 'It's your gaff man. You can come and go as you please.'

'Yea, but I told you I was stepping back and now I'm interfering again. I didn't intend to mess you around.'

'No worries. As it happens Angela's after me having a couple of days off. Wants to go up north for a funeral and I told her I could only spare one day. You'll be in her good books from now on.'

'As long as you're sure.'

'Aye, not a problem.' Ian's tone was reassuring but concerned. 'Everything ok?'

'Yes, thanks. Just going a bit stir crazy. A day or two back at the pit face will knock it out of me.'

Ian's chuckle was low and coarse. 'It's in your blood, Tone. You're a worker. A man like you can't be sitting at home on your arse. I'm only surprised it took you this long. See you in the morning? About ten? I'll bring you up to date then head off for Ayrshire.'

'Thanks, mate.'

He replaced the phone and moved through to the kitchen to grab a beer from the fridge. Immediate problem solved. If he was tied up at The Olive Branch for the next few days, he would have the perfect excuse to keep away from Ruth.

CHAPTER 21

Sunday afternoon in the restaurant was a busy, but relatively simple, affair, roasting meats and preparing vegetables for the carvery. Tony had avoided three calls from Ruth and two from Marco, replying strategically, when he knew Marco would be otherwise engaged, leaving a message explaining he was tied up with work for a few days, keeping the details vague.

He had arranged for Nina to join him and Jamie for a meal at the end of his shift, but she arrived an hour early, offering to whisk Jamie away from the staff room to the park for a while. Tony rushed around, finishing jobs he needed to get done, then disappeared into the staff room to change, his heart brimming with contentment. Within moments Lewis thrust his head around the door to announce a visitor, and Tony followed him out, a broad smile on his face, expecting to see Nina and Jamie. Instead, he strode straight into Marco.

'Here's the man.'

'Marco. Hi. What are you doing in this neck of the woods?' He hoped the awkwardness he felt was not visible externally.

'What else but cricket? A pal of mine invited me to a match. His son's a keen amateur. If today's performance is anything to go by, we'll see him at Edgbaston in a year or two, mark my words. I tried to call you to come along, but obviously you were otherwise engaged. I got your message about the emergency. Damned inconvenient with Jamie the way he is. Are you managing ok?' He glanced around the bustling dining area.

'Thank you, but yes, it's fine. Just a small staffing issue. It will sort itself out in a day or two and Jamie's back to school tomorrow anyway, so we'll manage. I'm sorry to have missed the cricket though.'

The door swung open, and Nina and Jamie returned in a flurry of giggling and chatter. 'Marco! Where's Max?'

Marco acknowledged Nina with a nod. 'Max is safely deposited in the car. He's had an exhausting afternoon chasing his tail. How's the arm?'

Jamie waved the offending limb in the air. 'It's good. I don't think it's broken any more, but dad says I have to keep the cast on 'til the doctor says. Are you having roast dinner as well?'

Tony bit his cheeks. He had given the false impression in his earlier message that he'd be working all day, but Marco didn't appear to notice.

'Not today, though it smells fabulous. Ruth's at home cooking up a storm, so I can't stop.'

'Why don't you and Nina go and sit down, and I'll be with you in a minute. Lewis? Is the table ready?' Tony urged Jamie on with a little push, eager to move him on before he could say anything untoward.

Lewis led them away, one hand on the small of Nina's back, leaving Tony to cover his tracks with Marco. 'Yes, we're having a quick dinner here, then getting Jamie home to bed. It'll be a long day for him, back at school tomorrow.'

'It's good to see him doing so well. He had us all worried last week. Ruth will be pleased. Don't forget though, if you need another pair of hands, we're only a phone call away – that is, if you trust us with him anymore.'

'Of course I do. Why wouldn't I?' They stepped to one side as an elderly couple entered and hovered, waiting to be seated.

'Well, after last weekend's shenanigans. Between you and me, Ruth's been rather concerned. I've never seen her in such a stew, but you know, she's so attached to the boy and she's afraid you'll not want her caring for him anymore. I tried to reassure her, but you know women.' Marco's tone was light, but his demeanour gave away the level of his concern.

As much as Tony wanted to create distance between them, he didn't want to cause hurt. 'No, no. Honestly, mate. Jamie can be such a menace. You have to have eyes in the back of your head. Please, tell Ruth, it wasn't her fault and I have no reservations about making use of your babysitting skills again. It's only with Ian away and Jamie being laid up, it's been easy enough to have him here. I'm just pleased to hear you're still prepared to look after the little terror.'

Marco's relief was visible. 'That's good to know. As it turns out, I had a call from Howard yesterday, you know, my historian friend. He's in town and would like a chinwag about your grandfather, apparently, he's turned up some interesting stuff. If you're up for it, we can meet him at the pub on Wednesday night. Ruth will sit with Jamie. Assuming the staff problem is sorted by then?'

Tony considered it. He'd be spending time with Marco, not Ruth, and he really was eager to know what Howard had dug up. What could be the harm? 'Yes, why not. Ian should be back up to speed on Tuesday, so that would be great. I do appreciate all you've done for me, you and Ruth.'

Marco patted his arm. 'It's our pleasure. Ruth will be over the moon. I'll text you the details once I've confirmed with Howard.'

Tony watched him exit. He wasn't sure he was doing the right thing, but never mind, there was nothing he could do about it now.

He turned to pick out Nina's head among the diners, the smile returning to his face when he spotted her, and he made his way to the table.

Lewis was presenting a full-on charm offensive, smiling and chatting with Nina, while Jamie stared at their exchange. Tony slid into the vacant seat, winking at Jamie and ruffling his hair, waiting for Lewis to realise he was there. When he did, he stepped back, quickly resuming a professional stance.

'I was just saying to Nina, the carvery is ready when you are. Make your way to the far end. You know the drill.'

'Yes, Lewis. I know what I'm doing.' Tony also knew what Lewis was doing, flirting with Nina, and he didn't appreciate it.

Oblivious to his employer's annoyance, Lewis presented Nina with a short bow. 'Passez une bonne soiree, belle dame.'

Tony watched, lips pursed, as Lewis walked away, before muttering quietly. 'The idiot obviously thinks you're French.'

Nina chuckled. 'I don't mind. He was only trying to be polite. Besides, I speak French well.'

Jamie was impressed. 'Can you really speak French, and Spanish and English? I went to French club at school once, but it was really hard.'

'You have to practice very much to learn a language well, but it's worth it. Do you remember any French words?'

Jamie shook his head.

'I learned a little of many languages because I have worked in lots of different countries. Perhaps I could teach you some?' Nina looked to Tony, checking she had not overstepped the mark.

Tony grinned at his son. 'What do you say, Jamie? You could learn to ask for ice cream in three different languages.'

Nina laughed aloud. 'I can definitely teach you that much, but not only in three languages.'

'How many can you speak?' Jamie was impressed.

She amused him further by counting on her fingers. 'Spanish, French, English, Italian and German, and a tiny bit of Swedish and Polish. That's seven.'

'Wow!' Jamie's eyes were wide.

'She's a very clever lady.' Tony chucked him under the chin. 'Why don't you show Nina where to go for her food? Go on. You lead the way.'

Jamie jumped down, took Nina by the hand and led her away. Tony stood to follow and spotted Lewis, loitering by the bar, focussed intently on Nina's behind. His first instinct was to punch him, but on second thoughts, he decided a more subtle lesson was in order. Trotting up behind her, Tony placed his hand on the spot where Lewis's eyes were resting, then turned to meet his gaze. Realising he had been caught in the act, Lewis coughed and turned his attention to the computer screen. Tony inwardly laughed at the young man's discomfiture. Perhaps now Lewis would realise she was spoken for.

CHAPTER 22

Howard was not what Tony had imagined. Exceptionally tall and wiry, the lecturer had stretched limbs, as if he had forgotten to stop growing. His voice was naturally booming, with an undercurrent of animation which never went away, but bubbled ferociously when he was excited, drawing the attention of all within earshot.

He was already seated when Tony and Marco arrived and welcomed them with an explosive greeting from across the room. A rumpus of introductions took place, drinks were ordered, and the party settled down to business.

Marco took a lengthy slurp from his glass, then began to pat down the front of his jacket. 'Ah, yes, before we start.' He extricated a flimsy plastic wallet from an inside pocket. 'This arrived. The elusive birth certificate from Scotland. Apparently, there was some sort of mishap at the sorting office, hence the delay and the state of it, but apparently you can claim expenses from the Post Office if you have to get it reproduced or whatever.' He withdrew the remnants of a tattered form and arranged them on the table.

All three crowded around the document. It had been ripped into several pieces and partially taped back together, but there were a number of loose fragments, and the size and shape of them suggested some portions were missing entirely.

Tony followed the main body of the text with his

finger. Staining had distorted the print and it was difficult to decipher, but he could read the name and date. The rest was mangled. 'I can't make much out of this. It's definitely for Antonio, but ...' He shrugged, disappointed.

'Howard? Cast your eyes across this. See what you can make of it.'

Howard pulled it directly in front of him and painstakingly smoothed the smaller pieces with his finger. 'This could take some time, but we'll see what we can do. So, Antonio Viscount was your grandfather?'

'Yes, he was, but obviously I never knew him. He died when my father was a baby.'

'So, I understand.' He continued to work as he spoke. 'Certificates like this are a great tool, but it's the stuff which happens between the births and deaths which are most interesting. Forms don't tell you anything about the man, do they?'

'No, but you've got to start somewhere, and I don't have much to go on, as my father also died when I was young. I desperately want to know where I come from, who my ancestors were.' He was surprised by how important the quest was becoming to him.

'I can understand that. Who are we if not a product of our predecessors?' He placed a couple of torn fragments alongside the bulk of the certificate, like a ragged jigsaw. 'And I must say you've done very well with such an inauspicious beginning.'

'Mainly thanks to Ruth. She's been great.'

Marco was proud. 'She loves a good mystery does my woman.'

Howard sat back to take a drink and straighten the curvature in his back. 'Yes, I've said it before and I'll say it again, goodness knows what she's doing with you, Rossi. She's clearly far too good for you.' He looked at Tony. 'She gave me some valuable details and I must say I was quite intrigued, with the disconnection, the strange migration pattern, but it quickly came together. You have a fascinating past.'

'Thank you, I think. Is fascinating good or bad? Is that your way of telling me I come from a long line of psychopaths?'

Howard guffawed. 'Not that I know of, but it's early days.' He continued with the jigsaw. 'First things first, there's the question of how Antonio came to move from Scotland to Wales. Not the strangest move, of course. People did move around post-war, but not usually without good reason. The big clue was the Isle of Man.'

Tony was muddled. 'The Isle of Man is a clue?'

'Yes, well, not in its own right, but that combined with the date.' He nudged Marco with a pointy elbow and winked, before turning back to Tony. 'Which would you prefer, Welsh ancestry or Scottish?'

Tony was happy to play along. 'Oh, I don't know. They both have colourful histories. I suppose I see myself more Robert the Bruce than Llewelyn Ap... whatever he was called. Go on. Break it to me gently. Am I English, after all?'

Howard rested his palm on the certificate and twisted to face Tony. It was far from complete, but in much better order than previously. He highlighted one area with the edge of his hand. 'What does that look like to you?'

Tony leaned forward to study it. 'It's a signature.'

'Yes, the signature of your great grandfather, but what does it say?'

'It's a bit of a scrawl, but I guess the end section says Viscount.' He frowned as he tried to make it out.

'You're seeing what you expect to see. Try again.'

Tony shuffled to prevent himself blocking the light and looked again. 'No. It's not Viscount, but similar. The handwriting's not great. Viscont with a flourish at the end or Visconti. Visconti?'

'Exactly.' Howard's tone reached maximum animation. 'Visconti it is! You're neither Welsh nor Scottish. You're Italian!'

'What?'

'Mmm.' He confirmed, pulling the document back towards himself and fiddling with the last of the piece. 'Your great grandfather was Italian in origin. During the Second World War, Italian ex-pats were impounded on the Isle of Man, to prevent spying. Many of them had lived here for years, saw themselves as British, but there was a great deal of suspicion and bad feeling toward them when Italy sided with the Nazis, and the Government decided that was the best course of action. Your grandfather was held in one of the Manx camps. It looks like he went on to work for the Allies and was posted down south, later in the war, transcribing Italian code into English, which is how he came to be awarded the commendation in the article Ruth found.'

'But how did Visconti become Viscount? And why would they have moved from Italy to Scotland of all places?' This was not a line of enquiry Tony had anticipated.

'I can't tell you exactly why they relocated, but they weren't alone. Italy wasn't a great place to live in the nineteenth century: their economy was dreadful and conditions dire. Millions upped and left over the course of a couple of decades. If they had any connections elsewhere in the world, or saw opportunity for employment elsewhere, they took it. As for the family name, you see it throughout history: changes of spellings or pronunciation, shortenings, sometimes accidental, but sometimes to oil the wheels of settling in a new place. No one wants to stand out as different when they're trying to fit in.'

Marco agreed. 'I can vouch for that. We've been Rossis for generations, but prior to that we were Rosenbergs. I'm guessing someone back in time wanted to conceal Jewish roots. We're such a cosmopolitan world these days it's difficult to see the point, but people aren't always as accepting, I suppose.'

Tony sat back and took a long draught from his pint. 'Italian. Who would have thought?'

'Several hundred miles south of where you thought you sprang from, eh? I'd like to say I'd traced back further still for you, but although I'd made the Italian connection, I didn't actually have the correct surname until now. I'll get back on to it over the next couple of days and see what I can turn up, but access to Italian registers isn't quite as simple as in the UK, so it may take a while.'

'No problem, I appreciate you taking the time. That's amazing.' He reached for his wallet, 'I certainly owe you a drink. What can I get you?'

Howard picked up his glass and downed the dregs. 'Go on, then. I'll have one for the road, same again please.'

Tony took Marco's order too and headed to the bar, his mind swimming with the facts revealed to him. It was incredibly exciting to discover he had links to another country, a country he had never even visited. Drinks collected, he returned to the others and regained his seat, ripping open a packet of peanuts.

Howard was waiting. 'I almost forgot to tell you.'

'What? Is there a relative in Outer Mongolia as well?' Tony was joking but would not have been overly surprised by anything now.

'Not that I know of, but I did dig up some information about your great grandfather, Leonard. Ruth told me you thought he died in the First World War, but that's not the case. He never was a soldier.'

Tony threw peanuts into his mouth and offered the packet around the table. 'But he died of a bayonet wound. How could that be?'

'Pub brawl. I accessed judicial records, though no one was ever charged.' Howard declined the nuts with a wave of his hand. 'The report showed witnesses had seen him at his local, in Glasgow, early in the evening, he was known as a heavy drinker apparently, and a row broke out. He was asked to leave, which he did, under duress, but his body was discovered hours later, after chucking out time, in the gutter down the road, the bayonet still stuck in his gut.'

'Good grief. That's brutal.' Tony threw himself back into his seat.

Marco hooted with laughter. 'Listen, Tony, no offence, but I'm glad we're not related. It seems everyone in your bloodline comes to a sticky end. You should watch your back, mate!'

Tony joined in with the hilarity, but his stomach clenched at the pattern which was forming. As much as the idea was farfetched, the facts couldn't be denied: his father died in a house fire; his grandfather killed by a train and now, his great grandfather stabbed and left in the gutter. It seemed the Viscount family were possibly the unluckiest family on the planet.

CHAPTER 23

His family's bad luck weighed heavily on Tony's shoulders. He turned each death over in his mind to make sense of it, but the bizarre nature of each still unsettled him. The deaths were unconnected, had happened years apart, in massively different circumstances, providing no threatening pattern, but nonetheless he would have been more comfortable had they lived to a ripe old age.

For the first time, he quizzed Trish about the fire which killed his parents. He'd been too young when it happened to want details, but now he felt remiss for not knowing more. Trish's response had been reassuring, but scant in detail. There had been an inquest and she still had a copy of the report somewhere, but there had never been any suggestion of foul play and, like him, she had been too wrapped up in loss to question the findings. She promised to dig out the file but urged him to concentrate on the present rather than dwell on old events.

He sensed she was worried about his growing fascination with the past, from the tight tone of her voice. Her anxiety was understandable, as he realised his interest could easily become obsession, but he was determined to keep it in check. With that in mind, when Jamie was invited to Charlie's birthday sleepover at the weekend, Tony embraced the unexpected freedom and made plans for a night out with Nina.

They went to a trendy diner on the corner of the

High Street, with outdoor seating, so they could people watch as they ate. The sun was strong and remained well into the evening, and the balmy fresh air was a welcome boon. A carnival atmosphere, seeded by the weather, had everyone in high spirits and conversation flowed, as did the wine, and by ten o'clock it was becoming rowdy. As the volume rose, they decided enough was enough and Tony settled the bill. He led Nina by the hand, weaving through the crowded pavement toward the town centre, the hubbub fading as they moved away.

'Man, it was loud back there!' Nina stumbled after him, a sudden breeze and the last glass of wine, both hitting her simultaneously.

Tony drew her into his side, an arm around her shoulder, though his legs were little steadier than her own. 'I know, but it's early yet. Let's find somewhere quieter?'

Clinging to each other, they bypassed a number of bars, all with joyful but noisy customers spilling on to the streets.

'Half the world seems to be out tonight.' Tony checked his watch. 'I know. I've got the perfect location for a nightcap.' They rounded the corner. 'It's classy, intimate, there's soft lighting and gentle music and it's very select in its clientele.'

He halted outside The Olive Branch. The lights were out, and the door locked, but he reached deep into his pocket for a set of keys and carefully selected one to gain entry. The alarm sounded and, giggling, he bundled Nina through the staff room door to the control box to deactivate it. He backtracked to secure the main entrance, then escorted her through to another door at the back, leading out onto the beer garden.

She laughed at the empty space which greeted her.

'Very select clientele, but I don't hear music.'

He bowed. 'Please take a seat, my lady. Your wish is my command.'

Returning inside, he slipped behind the bar and activated the exterior stereo system, then selected a good bottle of red wine from the rack and two glasses from a shelf above. Backing through the rear door, he turned to find Nina swaying to the music in the gap between the tables, short flowery dress shimmying around her thighs. He placed the bottle and glasses on the nearest table and joined her, slipping his arms around her waist. She opened her eyes, sliding her hands up his chest to the back of his neck, their lips meeting for a long, sensuous moment. They clung together, Nina resting her head on his shoulder as they moved to the sultry melody.

When the track finished, they pulled apart and Nina spotted the bottle on the table. She dragged him toward it. 'You are a very bad influence. Are you trying to get me drunk?'

'I think that boat sailed. You are definitely a little worse for wear.'

She held a glass up for him to pour into. 'That is the pot calling the… or the kettle calling the… What is it?'

'It's the pot calling the kettle black.' He assisted her into a chair, before sitting opposite.

'Well, I'm glad you admit to it.'

'I'm admitting nothing. Drink your wine.' Reaching across, he hooked a lock of hair behind her ear.

She took a sip and groaned. 'This is very good, Mr Viscount, very good indeed.' Tilting her head to one side. 'Should I still be calling you Mr Viscount? Or do you answer to Mr Visconti, now? How do you like being Italian?'

He shrugged. 'I don't like the idea my days are numbered.' Tony swallowed deeply, staring into his glass, as he rolled it between his hands.

'What do you mean?' She leaned across the table, frowning and gripped his wrist.

He shook his head. 'Oh, nothing. It's just, none of my ancestors lived into old age. My father was only in his forties when he died, my grandfather was forty-four and my great grandfather was younger still, not much older than I am. I've tried Googling further back, but Visconti seems to be a very common name in Italy, and I don't really know where to start, but from what I do know, it's like we're jinked.'

Nina slapped his hand playfully. 'Don't be silly. It means nothing. Your great, great grandfather probably lived to be a hundred years old.'

'I don't know if I'd want to live that long.' His mood had taken a dip and her simplistic reassurances were insufficient to rouse him.

She scrambled from her seat, onto the bench next to him, stroking his right earlobe between her finger and thumb, as she breathed words into the other. 'Not even with me, right beside you?'

He turned into her embrace. 'Maybe I could be persuaded.' As his mouth caressed hers, heat rose, the soft, gentle kiss becoming deeper, more intense with every moment.

'Are you coming home with me tonight?' Tony desperately longed for her to say yes.

'Are you inviting me?'

He replied with his lips on hers in another long, hot caress. 'I'll call a taxi.'

As he reached for his phone, she snatched up her handbag and rose from the seat. 'Which way is the ladies room?'

Tony gave her directions and watched as she negotiated the steps down to the entrance, then dialled the cab service, sat back and waited, enjoying the subtle breeze sneaking round the main building, making feathers of the hair on his forehead. There was little noise here, although if he listened hard, he could still hear muted revelry from the main street. The walled courtyard held everything outside at a distance, making it feel private and protected, a secret haven.

A sudden sound from the brick outbuilding, attached to the back of the kitchen, drew his head round in a snap. Over previous months, several incidents of damage to goods stored inside had occurred and the staff suspected vermin but had found no evidence. In the meantime, they had moved perishable items, storing only solid goods, kegs, used crates and the like out there.

The only way in was through a wooden slatted door on the side, from the courtyard, which was kept padlocked, and there was a narrow window high up, close to the flat roof, which provided natural light. Tony sat in silence, eyes fixed on the door, holding his breath, listening for a repeat of the sound, to pinpoint its origin. There was none and he was beginning to think he had imagined it, when a quiet shuffle sounded from inside. He jumped to his feet and tiptoed across the slabs. The padlock was missing, and, after a quick search, he spotted it, resting on an empty oil drum to one side, under the window of the kitchen. He made a mental note to mention it when next in contact with Ian. Although it was a tucked away spot, you could never be too careful.

Edging back the bolt, he bolstered himself for rats or other creatures to scurry past as he threw open the door but, as he gazed in, there was no sign of movement, just an unnatural stillness, as if something was watching and waiting. He picked up a broom, leaning against the shelving units which lined the walls, and tentatively stepped further in, jabbing out with his makeshift weapon at a sack of potatoes in the far corner. The sack fell over, spilling its contents, but nothing untoward emerged. Relieved, Tony dropped the brush and set about collecting up the escaped tubers, piling them back into their bag. As he stretched over the top to the furthest corner, the door swung shut, leaving him in relative darkness.

Straightening up and swearing under his breath, he grasped the shelves on either side to gain his bearings and allow his eyes to become accustomed to the dim. He presumed the door had been caught by the breeze and a firm hand would be enough to push it open, but as he leaned against it, it remained sealed. Placing both hands flat on the crossbar, he pushed again, but it was stuck fast, and he began to suspect horseplay, rather than nature.

'Nina! Very funny, now let me out.' He waited and listened but could hear nothing beyond the door. 'The taxi's on its way. We need to go through to the front to keep an eye out for him.'

There was no response and he leaned back against the shelves, waiting for her enjoyment of the prank to wear off, but his patience wore thin first. 'Nina?' He listened as hard as he could, his senses heightened by the isolation. An acrid smell tickled his nose and he inhaled deeply to identify the aroma. It was warm and sharp and his eyes smarted as it built around him. Smoke.

He pounded on the door, any residue of amusement dissolving. Smoke was billowing under the door into the confined space where he was trapped and there was nothing he could do about it, no way he could escape, except through the blocked portal. His chest bubbled with the contaminated air, and he coughed into his sleeve. If he couldn't get out, he had to stop the smoke coming in. He grabbed the potato sack, wrenching it on to its side so the contents emptied onto the floor. Then he took the empty bag and pushed it into the crack at the base of the door. His lungs began to hurt, and he felt panic rise within him, but swallowed it down, knowing if brute strength could not help him, then a clear head was his only hope.

The window caught his attention. It was too small for a human to climb through even if he could somehow get his body up to its level, but if he could smash it, it would allow fresh air back into the space. He grabbed the long-handled brush from where it had landed and, holding it by the bristle end, thrust it up, past the goods on the shelves, into a gap where the glass was exposed. The first hit created no more than a dull thud. The second, more powerful impact, spread a spider's web of cracks from the corner of the pane. He pushed the end through and swept the fragments aside.

Before he had time to consider further action he heard Nina's voice shouting, becoming louder as she came closer. 'Tony? Tony? What are you doing? Are you in there?'

'Yes, I'm in here.' Relief washed through him. 'The door's stuck. Can you see what's blocking it?'

He heard her muttering loudly, a heaving and shoving accompanied with pained squealing, as the door flew outwards. His body fell through the gap onto the grass, and he gulped at the clean air.

Nina was clasping her left hand with the other. 'What were you doing? I burnt myself. This thing is hot.'

The oil drum was lying on its side against the wall, smoke pouring from under an ill-fitting lid. The padlock was lying next to it.

He jumped to his feet. 'I thought I heard a noise inside. When I went in the door banged shut and I couldn't get out. I thought it was you, playing games.' Taking her damaged hand, he examined it. The skin was pink and puckered. 'Come on, let's get that under the cold tap.'

'Some game!' She muttered through clenched teeth, as they moved back inside and through to the kitchen. 'The drum was in front of the door. Who would do such a thing?'

'Keep that under the water. I'm going to check out the back and make sure there's no one there. Will you be all right?'

She nodded brusquely. 'I'm fine. Be careful though. Should we call the police, do you think?'

'Yes, but I want to be certain there's no one out there doing more damage. I won't be long.'

Tony slipped a long knife from a block, before hurrying back outside. There was nobody there. He sensed it. Everything was quiet and still, the only sign of anything untoward the smoke still seeping out in thick, black clouds. He gave the drum a wide berth, circling all four corners of the garden, the knife held out like a talisman. The area was empty. There were few places a person could hide, and they were all vacant, but the rear gate, which opened onto a delivery area, servicing several units along the street, was unlatched and swinging against its frame.

He stepped through and glanced up and down the concreted area outside, but there was no sign of anyone or anything out of the ordinary. He breathed deeply as he scanned the horizon. Whoever had been there was gone now. Back in his own grounds, he pulled the gate closed, shaking it firmly to check its stability and cast his eyes across the whole space. He had never felt anything but safe here. Suddenly that was no longer the case.

Inside, Nina remained at the sink, a gentle flow of

water running over her injury, all the earlier joy of the evening drained from her face.

'Whoever it was has gone. Are you ok?' He kissed her forehead.

'I'm fine. I've had worse burns making dinner.'

'Ok. I'm going to phone the police.' He paused at the door to the dining area. 'I'm sorry the evening ended this way.'

She shook her head. 'It's not your fault, is it?'

'No, I suppose not. I'm glad you were here though. Goodness knows what would have happened, if you weren't.' His frown deepened as he considered the alternatives.

'Don't even think about it. Go on. Make the call.' She urged. 'I want to go home.'

'Of course. Sorry. The taxi will be here any minute. I guess you could go if you want to. I can deal with the police.'

'Tony, I don't want to be alone tonight. Can I still come home with you?'

He left the door and stepped toward her, wrapping his arms around her body, carefully avoiding the sore, outstretched limb. 'Of course you can. It's what I want more than anything.'

As he dialled the police, his mind flicked back over the events of the last hour, checking the facts and the order they'd happened, from deactivating the alarm to dancing on the lawn to breaking free from the storeroom. He hadn't sensed anyone else in the garden, it had just been him and Nina, hadn't it? But it couldn't have been. Someone had closed the door. Someone had tipped the oil drum in front of it, and someone had started the fire. But who was that someone and why on earth would they want to do him harm? A voice announced the emergency services at the end of the line and Tony's thoughts switched to the task in hand.

CHAPTER 24

Tony lay awake, listening to Nina's soft breathing in the bed next to him, as he ruminated over the night's events. The police had kept them busy well into the early hours, looking around the place, filling in forms. Their conclusion was there had been an intruder, interrupted by Tony and Nina's arrival, who had seen a chance for escape when Tony entered the storeroom and gone for it, disregarding possible repercussions in their eagerness to get away.

Tony had been shocked and frightened by the experience. He shuddered to think how easily he could have joined the list of Viscount men who died young. What would have happened to Jamie? Who would have been there to protect his little boy? After a while though, it occurred to him, perhaps this had been his brush with death; some sort of supernatural test of his mettle and he had passed, unlike his ancestors, he had come through, unscathed.

His mind circled these views all night but, as early morning light filtered through the curtains, he finally reached a conclusion. It had been a terrifying experience, but he had survived and was grateful. He would try to ensure nothing like that ever happened again, but, if it did, he would have backup systems in place. He needed to secure his son's future, but in a way that didn't compromise his own happiness. It wouldn't be easy, and he suspected it would mean those around him having to do some compromising of their own:

Ruth and Marco accepting Nina; Nina accepting she was a part of Jamie's life as well as his own and Trish accepting Ruth was one of his best friends, even if she had doubts about Ruth's motives. All these people were important to him, and they played a vital role in the future of his son. Mindset, he felt his shoulders relax and, at last, he was able to sleep.

The morning was a rush of phone calls, to Ian and the insurance company, to explain what had happened, and to his closest friends, to invite them to a barbecue that afternoon. A few hours of slumber had not reduced his determination to knock the corners of his life into shape. He left Nina at the house, stretched out in the sunshine in the back garden, having returned home for shower and fresh clothes, while he made a swift circuit of the supermarket and collected Jamie from Charlie's house.

A few minutes down the road, Tony pulled over to talk to Jamie face to face, bubbles of nervousness rattling inside him.

'Why are we stopping here?'

Tony climbed from the front seat into the back, next to his boy. 'I wanted to have a quick chat with you, that's all.'

A frown appeared on Jamie's forehead. 'Have I been naughty?'

Tony laughed and his anxiety dissipated a little. 'Not that I know of. No, I wanted to have a chat about Nina.'

The boy sat in silence, waiting.

'I like Nina.' There, it was out there, plain and simple. 'I like Nina quite a bit and I was hoping you liked her too, because she might be coming to visit us more often. What do you think?'

Jamie seemed to consider the implications. 'Nina's very good at games,' he paused, 'and she did say she would teach me some Spanish words.'

'Good. So, you don't mind, if she comes around the house sometimes?'

'No, I don't mind.'

Thinking the conversation was at an end, Tony reached for the door handle, but was pulled up short.

'Dad?'

'Yes?' He looked over his shoulder.

'Is Nina your girlfriend?'

The question was innocent enough, but Tony suspected how he replied could affect everything. He decided honesty was the best policy. 'Yes, Jamie. Yes, she is. Is that ok?'

The child nodded and, as he appeared to have nothing more to add, Tony once again moved to leave the back seat.

'Dad?'

'Yes?' Again, he turned back.

'I have a girlfriend too. She's called Jessica. Is that ok?'

Tony had to stop himself laughing aloud. Jamie clearly considered this a serious question, by the expression on his face. 'Yes, Jamie. That's absolutely fine.' He didn't quite know what else to say. 'Did you want to invite her over sometime?'

The boy made a disgusted noise and shook his head vigorously. 'No!'

'Oh, ok. Well, thanks for telling me then.' He climbed back into the drivers' seat. 'Nina's at the house now. We're going to have a barbecue later.'

'Ok.' Jamie's attention was back on a collection of Lego he was busy deconstructing and rebuilding on his lap.

Tony watched in the rear-view mirror with a light heart. If only all his friends would accept his life decisions so easily.

Trish was first to arrive, and Tony was glad. It gave him the chance to introduce her to Nina without onlookers. The two women warmed to each other instantly, bonding over their common interest in Jamie and love of travel. When she heard that Nina and Marco were to join the party, Trish eyed him curiously, but said nothing.

He acknowledged the look with, 'It'll be fine.' And it would be fine, he was sure. Trish was mature enough to keep her opinions to herself and would provide a good buffer between Ruth and Nina. What could possibly go wrong?

When the Rossis arrived, any potential awkwardness was avoided by an overenthusiastic Max, who rushed through the house to the patio and almost launched himself onto the smouldering barbecue. The ice was broken, if not completely melted.

Jamie disappeared with Max into the trees at the bottom of the garden, close enough for their play to be heard, without interfering with grown up business. Tony ensured everyone had a drink in their hand, then made a start on his personal agenda.

'Ok, guys. I know most of you have met before, but I thought we should do this properly.' He passed an arm around Nina's shoulders. 'As you know, Nina and I haven't known each other for long, but she's become quite important to me and I'm hoping you'll all welcome her into the…' He searched for the right word. 'What? Pack? Group? Family? Whatever you guys consider yourselves to be.'

There was a short silence which Trish hurried to fill. 'Of course.' A ball bounced into their midst, closely followed by Max, who back flipped, caught it between his teeth and bounded away. 'Welcome to the madhouse.'

They all laughed, but Tony wasn't finished. 'Yes, it is a madhouse, most of the time,' He smiled at Nina directly. 'But you know that already.'

He pointed at Trish. 'Now, you've met Trish already, but I should clarify, she is my aunt, but has cared for me for much of my life, and although I often ignore her advice, I must acknowledge, she is probably the wisest person I know.'

Trish pooh-poohed his comments with a wave of her hand.

He turned to the Rossis. 'And this is Marco and Ruth.' Marco lifted his glass in a silent greeting, while Ruth stayed steady, waiting to hear what he had to say. 'They are the best friends a man could have. They've been there for me, particularly over the last few months, when I simply couldn't have coped without them. At times, they've fed me, clothed me, even got me drunk once or twice, I think, Marco?'

Marco coughed. 'Only when absolutely essential, old man.'

'And they've been real stars as far as Jamie is concerned. Nobody could ask for better friends.'

'All right. Rein it in, Tony. You'll have us blushing.' Marco wriggled in his seat.

'Yes, yes. I know. You can't bear anyone singing your praises, but there are times it needs to be done. Look, I've asked you all here for a reason, and I don't mean just to meet Nina, although she's definitely a good reason. Something happened yesterday which really got me thinking...'

Trish interrupted. 'What's happened?'

He held up his hand. 'I'll tell you all about it later, but it doesn't matter. What does matter is Jamie, and I need to be sure he's well looked after, no matter what. Now, me and Vicky were never very religious, so we didn't go in for christenings and all that, and we never really considered Godparents or suchlike, but I think we were remiss. I'm still not religious, so I'm not going to be dragging you down to church next weekend or anything, but I wanted to ask you, Trish, Ruth and Marco, if you would agree to be guardians, legally, I mean? I've also asked Vicky's sister, Sarah, but she couldn't make it here today.'

Silence reigned.

'I understand if you need time to think about it. It's a big ask, and if you'd rather not, that's fine. I don't want you to agree to anything you're not sure of, because I need to know Jamie would be well cared for, if anything were to happen to me.'

Trish leaned forward and patted his knee. 'It goes without saying. I love the little monkey to bits, and I would be more than happy to make it official, though I'm sure it'll never be needed. We're family.'

Tony squeezed her hand and turned to his friends. Marco was gazing in concern at his wife, whose hand had flown to her mouth at the request, her eyes full of tears. She nodded at her husband, unable to speak.

Marco coughed; his face more serious than Tony had ever seen it. 'Tony, we would be honoured. He's a smashing young chap and we absolutely adore him. Thank you for asking.'

Ruth continued to nod, silently agreeing with everything her husband said and Tony, not wishing to cause further embarrassment, changed the subject.

'Good. In that case I'm going to get the steak on the grill. Come on, Marco. Give me a hand.'

Within seconds the tension had lifted. They were all amused by Tony's downplayed and comical retelling of the events of the night before and even Tony began to feel better about it, suspecting excessive alcohol had played a part in the gravity he had viewed it with before. Games were played with Jamie and Max. Conversation flowed between all parties. Excellent food was served and eaten, and they lolled around the garden well into the evening, when Tony, aided by Marco, began to move dishes through to the dishwasher.

Several trips in, the phone rang, and Marco leaned through the patio doors to alert Tony, who was chasing Max away from leftover kebabs.

'Tony. Phone. Do you want me to get it?'

'Yes, please.' He gave up the chase and strolled inside to hear the tail end of Marco's dialogue.

'Good man. Yes, he's coming now. Definitely, soon.' He handed the handset to Tony. 'It's Howard. Got an update for you.'

'Hi, Howard. What have you got for me? Anything exciting?'

Howard began to speak, and, after a few moments, Tony reached for a pad and pen so he could jot the details down. The call was brief, but by the time it finished Tony had a page of notes and a thumping heart. He returned to the garden and slumped into a chair. Marco glanced around from the lawn, where he was wrestling a football away from his dog.

'What's new?' He tucked the ball under his arm, having won the round, and returned to the patio. Then, noticing the pallor of Tony's face, his enquiry took a serious note. 'Is everything all right?'

Tony shook his head in astonishment. 'Yes, yes. Everything's fine. It's just this.' He waved the notepad in the air. 'It gets worse.'

'Why worse?' Nina had been chatting to Trish, but her attention was caught by his tone.

'You know you thought my great, great grandfather lived to be a hundred?'

She nodded.

'He didn't.' Everyone, except Jamie, who was diving around the grass, imitating a jet plane, turned their attention to Tony. 'Get this. Leonardo, my great, great grandfather, died age twenty-eight. Death by hanging. His grandfather, Alessandro, died age thirty-six. Death by drowning.'

'What about the one in between? Leonardo's father. I bet he lived to be old and hearty.' Nina was determined to find a silver lining.

Tony shrugged. 'We shall never know. Apparently Tonio disappeared in eighteen fifty-nine, aged thirty, but his body was never found.'

'Is there any good news?' Trish studied his features, a crease between her eyes.

'I suppose, but not in relation to life expectancy. Howard managed to decipher more of the damaged birth certificate and found the town of birth for Leonard, which is how he came across the other information so quickly. It's in the southwest corner of Italy, so I've got a base now. Somewhere to start looking.'

'Looking for what?'

'I don't know. Reasons? Reasons why we came to the UK? Why we all die so young? I've got to go there.' He looked up to meet the eyes of those crowded around him but received no response except veiled glances at each other. 'You do see that, don't you? I have no idea what I'm going to find, but I've got to go.'

CHAPTER 25

As the plane banked to land at Brindisi Airport, Tony still wasn't sure he had the full backing of his friends for this pilgrimage. They'd rallied around to care for Jamie for the few days he would be absent, but there'd been an abundance of raised eyebrows. He had the feeling they thought he was taking his quest too far. Jamie had initially been disgruntled at being left out, but the promise of term end celebrations at school had persuaded him he was best off at home, so Tony had been able to leave with a clear conscience.

Howard had cobbled together a file of information to help him, places to visit, people to contact, and Tony had thoroughly absorbed it in preparation, determined to make the most of his time. He'd found very reasonable lodgings, close to where his great grandfather had been born, off the beaten track for the majority of travellers.

The journey from the airport lasted half an hour, firstly on multi-laned, busy roads, but the last few minutes saw them turn off to a narrower, quieter route. Glimpses of the choppy Ionian appeared between trees and houses, coastal lights bouncing off the waves, before the minibus turned inland, leaving the ocean behind. Tony absorbed everything he could see in the poor light, trying to identify anything which would call this place home, but there was nothing. It was very different from the English environment he had grown up in. By the time he arrived at the bed and breakfast, he was tired and disappointed by the lack of a natural connection to the place.

He rolled into bed without unpacking his bag, sleeping deep and dreamless, until the early morning sun glared through his uncovered window, disturbing his rest. A full eight hours had passed and the bubble of excitement within him was renewed and refreshed. Today was the day he would find his roots, find them and explore them, until he finally understood what the Visconti family was about.

Jumping out of bed, he peered through the window and found himself overlooking a quadrangle, hemmed by rustic old walls, and laid out with wooden bench tables. A few people were milling around, and he guessed this was where breakfast was served, so he quickly showered and dressed, eager to begin the day in earnest. He had a tight schedule to achieve all he wanted to in the time available, starting with a grilling of the guest house staff, who were sure to have local knowledge.

Signage directed guests from the lobby, along a terracotta tiled corridor and through double doors, propped open, affording entrance to the outside dining area. The air was already heavy with heat and the scent of jasmine, but the sun was kept at bay by the high surrounding walls.

A middle-aged woman, wearing an apron and with dark hair swept back in a bun, waved a greeting from where she was attending other guests and gesticulated for him to take a seat. He chose a seat on the perimeter, where he could take in the whole square, with its colourful potted plants dotted between tables, providing an idea of privacy from other diners. When the hostess arrived at Tony's table, he was disappointed to find her English poor, though far better than his Italian, and any idea of quizzing her fizzled out.

He had brought the dossier of information down with him and now spread the documents out, poring over them, wondering what to do first, while he sipped fresh orange juice and waited for his food. The Tourist Information centre seemed the best place to start. There, he should be able to buy a map, so he could work out a route to cover all the locations he wanted to visit; the address where his great grandfather lived prior to emigrating; the civic buildings and the museum of local history, among them.

A younger woman delivered his breakfast, and he scrabbled the paperwork out of her way, but it had obviously caught her eye.

'It looks like you're on a mission?' The heavily accented English was clear and fluent and took him by surprise.

'You're not Italian?'

'Yes and no. My father was Italian, but I grew up in Sweden, where my mother's family live. I spent a couple of years in England studying, but I'm having a gap year, travelling all over Europe, so here I am, in Italy.'

'And do you like it? Here, in Italy?'

Her smile was wide and genuine. 'I like it everywhere. Wherever I go I want to stay. Then I move to the next place, and I want to stay there, as well. I only meant to stay here a week, but they needed help in the kitchen, and I thought, why not? Croatia will wait. It's not going anywhere, and I have another two months before I have to go back to college.'

Tony envied her free spirit. He rarely did anything without extensive planning and cogitation first. Although, he had never heard of this place until ten days ago and here he was. Perhaps he did share a portion of her spontaneity, after all.

Wiping a hand on her apron, she proffered it to shake. 'I'm Sonya, by the way.' She tapped his file. 'You are looking for something here? It is not a holiday for you?'

He grabbed at the opportunity to get help in his search. 'Tony. Yes. I am looking for something. My family came from here years ago and I'm here to find out as much about them, and the place, as I can. Would you know any locals? Are there still any Visconti's living here, do you know?'

'I'm sorry.' She shrugged her shoulders. 'I haven't been here long enough to know these things. I could ask Renata if you wish. She is native here.'

'Would you? That would be great if you don't mind.'

She tucked the empty tray under her arm. 'Of course. Give me a few minutes. When I have a chance, I'll speak to her.'

Tony sat back and sipped at the strong, black coffee. The caffeine zinged through his bloodstream, and he simmered, waiting for her return. Absent-mindedly, he observed the staff flitting from table to table, busy about their duties, hungry sparrows skilfully playing chicken around their feet as they moved.

At last, he saw Sonya pause by the beaded curtain to the kitchen, allowing Renata to pass the other way. She touched the older lady's shoulder to delay her, and they both glanced his way. He guessed the question about his family was being relayed. He saw Renata's head snap around at whatever had been said, her hand flicking up to create a vehement stop sign. There was a brief, but emphatic interaction between the women, before Renata stalked away, shaking her head, Sonya left staring after her. Tony straightened up in his seat, the communication between the pair piquing his interest. What had been said to cause such a strong reaction? He was sure they'd been talking about him.

In the few minutes it took for the young waitress to return to his table, he watched Renata rushing between guests and, unless he was imagining it, avoiding eye contact with him.

When most of the quadrangle had cleared, Sonya sidled next to him and slid into a chair. 'Sorry, Tony. Renata is not able to help, but here…' She handed him a leaflet, unfolding it to reveal a map of the town. 'This should help. We're here.' She marked the paper with a fingernail and traced a route with the digit. 'If you walk down here, you will find the Tourist Information. They are good, but not always open, so talk to someone there, maybe.'

Watching her face intently, he asked the question burning inside him. 'Renata seemed… annoyed? Is there a problem?'

Sonya darted a glance over her shoulder, locating her employer. 'No, no. Not at all.' She lowered her voice. 'She is not always as helpful as she could be. She doesn't like to get involved. You know?'

'Not really. Involved? Involved in what?'

'I don't know.' She shook her head and shrugged. 'Renata is just Renata. Listen, see what they can tell you in town and let me know what you learn, at breakfast tomorrow. I work at the bar next to the library in the evenings and I will ask around, see what I can find out.' She stood to walk away. 'We'll speak tomorrow, yes?'

'Thank you. I will.' He had a feeling there was more to Renata's reticence than Sonya was letting on, but there was nothing he could do about it, and he'd find answers from somewhere. Lips pursed; he studied the map. A quick perusal highlighted several landmarks he wanted to visit, so he gathered his things together and headed out.

He turned out of the lodgings and downhill, past outlying stone villas edged with large vibrant gardens, towards the whitewashed flat roofed houses in the main town. Pavements were sparse, and he was forced to hop into broad, shallow gutters whenever a vehicle passed. The lower town was a higgledy-piggledy mass of tombstone buildings, clinging to the hill, with narrow stepped walkways joining upper to lower levels, opening out onto pleasant squares, where people sat, drinking coffee and watching the world go by.

A tall, spluttering fountain indicated he was in the right place, and he ambled towards the far corner, where the map showed the Tourist Information office would be. Two large jardinières marked either side of the entrance, but the blinds were closed and the lights off. A small sign propped up inside the window displayed what he presumed to be opening hours and, after checking his watch, he surmised he had another hour before anyone would turn up. Frustrated, he re-examined the map and followed a side alley around the side of the office, to a large intricately embellished civic building, his fingers crossed that this would be open. It was.

Broad steps led up to a triple set of double doors, all smoked glass and chrome, completely out of keeping with the architecture, and as Tony jogged up, the centre pair automatically swung inwards, drawing him into a lush lobby. The doors closed behind him, creating a respectful hush, and when the smart young male receptionist looked up to greet him, Tony hurried to the desk rather than raise his voice.

'Hello. Do you speak English?'

'Yes, sir. How can I help you?'

'I believe Mr...' He referred to Howard's notes. 'Stefano Esposito works here. A friend has arranged for me to collect some forms from him.'

The assistant tapped the keyboard on his desk. 'Mr Esposito, yes. It will be necessary for you to make an appointment.'

'Oh. Ok.'

The man tilted his head as he studied the screen. 'Thursday? In the afternoon?'

'Oh.' Tony's heart sank. He flew home on Thursday and had hoped to have the promised certificates earlier, to assist with his investigation. 'There's nothing sooner?'

'Mr Esposito is a very busy man.' He did not crack a smile.

Tony had a feeling the receptionist was being obstructive, but what could he do? He was at the mercy of the Italian Civil Service. 'Ok. Thursday's fine, thank you, but could I leave my mobile number and if there are any cancellations, perhaps Mr Esposito would call me. I would be happy to come in at short notice.'

The man shrugged. 'If you wish, but I think it unlikely.'

That was all Tony could ask. He provided the necessary information, pocketed an appointment card, and backtracked through the doors to the steps. At the bottom he paused, pulled the map from his file, and looked around for inspiration. No luck with the Tourist Information. No luck with the Civic Centre. What next? The local museum was only across the square, and it seemed logical to make that his next stop, though he was unsure if it would be much help.

He set off in its general direction but was pulled up short by a stranger's voice calling his name from behind. A short, round man with very little hair and an affable manner greeted him.

'Mr Viscount? Tony Viscount?' He held out a hand. 'Stefano Esposito. You are a friend of Howard Shoreland, I understand.'

'Yes. Very pleased to meet you. I've made an appointment to see you on Thursday.'

Stefano waved the idea away. 'No, no. Not necessary. Romano can be a little overzealous about guarding my diary. Listen, I do have a meeting this morning, but if you can come back in...' He studied his watch. 'Maybe an hour? An hour and a half? Yes, an hour and a half, I will see you then. Is that acceptable?'

Tony grinned. 'That would be fantastic.'

'Good.' Stefano began to walk back up the steps. 'Go to the museum. Go for coffee. I will see you later. Ok? Ok!'

Finally, something was going Tony's way. He smiled as he headed off in the direction of the museum.

CHAPTER 26

Inside the door of the museum was a gift shop, manned by a leathery old man, busy stamping prices on postcards. He looked up as Tony entered but returned to the task at hand when he decided his services weren't required. Helpfully the signs were in several languages and Tony soon identified the different areas of the centre. Straight ahead was a gallery of artwork and local crafts, and a side door gave way to a small, dark cafeteria, which appeared to be closed, while a chunky wooden dogleg staircase led up to historic artefacts.

He took the stairs two at a time and found himself in a wide corridor, the walls marked up with a graphic timeline, interrupted at intervals with glass topped display cases. The first part of the exhibition related to ancient history, and Tony hurried through the ages. Black and white photographs showed people at work and, although Tony was unable to read much of the text presented alongside, he surmised the wealth of the town had been built on olive cultivation, wine making and fishing. A gap, midway down the first corridor, opened into a box room with a television replaying a short video of a toothless old man hand knotting fishing nets, his gruff Italian voice repeating the intricacies of the ancient craft.

Another area was given over to law and order, and the methods used to encourage adherence to the straight and narrow, and Tony viewed the gruesome devices, presumably used to extract confessions, with horror. He enjoyed looking at locally made wickerwork and wood carving; maps and plans of the borough across the ages, expanding from a few houses to the busy town it now was. Nowhere did he find mention of the name Visconti among the exhibits. He headed downstairs, checking his watch along the way. He still had half an hour to kill before going back to see Stefano.

The old man was still busy, dusting shelves, and a couple of other visitors had wandered in and were browsing through guidebooks propped against a wall at the back of a narrow pine table. Tony thought about trying to speak to the curator about the Visconti family. If anyone would have good local knowledge, surely he was the man, but the presence of the other visitors made Tony self-conscious and he stepped back into the square, deciding instead to enjoy a walk in the sunshine, prior to his appointment.

By the time he re-entered to the Civic Centre, his cheeks were tinged pink by the sun and his lips were dry. Romano pointed him toward a cluster of cream and chrome chairs and a smoked glass coffee table, which served as a waiting area, but Tony barely had time to sit before Stefano appeared from an office at the rear, greeting him like an old friend, waving him through.

'So, Tony. How do you like your Mediterranean roots, huh? It's good to be Italian, no?' He poured coffee from a percolator into tiny cups and pushed one in front of Tony, before sitting behind his desk.

'Italy's a beautiful country.' He figured a little national flattery would do no harm. 'It's a bit of a shock to find out about our history here though, I had no idea.'

Stefano raised his cup and his eyebrows. 'Who can tell what our forefathers got up to, hey? I could tell you many stories, believe me.' He opened a drawer and pulled out a stack of papers. 'Since talking to Howard, I have dug a little deeper and have more information. Another generation. I hope this will please you.'

Tony was over the moon. 'You have? Thank you.'

'Howard has done much for me in the past and I like to repay my debts. Now, I should explain. In Italy, all certificates, must be requested by post and provided by post, so these...' He waved the papers in the air. 'These must be sent to you, once I have a signed request. Here.' He slid a form across the desk. 'If you sign this letter, I have prepared for you, it will seem as if you wrote to me yourself, so everything looks correct.'

Tony reached for a pen and signed where Stefano had indicated. 'Thank you, but I don't want to get you into trouble.'

Stefano waved away his concerns. 'It's all paperwork, you know, bureaucracy, but it's not a problem. Do you have ID with you today? Your passport perhaps?'

'Yes.' He pulled his passport from inside the file he was carrying and handed it over.

Stefano examined the photograph and laughed. 'These pictures, they are never like the real man, are they? At least, I hope not or there are some strange people out there.' He carried it to a scanner at the rear of the room and photocopied the page before handing it back. 'Ok. That's all I need from you and this...' He shuffled the papers again, 'is what you need from me.'

Tony took them and glanced through the information. It was all in Italian and made no sense to him whatsoever.

'As I say, the certificates must be posted, so I have put originals in the post. There's nothing I can do about that. They are entered in a register when they go through the post room so some things cannot be overcome. But what you have are very good copies. Our secret, yes?'

'Yes, of course. Thank you. I am grateful.' A frown gave away his confusion.

'You need me to explain?' Stefano nodded at the forms.

Tony was ashamed of his ignorance, but in their present state, the certificates were useless to him. 'Would you?'

'No problem.'

Stefano first went through the birth certificates, translating them from top to bottom, while Tony made hurried notes. The further generation took him back to the eighteenth century and he added the new name to the sketch of his family tree he was carrying. When it came to the death certificates Tony paid close attention. He questioned Stefano on the facts, but there were so many missing details it was impossible to create a clear picture.

'I don't understand how all these early deaths could have happened and not caused suspicion. Is that normal for Italy?'

'Italy does not do normal. But look, when you see all this on paper it seems shocking, but remember these things happened many years apart and maybe it was not seen in the same way. It may be there was nothing suspicious at all. Let's look more closely.' Stefano selected a form and ingested the details. 'Like this, Alessandro, died by drowning, but this is not a surprise. He was a fisherman in the nineteenth century. Many, many fishermen died in this way. The Ionian can be a cruel mistress. Nothing suspicious.'

He reached for another. 'And Leonardo, died by hanging, but they were hard times. People suffered much from the poverty and the difficult circumstances in which they had to live. Sometimes it was just too hard to keep going and people hang or take poisons or do something to harm themselves. Sad, but not suspicious.'

Tony pursed his lips, considering Stefano's words. 'What about Tonio? His disappearance? Is there information about what happened to him?'

Stefano drummed the table with his fingers as he read a different, longer document with small, closely penned notes. 'There is little to say about Tonio. He was reported missing by his wife when he did not return from a fishing expedition. You see? Again with the fishing. It's a dangerous occupation. The authorities declared him dead after two years, but the body was not found.'

'So, you don't think there was anything untoward going on?'

'Not at all.' Stefano placated. 'Remember, this was a hundred fifty years ago. Things happened.'

Perhaps Tony had blown the whole thing out of proportion. There was one certificate left to be examined and he hoped this would further quash his concerns. 'What about the last one?' He referred back to the family tree. 'Benedetto, wasn't it?'

'Yes, Benedetto, and of course we have his father's name from the birth certificate, another Alessandro, but unfortunately, I have not been able to locate documents for him yet. This is not so much a surprise considering the dates and I am sure something will come up soon. Now, Benedetto.' He ran his eyes over the document and his eyebrows sprung up his forehead and he looked at Tony. 'You wanted scandal. Now you have it for sure. Benedetto was killed. His throat cut.' He ran his finger in a cutting motion around his own neck in demonstration.

'What?' Tony was horrified.

'He was murdered. It is here, in black and white.' He slapped the form with the back of his hand.

'Who did it? Why did they do it?' This news had

slapped the growing optimism right out of him.

'I don't know. It doesn't say. There would have been official papers, an investigation, a report, I guess, but that sort of thing is not stored here. Also, it was eighteen eleven and records were not so reliable. I don't know if it would even be possible to find out. I can try. Make some calls.'

'I would really like to know, if it is possible. I'm sorry, I know you've gone to an awful lot of trouble already.'

Stefano shrugged. 'It's ok. It is my job. I will see what I can do, ok?'

Tony gathered his things together and piled them into the file, then rose to his feet. He held out a hand to his new friend. 'Thanks again. You've got my number, haven't you?'

'Yes. I have it. I will let you know what I find.' He followed Tony to the main doors and waved as he stepped into the sunshine.

Tony made to walk away, but suddenly back tracked as a thought occurred to him. 'Sorry, Stefano. I should have asked before. You're a local man, I guess. Do you know if there are still Visconti's living around here?'

Stefano rubbed his chin, considering the question. 'It's not a name I have heard, and I've been here for ten years. Before that, maybe, but I wouldn't know.' He turned to walk inside. 'I'll call you when I speak to my friends, yes?'

Tony gripped the file under his arm and wandered away. His imagination was full of unexplained murder and mayhem, and he felt drained. Glancing at his watch, he realised lunchtime had come and gone while he had been at the Centre and decided to find somewhere to sit and eat, while he came to terms with it all.

CHAPTER 27

Tony spent the rest of Monday afternoon searching the cemetery for the family name, but there was nothing, nothing to show the Visconti's had every existed, let alone inspire further investigation. The trail was cold.

At breakfast, Renata gave him a wide berth, so much so he began to despair of being fed, until Sonya appeared and was pointed in his direction, which went to prove Renata had been aware of his presence all along and chosen not to serve him. He wondered what he'd done to upset her.

Sonya was as amenable as ever and assured him she hadn't forgotten his mission but had mostly drawn a blank. One man had admitted recognising the name but confirmed the Visconti family were long gone. He had mentioned an address though; a vineyard outside town, which had been connected to the family, but had fallen into disrepair when it was abandoned, years ago. Sonya had scribbled the location on a napkin. Tony soon located it on a map on his phone, but with no idea how to get to it, he decided to head to Tourist Information for guidance.

Although there was little to go on, Tony felt a new glimmer of hope and eagerly set out, only to find the office locked, like the previous day. He kicked around, aware he had at least an hour to waste, but then remembered the bar Sonya worked at, next to the library and decided to find it, with the intention of going there that evening to speak to the locals himself.

He soon found it, his natural compass beginning to understand the maze of streets, but the shutters were padlocked so he strolled into the only building which appeared to be open so early in the day, the library.

It was compact, high shelves stacked with books of all sizes and genres, lining the walls. He wandered from one aisle to the next, running his eyes over the titles, wishing something would jump out and grab his attention. A petite woman, with wire rimmed glasses and a lanyard, spotted his aimless wandering and, after she had stacked an armful of books on a wheeled trolley, backtracked and spoke to him in rapid Italian. He shrugged, apologising in English, and she stood still, frowning as she searched for words.

'I help?'

He shrugged again, not knowing what he was looking for, let alone what to ask for. Eventually though, as she seemed intent on staying right where she was, he simply muttered. 'Visconti?'

She shook her head, her expression blank, but all he could think to do was repeat the name. On second hearing, she repeated the word to herself several times over, looking around the room for inspiration, which must have struck suddenly as her hand flew into the air like an exclamation mark. 'Aah!' She walked away, beckoning for him to follow. 'Come. Come.'

Stopping at a shelf to the rear, away from the colourful dust jackets of the fiction section, the woman ran a finger over the spines of a selection of tomes, pulled one out and inspected an index at the front. 'Yes.' She flicked forward to a point midway through the book and read the text for a few moments. 'Here. Visconti, yes?'

He looked at the line to which she was pointing and sure enough the name Visconti was there in clear print, but he could make nothing of the rest, not even the genre. He took the book from her hands and concentrated on it, frowning in frustration. The only way he would be able to translate the writing to English would be via a translator or the internet and clearly the librarian's language skills were not up to the job. Sonya would help, he was sure. He turned to the woman, who was watching him closely.

'Can I take this? Bring it back tomorrow?'

Her face was blank, but for mild suspicion.

He reverted to hand gestures and pidgin English to help her understand, tapping the book and pointing to the door. 'I take? Domani?'

Her face flew into a vivid, emphatic negative and she snatched the book from his hands, as if he were liable to make a run for it if he held it a second longer. 'No, no, no.'

She walked away, and he sensed the first piece of written information he'd found slipping from his grasp. He followed her, trying to remember any Italian he had stored in the long-closed vaults of his brain, drawing a blank. 'I'll bring it back. I promise.' It suddenly occurred to him the value of the book could be the issue and reached for his wallet, pulling out a handful of Euros. 'I can pay.'

The action drew her attention, and she stopped him, patting his hand. 'No, no, no.' Once again, she beckoned for him to follow, stopping at an oak island set up with office equipment. Opening the book out, she laid it flat on a photocopier, pulled the lid down as far as she could and set it going, physically blocking light entering around the gaps at the edges with her body. A sheet of paper whirred from the other end of the machine and grabbing it, she checked the quality of the print. Showing it to him, she again pointed out the name Visconti, so he could see the correct portion had been duplicated.

He took it from her. 'Thank you.' He couldn't wait to find out what this was all about. Waving the sheet, he began to walk away. 'Grazie!'

She stopped him with an urgent tap on the shoulder and an open palm. 'Euro.'

'Sorry.' Of course, he had to pay for the copy. He handed a coin over. 'Sorry. Grazie.'

Leaving the library, he took one more look at the document, before folding it and thrusting it into his back pocket. It felt good to know someone connected with him, somewhere in the past, had warranted a mention in the history books, whatever it may be for, and in a short time he would find out who and why. At last, here was something.

The front door of the Tourist Information Centre was open when he returned to it, and he brushed past the foliage marking the entrance into a busy room. A party of four had arrived ahead of him, and were browsing through leaflets and trinkets, chattering cheerfully in a language he guessed was Eastern European. Two members of staff, a young man and an older woman, wearing matching cravats and trouser suits, eyed the group, eager to be of service. Tony hung back, waiting for them to finish, so there'd be no pressure to hurry his own questions. When, finally, they left, he approached the desk.

'Do you speak English?'

The young man spoke. 'A little, yes.'

Tony let out a sigh of relief. 'Great. I hope you can help me. My grandfather's family came from here. Someone told me they once lived at this place.' He handed over the note on which Sonya had written the address. 'I'd like to visit it if I can. I don't have a car; do you know how I can get there?'

The couple came together to study the writing, muttering to each other quietly in Italian. The woman reached for a computer tablet and called up a map. They both perused it, expanding the view until the correct location came into view. She glanced up abruptly and uttered something sharp and short. The man chuckled and turned the map to face Tony.

'The house is here, you see? It is not on the main road and there are no signs. It is very private. Are you sure this is the place? It has been empty for very long. No one goes.'

Tony shrugged. 'No, not sure, but a local man said so. How could I check?'

The man muttered to the woman again, pausing for instructions before replying. 'What name is your family?'

'Visconti.' As the word left his mouth, the woman inhaled sharply. 'Have you heard of them?'

'I don't know. My colleague...' He turned to the woman, and they held a brief conversation, the man's face breaking into a condescending smile. 'My colleague knows a little. Only stories, you understand. She is very... um... superstitious.' His tongue stumbled over the word.

'Superstitious? I don't understand.'

'The house, it is part of an estate.' He explained. 'Once very rich. But now, it is known as Ghost House. Growing up, there are many stories about Ghost House. All made up, of course. It is just an empty old house, and mothers, they don't want the children to play in the ruins, so they make up horror stories. We all know the Visconti family lived there. It is like legend, you know? They lived there, they died there, then they are not there anymore. We didn't know any family are still alive. This is a surprise to see you.'

'My great grandfather moved to Scotland before the

Great War. I've only recently discovered he came from Italy. So, the Visconti family are all gone?' Tony felt strange, being the foundation of tales told to scare children into good behaviour.

'Yes, all gone, but not completely forgotten, as you see. They are remembered around campfires, whispered stories. Such things keep the name alive, particularly for people like my colleague.'

She had taken a step back but listened intently to their conversation.

'Can I visit the Ghost House? Or is it unsafe?' Tony wanted to see it for himself.

'No, you can go there, with care, but no bus goes that way. You could hire a car, but it's not far out of town. It would be less Euros to take a taxi. Not all drivers would go there, but it should be possible. Do you want me to arrange this? Today?'

'Please. That would be great.'

The man stepped back and pulled a small address book from next to the till, flicking through the pages, before picking up the phone. The woman muttered under her breath, but he waved her away and she stomped to the other side of the room, rearranging leaflets, tutting and huffing at regular intervals.

Tony listened to the man's telephone call but was unable to pick out more than a handful of words.

Covering the mouthpiece with his hand, the man leaned forward. 'You want to go now? Or after siesta?'

'Whenever I can. Now, I guess.' A piece of the jigsaw seemed about to fall into place.

The conversation resumed briefly, before the handset was replaced. 'Mario, the driver, will be here in five minutes. You discuss the fee with him, but don't pay more than thirty Euros. If he asks for more, tell him to talk to me.'

'Thanks.' Tony quickly pulled the folded paper from

his pocket. 'Just one more thing.' He smoothed it out with the heel of his hand and pointed to the sentence where the family name appeared. 'Do you know what this is about?'

The young man took the page and studied it, running his finger under the words. When he finished the sentence, he hummed to himself and looked wider, reading the whole paragraph for clarity. 'Aah! I see. This is about art.'

'Art?'

'You know, pictures. It talks about an artist from years ago, a local man, not very famous. He paint many people from this place. I think there is one painting, maybe more, of the legend of Visconti. This man's work is displayed at the museum. If you go there, perhaps you see a picture of your ancestor.'

Tony took the sheet back and replaced it in his pocket. 'In the museum? Thank you. I'll have a look.'

Returning outside, he stepped away from the entrance onto the square, waiting out of the flow of pedestrians for his driver. He mulled over what he'd learnt. For every answer he received, another question formed, and he wondered if he'd ever truly understand his Italian history, but perhaps understanding wasn't necessary. Understand it or not; like it or not, he simply had to accept it.

There was more wilderness about the estate than garden, the gateless entrance the only defined feature of otherwise blurred lines. Mario declared he would go no further in actions rather than words, halting the vehicle by the verge, reclining his seat and pulling a cap over his eyes.

Bemused, Tony got out and wandered down the overgrown path, checking behind at intervals to ensure the taxi was still there. Though it was unlikely Mario would leave without him, as no fee had as yet exchanged hands. About a hundred yards along the track, it veered left, around a patch of overgrown bushes and trees, and what remained of the building came into view. Wire netting fences squeezed the pathway here and there, and he suspected, over time, parcels of unworked land had unofficially been claimed by adjacent farmers, but having stood empty through two world wars, it was hardly surprising. The house itself had not been taken over, possibly due to its spooky reputation or, perhaps, the theft of bricks and mortar was not as acceptable.

There wasn't much left. It must have been magnificent once, but now the roof and upper floor of one wall were lying at the foot, splattered across the ground. Tony tiptoed to the gap where the front door once stood. All the doors and windows were gone, not broken or decayed, but missing entirely, leaving nothing but gaping holes, exposing the interior to the rigours of wind, rain and creatures who chose to make it home. He hesitated to enter. There wasn't even a breath of air to disturb the obviously unstable masonry, but the high walls loomed threateningly, and he felt safer outside. The floor inside was an uneven carpet of shattered stone, interrupted by various shades of green, and foliage had climbed the brickwork to the sky, unhindered by anything but gravity. Something moved in the far corner and Tony backed out, unwilling to share the space with whatever wildlife had staked claim to it.

He made a slow circuit of the ruin, picking his way along broken paving and stepping gingerly over tree roots to give a wide berth to sections of fallen rubble. His heart felt heavy. This pitiable shell had been a home once. Children had played here. People had laughed and loved, been happy here, but now it was cold, empty and abandoned. There was no atmosphere, no sensation of foreboding, but he could understand why the locals described it as a ghost house. It wasn't the presence of spirit, but the absence of it.

When he reached the drive, he turned his back on the house and didn't look back. He climbed back into the car and Mario woke from his slumber, readjusted the chair and his cap and drove away.

CHAPTER 28

Tony picked up a sandwich and a bottle of wine from the supermarket in lieu of lunch and took them back to his room. The afternoon was well underway by the time he mounted the stairs and exhausted from the morning's excursion, after eating, he followed the custom of siesta and slept into the early evening.

There was nothing to rush for when he woke up, so he took a long cool shower before checking in, first with Jamie and Marco and then with Nina. Jamie was so excited over the end of term assembly that morning, Tony hardly had to speak at all. Nina had been a balm to his weary spirit and listened to the sparse detail he felt able to share. He was still processing what he'd seen and heard. By the time he returned home, he should have a wider picture, hopefully with good news to balance out what, at the moment, felt like an overwhelming amount of bad.

He intended to go back to the museum tomorrow, to search out the artwork the tourist guide had mentioned. That was a promising source for information. Hopefully, the paintings would be accompanied by some provenance. Looking over his notes, he considered what more he hoped to uncover during his stay. He had the certificates, which also meant he had all the important dates he needed, and the causes of death, though no matter what Stefano Esposito said about dangerous professions and the fragility of life in times gone by, they still didn't sit well with him.

Things just didn't add up, not in a clean, clear way. There were too many anomalies: for a start, the drowning and disappearance of Alessandro and Tonio. Their family owned an enormous, wealthy estate, so why would they have become fishermen? Perhaps it was as simple as farming life not being for them, but that didn't ring true. Surely, historically, sons followed fathers into the family business. There weren't the choices or the expectation of choice, people had in modern times. Secondly, Benedetto, murdered in a most gruesome manner. Who was responsible for that vicious act and why had it taken place? Fights happened, accidents happened, but to cut someone's throat was a premeditated, deliberate act. He desperately wanted to know what had incited someone to do it but didn't have a clue where to start looking online.

Tony shuddered. It wouldn't do to sit in his room ruminating. He needed to be out, mixing with people, hearing them talking and laughing. He needed distraction.

Making the conscious decision to leave his file behind, he grabbed his wallet and headed into the heady warmth of the night. With no solid idea of where he was going, he wandered into town, enjoying the sights, altered and ethereal in the half light. The bars and restaurants took on a new lease of life after dark, and music and chatter spilled onto the streets. There were people everywhere, but Tony felt separate, alone, and he yearned to spend time with somebody he knew. The best idea he could come up with was to call in at the bar where Sonya worked. She at least would be a familiar face.

The front of the establishment was wide open, tables and stools huddled on the pavement as well as inside, but most had been shifted to the far end, circling a large screen television. Customers were heckling the football match being shown, so Tony chose a seat a safe distance from the crowd, but not so far away as to feel isolated. Sonya was carrying out brisk business at the counter but spotted him not long after he sat down and moved toward his table as soon as she was able.

'It's busy.' Tony nodded at the rabble.

She wiped the table with a cloth and tucked it back in her apron. 'It's always busy when there's a game. The men become a wild pack. They're not permitted to be this noisy at home. Did you want to eat? The steak is good.'

He plucked the menu from its holder, but, spotting the exclusively Italian writing, immediately replaced it. 'Steak would be great, thanks. And a pint of something cold.'

She began to walk away. 'Lager or ale?'

'Lager, please.' He sat back to wait, one eye on the television, trying to surf the excitement of those around him.

Sonya returned with his drink but was called back almost instantly as the half time whistle blew and the throng turned as one to the bar. It was lonely being the only one in the middle of a hectic room who couldn't speak the language.

The match had restarted by the time his steak was prepared and in the lull which followed, Sonya delivered the sizzling plate to him and sat down. 'You don't mind if I join you? I'm taking my break now.'

'No, please do. I could use the company.'

She drank from a tall glass of fruit juice and sighed. 'How is the search going? Was the address helpful?'

'Yes, it was. I went to see it today. It's a ruin but would appear to be the right place. Tourist Information confirmed that for me. It turns out the Visconti family are celebrities around here. Or were, I should say.' He sliced a thin piece of steak and chewed slowly.

'Really? Celebrities, huh?'

'Not in a good way, unfortunately. They're seen as a jinx or something. The house is known as the Ghost House. Not a very auspicious history.'

She shook her head. 'What is jinx?'

'Oh, sorry. It's like very unlucky or a bad omen.'

A frown formed on her brow as she concentrated. 'How so?'

Tony downed what was left of his pint and stroked his chin dry of moisture. 'I assume it's because all the men died young. Knowing what I know now, I think I'm lucky to have made it this far.'

She laughed aloud at his solemnity. 'You look pretty healthy to me.'

Joining in her levity, he raised his eyebrows. 'You can be as healthy as you like, but you're not likely to survive a knife to the throat.'

Having taken a sip of her drink, Sonya swallowed hard on the guffaw which threatened to erupt. 'Oh, I see. Well, in that case you had better watch your back.'

'Only one went that way. There was a drowning, a hanging, all manner of sticky ends. The family seem to have just faded away. I think me and my boy are the only ones left.'

'Would you rather they all lived long, dull lives? I bet your son will love the drama. It will be something to show off to his friends.'

'He's a bit young for that. If I told him the details, it would probably give him nightmares.' He pulled out his phone and clicked on a photograph of Jamie, smiling with pride as the image beamed from the screen, and turned it so she could see.

She took it from him, and her face softened. 'He's very handsome. How old?'

Before he could reply, his phone rang, and she handed it back.

Apologising, he answered it, and she picked up her drink, taking it back to the bar to give him privacy.

It was Stefano Esposito. 'Ah, Tony, my friend, I have news, not much, but some. I spoke to colleagues about Benedetto and the feeling is, it will be difficult to find anything official from that era. Very much documents were lost during the war, you know? But we will keep trying.'

'I appreciate you taking the time. Thank you.' Tony held one hand over his other ear to cancel out the noise from the football crowd as a goal was scored.

'The good news is one colleague recognised the name. Apparently, the Visconti name is infamous around here. I did not know this.' His tone was jolly. 'My colleague, she says there is a play, at the open theatre. Every summer it is different local stories, but this year it tells again the Visconti legend. The woman who organises this is an historian. I don't have her contact details I am afraid, but she will be at the next performance on Thursday night. I am sure if you speak to her, she will be happy to help. You don't need a ticket. You just go to the theatre at eight o'clock.'

Tony was blown away by this information, the possibility everything could be explained in one sitting. 'That's fantastic. Thanks, Stefano. My flight is at midnight, but I should be able to go to the play and still make it. Do you have the woman's name?'

'Yes, yes. She is Paloma Bianchi. A very nice woman. I met her in the past once or twice. I think everyone knows her. You should find her at the theatre very easily.'

'That's great. Thanks, again.'

Stefano ended the call and Tony looked at the handset in his hand.

Sonya returned to the table with another beer for him. 'Everything alright?'

'Yes, more than alright. Apparently, there's a play about my family at the open theatre. Is that down past the fountain? Yes, I'm sure it is.' He answered his own question, without pausing. 'There's a performance on Thursday evening. I should be able to make it before I fly home. This is amazing. It should tell me everything I want to know.'

'You realise it will probably be in Italian?'

Tony slapped his hand to his forehead. 'I hadn't thought of that. It's all right, I've been to operas and things before which are in different languages. You can usually work out what's going on.' He refused to have his spirits dampened.

'I could come with you, if you like?' She offered. 'I can translate, maybe?'

'You don't have to work?'

'No.' Sonya leaned in confidentially. 'I have told my boss this is my last night. I had a call from my friend. She is in Skopje and will be in Tirana at the weekend, and I'm going to meet her there.' She shrugged. 'Time to move on.'

'Then I'd love you to come. Thank you.'

She stood as a voice behind the bar called her name. 'Listen, don't tell Renata. I haven't had the chance to let her know yet. I wouldn't want her to find out from someone else.'

'Don't worry.' He chuckled. 'Renata and I don't appear to be on talking terms.'

CHAPTER 29

Wednesday began overcast and much cooler than previous days, a relief after such relentless heat, but as the day wore on the sun burnt off the cloud and the intensity of the rays returned with a vengeance. Tony intended to take things easier: a long, lazy breakfast; a visit to the gallery at the museum and a walk around the open-air theatre to ensure he knew exactly where he was going on Thursday night, vital as time would be tight and he didn't want to risk missing the flight home.

He entered the museum with a real sense of purpose. The same old man was leaning on the counter, muttering as he ticked items off a manifest on a clipboard. As before, the building appeared empty apart from the two of them and Tony felt obliged to speak as he passed into the gallery. The man acknowledged his 'good morning' with a nod and watched as the swing doors closed behind him.

The size of the gallery took Tony by surprise. The cavernous space was broken up by mismatched pillars, creating intimate corners and alcoves within the whole for various displays. All manner of artwork hung from the walls, and a large paper-craft giraffe hung from the centre of the ceiling, swinging gently in the waft of air Tony had created by entering. The room was awash with colour and texture, thanks to light flooding through overhead skylights.

As much as he had a mission to fulfil, Tony felt

himself drawn to the vibrant displays and, as he had time, he began a logical and thorough exploration of the room, playing tourist as well as detective. The first wall was layered with a collage of paintings and drawings, all of a similar ilk, crude in delivery and childlike. Each was marked with a name and age and Tony assumed they were probably produced by local children. He smiled at the touching naivety of the creations and could imagine work of his own son sitting comfortably alongside. The next section was an eye-catching array of distant horizons, from sunsets on water in vivid oranges and reds to twilight shades of purple and navy, made from textiles to provide layers of depth and texture.

A display of wooden grotesques, all protruding tongues and bulbous eyes, made for a much darker show of creativity and Tony moved swiftly past to a small, but even darker collection of oil paintings. Horrific images of torture and murder groaned from the canvases; blood dripping from sharp knives; bodies hoisted by ropes around the neck, hands secured behind backs, faces contorted in agony and fear. Part of him wanted to look away, ignore the pain in the eyes of the victims, but the other part was transfixed by the horror.

He couldn't help but wonder who would hang one of these monstrosities on their wall, let alone what type of character would have the imagination to create it. The artist's name was displayed on a plaque, together with the titles of each individual piece, but it was nothing Tony recognised. He moved along, a need for fresh air, clean of the awfulness of the atmosphere conjured by the evil images, driving him on. He studied a wall of head and shoulder portraits, checking individual names allocated to them, but drew a blank.

A cursory glance at the rest of the pieces left him

frustrated. Nowhere could he see any reference to the name Visconti. Either he was missing something, or they were no longer here. He considered a second circuit of the room, but an attempt to communicate with the curator seemed a more time efficient option.

Walking back into the museum lobby, Tony waited patiently at the till for the old man to look up from his paperwork.

'Do you speak English?' He asked hopefully.

The man shrugged and shook his head and Tony thought about giving up, but in view of recent experience decided to persevere.

'Visconti?' He sounded the consonants slowly and clearly.

The man gave a brief nod and waited for more and Tony, encouraged, pointed towards the swing doors and repeated, 'Visconti?'

The curator nodded again and sidled out from behind the counter. He led Tony back into the gallery, straight down the middle of the room, bypassing the gambolling giraffe to the terrifying oil paintings along the back wall.

Tony couldn't understand. He reread the signage, but there was no sign of the name he was looking for, but the man stood watching and waiting.

Tony pointed at the artwork. 'Visconti?'

The man nodded and smiled broadly. 'Si.' He muttered. 'Visconti.'

Examining the works again, Tony glanced from the guide to each of the paintings and back again, a confused frown marking his forehead. The man beckoned for Tony to follow him back into the entrance hall. When there, he rummaged behind the desk and pulled out a small box of leaflets, selecting one from the top and slid it across the counter. Tony took it. The front showed a pale portrait of a man with a curly moustache and an old-fashioned hat, staring into the mid distance, and a title, an unfamiliar name. Inside were miniature reproductions of some of the paintings in the gallery and a single leaf of notes, in Italian, in French and English. Tony fell on the familiar lettering with relish, but the complicated way the different languages were laid out on the page made it difficult to absorb immediately, so he thanked the guide, dropped some Euros into a Perspex box on the counter, and moved out into the street, in search of a cafe.

As soon as he had purchased a drink and settled at a quiet table, he opened the leaflet and followed the English words with his finger. The information was brief. The Condemnation of Gjeshe, was the official title of the collection, whoever or whatever Gjeshe was - he would Google that later, but an alternative citing referred to them as The Anguish of the Viscontis. They'd been painted decades ago and were the most well-known works by the man on the cover.

He looked again at the thumbnail pictures depicted in the leaflet. The first showed a character lying on his side, blood oozing from a wound to the chest, while a second character stood away, arm outstretched, a pistol in his hand. The second had a man splayed across a bench in a pool of gore, his throat agape, while two conspirators grinned madly at the body, one wiping a sword with a rag. The third displayed a figure tied to the strut of a bridge, his mouth bound with a gag, as water rose to thigh level. One man on a horse watched from the shore, while another leaned over the bridge, pointing in glee. The last of the collection showed two men physically hurling a screaming figure from a cliff top onto razor sharp rocks below, where the waves crashed and heaved.

With all his heart, Tony prayed the tortured figures depicted were not real people, not recreations of actual history. He weighed up what he knew about his ancestors alongside the art. One had had his throat cut and one had drowned, which would fit, but there was no connection to the other pictures, so in his mind he refuted any correlation as accidental. They were surely simply the works of a skilful, but troubled, soul.

Finishing his drink, he tucked the pamphlet away, settled the bill and strolled away to find the theatre. He had an uncomfortable feeling the play would not be a light-hearted study of Victorian Italian life. To warrant an annual re-enactment there must be a bigger and, in all likelihood, grimmer story to be told. As soon as he was sure of the location, he intended a change of tack. The investigation, and the insights he had uncovered, were weighing heavy on his shoulders and he needed a break from the bleak. For the afternoon and the following morning, he would put it to one side. He'd go back to the hotel, grab a towel and head for the beach, to let the sea air and the saltwater cleanse it away.

CHAPTER 30

The amphitheatre was buzzing when Tony and Sonya emerged from the narrow streets leading into its wide-open space. Although sited outdoors, the steep ascending rows of stone seating, rising from the crater of the stage, and high-sided buildings beyond them, held sound captive within its confines, bouncing off the uneven surfaces. There was an air of festival, and it seemed much of the town were in attendance, milling around, setting down picnic blankets and hollering greetings to friends from one side of the arena to the other. Rows of plastic chairs had been placed at the base, enclosing the performance area, maximising capacity. Tony selected a space close to the exit, mindful of the taxi he'd booked to take him to the airport and the possibility of having to leave briskly later.

A column of players in costume paraded past the audience onto the stage, signalling for a cease to the clamour. An expectant hush fell, and a tall, blonde woman came to the fore, addressing the crowds.

Sonya leaned in. 'The lady is Paloma Bianchi. She's thanking everyone for coming to the opening night and introducing the actors and thanking others for support, costumes, etc.'

The woman talked for a few moments, the actors bowed and disappeared into an alcove to one side, then her tone changed, less chatty, more momentous.

'It's going to begin. The Visconti's Fall from Grace.'

Sonya rested back in her seat, ready to take it all in.

Tony raised his brows at the title of the play and watched the action with a growing sense of foreboding.

There was a great deal of shouting from the main character, a young man surrounded by a group of cronies in tight trousers and flouncy shirts, loud, showboating, with much waving of swords and preening of costumes.

'He says, he is Alessandro Visconti and he can do whatever he wants. No one will stop him because he owns the world.' Sonya's narration erupted intermittently in rapid bursts.

'Nice guy!' Tony did his best to follow the action, as well as listen to Sonya's asides.

A woman entered, strolling the perimeter of the stage, a basket swinging from her arm. The male entourage, spotting her, sidled towards her, yelling obscenities. The girl turned, shouting back and made to escape, but Alessandro planted himself firmly in her way.

'She's not interested, but he won't listen. He says he will teach her to listen to her Lord and master.' Sonya bobbed in her seat, trying to hear the words as the cast moved to the other side of the stage. 'She says she's only fourteen and he must not disrespect her. Her family, the, umm, Tagliabue, will not stand for it. Fourteen? She's at least thirty!'

The men snatched up the girl and ran from the stage amid much screaming. A pause followed, then the same girl re-entered, now heavily pregnant. An imposing older woman approached her and grabbed her arm.

'It is the girl's grandmother. She is asking what the girl has been doing. How has this happened?'

The girl broke down, sobbing and hiding her face. The older woman stood very upright and made a declaration to the air.

'She says, Alessandro must pay for his disrespect. The Tagliabue men must find him and make him pay.'

A period followed of men running to and fro, crossing paths in their hunt for the perpetrator, until Alessandro was manhandled to centre stage and held by the arms, while a man poked his chest with a sword.

'It is the girl's father. He is challenging Alessandro to a duel. He says Alessandro may behave like a rogue, but the Tagliabue family are gentlemen, and he will meet him at dawn with… I think he said, with pistols.'

The stage cleared of actors again and unwieldy props were positioned.

'Great start.' Tony whispered. 'It looks like Alessandro was a rapist and a paedophile. What fantastic genes I have.'

Sonya giggled. 'It's all right. I don't think being an ass is hereditary.'

A smoke machine emitted wisps of gas across the stage, producing an eerie atmosphere and two groups of men entered from opposite sides, until facing each other, an arm's width apart. There was a lot of pushing and shoving and roaring, and Sonya frowned in concentration.

'I think the old man, the one with the long grey wig, is Alessandro's father. The one with the girl's father is her brother or her uncle, I'm not sure which. Ah, it is her brother. Alessandro and the girl's brother are to fight the duel. The others are in support. The one at the back is like a judge, to make sure all is fair.'

The men stood back-to-back, then paced away from each other. The crowd fell silent in anticipation. Alessandro turned prematurely, before the order was given, and fired at his opponent's back, but missed. The other man swivelled and held up his pistol to return fire, aiming at an open target and it seemed Alessandro was bound to fall, but his father suddenly pulled another gun from his cloak and fired first, flooring the Tagliabue man with a single shot. Then, Alessandro and his father fled together. The father of the shot man and the judge attended the crumpled body, with much wailing and weeping.

'The boy is dead.' Sonya whispered.

'I gathered as much.'

'The Visconti men are declared cheats and murderers, which makes them subject to penalty of death. The Tagliabue father vows to track them down.'

The body on the floor regained life long enough to scamper to the wings through the vapours and the other actors marched away, only to return in a new scene with the old woman, perched on a sturdy wooden throne. She slammed both fists violently on the arms of the seat and threw her arms around.

'She says, they must wipe the Visconti men from the face of the earth. They are agreeing. They are calling her something, a name, I don't understand. Jeshe? I don't know this word.'

'It could be Gjeshe. It's in the title of the paintings. I looked it up, but I couldn't find out what it means.'

Sonya held her hand up to silence him. 'A messenger says Alessandro is drunk in the town. They're going to get him. Oh dear, I don't give much for his chances.'

The drunkard was carried to the stage and deposited at the feet of the other men, whimpering and incapable.

'The Tagliabue men have called for their pistols. It is the only true justice, for Alessandro to die in the way he would have if the duel had been uninterrupted. No, wait, the grandmother is taking the gun.'

The woman strode from her throne to the quivering man and shot him in the chest, then turned to face the audience.

'She says, the Tagliabue family will not be shamed, and justice belongs to them.'

An energetic round of applause filled the stadium and Sonya glanced around. 'I think this could be the end.'

Tony blew out a breath from between pursed lips. 'I know Alessandro was an idiot, but it doesn't seem right for me to applaud my ancestor's murder, even if he deserved it.'

'There's more. Hang on.'

Tony shot a quick glance at his watch. Only twenty minutes remained before his taxi would arrive and he was beginning to get twitchy. He wanted to hear the whole story, but he couldn't miss his flight.'

A makeshift bed, holding the pregnant girl, was carried centre stage. She was in the throes of childbirth and a number of people attended her, mopping her brow, giving her water, while the grandmother watched from her throne. A doll was held up, representing the baby's arrival and wrapped in blankets. Suddenly, the young girl cried out and the old woman stepped down from the seat.

'The girl is dead. The woman says her death too lies at the feet of Alessandro and his kin. The justice they have had is not sufficient. She must have more.'

At that, Alessandro's father was carried in, restrained by the Tagliabue men and the woman collected a sword from beside her chair and prodded him in the chest, in the shoulder, in the groin, as if she couldn't decide where to inflict damage.

'She says, she could take his arm, but it would not pay for the life of her granddaughter. She could take his leg, but neither would that be enough. Not even his life. Oh no!' Sonya grimaced at the next speech.

A servant figure brought the baby and laid it on the ground at the man's feet.

'She says, this child is not a Tagliabue child. It is the work of the devil, forced onto the body of the girl and tainted blood flows through its veins. It can never be clean. It is a Visconti child...Wait. Yes, it is a Visconti child, and the man must not be allowed to see any Visconti children grow and prosper, but she will allow the man to live to see his children and his children's children ripped apart.'

The woman raised the sword above her head and brought it down on the baby, rending it in half. A horrified silence spread throughout the arena. The man was released, and he fell to the floor, grasping the woman's ankles.

'He is begging for mercy.'

The woman stepped out of his grip and both she and the remainder of the cast left the stage, leaving only the Visconti man on his knees, hands clasped in prayer.

'He says his life is over. He will never stop paying for his weakness. He tried to save his oldest son, only to pay with the lives of his other sons and grandsons. May all those who follow forgive him because he will never forgive himself?'

He limped from the stage and the audience sprang to their feet, clapping wildly.

'This time it's definitely the end.' Sonya rose to her feet with everyone else, but her applause was unenthusiastic. 'Not to my taste, I'm afraid. A little too Shakespeare tragedy for me. I like a happy ending.'

Some of the crowd began to pack up and wander away. Others took the opportunity to mingle. Paloma Bianchi was joined on stage by well-wishers, shaking her hand and congratulating her. Tony checked the time. He had five minutes before his transfer to the airport. Although he now knew more of the family history, there were so many unanswered questions he wanted to discuss with her.

'What are the chances of me getting to talk to her before my taxi gets here?'

Sonya stood on the seat to get a good view of the crowd. 'Not very good, I think. If you get to the front of the queue, you will probably have to leave before you can speak properly. Do you want me to try? I can phone you or email you. Or I can pass your contact details to her. I bet she would love to talk to a living Visconti.'

He glanced at the stage, to the exit and back again. There was no choice if he didn't leave soon his flight was in jeopardy.

He hitched his rucksack over one shoulder. 'Would you? You've been such a great help already; I feel guilty asking.'

'I offered. Anyway, I'll look you up when I'm back in England and you can buy me a drink.'

His eyes flew to the gate again. 'Ok. Thanks.' He gave her a brief hug before darting away. 'Call me.'

'Go on. Catch your plane. I'll call you.' She hollered at his back, then walked towards the stage.

CHAPTER 31

Tony spent the taxi ride running over the information he'd collected. The evidence backed up his opinion that the Visconti men were uncommonly unlucky, although this was sometimes accompanied by bad behaviour and risky business. Maybe there was truth in the ethos, people were responsible for their own good fortune. Paloma Bianchi seemed to be an authority on the subject of his family, and he was disappointed not to be able to speak to her face to face.

A mile from the airport, Tony's phone rang. He expected to see Sonya's number, but the caller was unidentified, and he answered with interest.

'Mr Viscount? Or should I say Mr Visconti? Its Paloma Bianchi.'

He was surprised by the accent at the end of the line. 'Yes, Tony Viscount. Paloma, how great to hear from you. You're American? I had no idea. I thought, listening to you on stage earlier, you were Italian.'

'Aha, but you're English. I suspect the Italians who were watching are slamming me.' She laughed. 'I grew up in the US, but my father was Italian, so we spent vacations over here. I was so interested to hear from your friend. I truly thought all the Viscontis had been wiped off the face of the earth by order of Nonna Tagliabue. How did you come to be in England?'

Apparently, it wasn't only he who had questions. 'My grandfather emigrated in the early part of the twentieth century. We thought he probably moved for economic reasons, though there's nothing solid to back the theory up.'

'Yea, you could pretty much come and go as you pleased in those days. If you didn't want people to know where you were they didn't have to. Not like nowadays, with the World Wide Web. Would your grandfather be Leonardo, born late nineteenth century?' She seemed to be reading from a list. 'I followed the tree forward from Benedictine as far as him, but then my trail went dead.'

'My records show him as Leonard, but I guess that could be an attempt at sounding more English, like changing the surname to Viscount. His father was Leonardo.'

'Yea, that sounds right. How exciting. So how much do you know about the past? Had you heard about the vow before tonight? The wrath of Gjeshe?'

'I saw the artwork at the museum, but I'm still not quite clear. What is Gjeshe?'

'Gjeshe is Albanian for grandmother, because this particular grandmother was originally Albanian. She married into the Tagliabue family, but she brought the Albanian codes of conduct with her. I must say, she was particularly vicious. It was she who declared the oath and began the vendetta, which ran through the generations, much as you witnessed in the play tonight. The persecution of the Visconti clan was all down to her.'

The taxi pulled into a drop off point outside the airport and Tony gathered his things, ready to exit, apologising to Paloma for the disruption and settling the bill with the driver. He walked into the departures lounge and checked the boards. 'I'm sorry about that. I know it's late, are you ok to talk. I could call you tomorrow if you'd prefer.'

'There's no chance I'm letting you off the phone until

I hear your story, even if it's the wee small hours.'

He laughed, understanding how she felt. 'That's great. It'll kill time while I'm waiting to fly. Just a minute, I'm going through security.' His belongings floated along the conveyor belt and out the other side, where he took possession again.

'Look, can you clarify for me, you said she began the vendetta? Were the Tagliabue responsible for more violence against the Viscontis, after they killed Alessandro and the baby?'

There was an extended pause before her shocked voice continued. 'Oh, Tony, that was just the beginning. Do you not know the rest?'

'What rest?' He waited; breath held tight in his chest.

'The Tagliabues hounded the Viscontis down through the generations. They allowed the family line to continue, but as soon as the continuance was established, in other words, when they were satisfied another generation was assured, the adult males were murdered. They were beaten, drowned, hung. Their imagination and cruelty knew no bounds.'

Tony felt sick to his stomach. 'So, all these death certificates I have, for Benedetto, Leonardo, Alessandro, they weren't accidents?'

'Not at all. The official documents may say one thing, but it's an open secret. The whole town knew these men were being killed. No one would work for them, associate with them, because it was more than their lives were worth. The Viscontis were isolated, abandoned by what had once been their people. They couldn't continue to work the vineyards because they didn't have the manpower, they lost their friends, their money. They were outcasts.'

'Which is why the estate was abandoned.'

'And no doubt it's why your grandfather left the Country. It was the only chance he had of saving himself or his children.'

Tony's head was spinning. 'Are you telling me this ... vendetta, continued right up until the twentieth century?' Surely, it was unbelievable a feud could be sustained so long.

'Tony, it's endemic of the Albanian culture. You really don't want to get on the wrong side of them. Families face years of suffering if they do. They run and hide, but their enemies lie in wait, for years, decades, generations even. It's described in Albania as living "in blood" - alive, but death always lurking around the corner. It's an incredibly brutal kind of justice.'

'Can the authorities do nothing about it?' He found the whole idea incredible. It made him angry to think this sustained campaign could have continued in such a way, because of the actions of one man.

'It's like the mafia. You're a brave person if you're prepared to stand up in court against them. Without witnesses, the authorities can do nothing. Look, it's a terrible thing, but it's over now. Your grandpa got away from all that, gave you a new start. At least you know it's in the past.'

He mulled her comments over in his mind. Had Leonard got away? Or had he simply carried the weight of the grudge into another Country. 'Is it though? Is it all over?'

She sounded confused. 'You're alive, aren't you? Your family survived!'

Tony felt a wave of cold spread from the tips of his limbs to his core as the pieces locked into place. 'Leonard was stabbed to death with a bayonet outside a pub in nineteen fourteen. My grandfather Robert was hit by a train the same year my father was born, and there are reports to suggest he was helped into its path. My parents...' His voice cracked and he felt himself inwardly crumple. 'My parents died in a house fire when I was a child. Did somebody do that to them? Did somebody kill my parents?'

'Hang on one minute.' He could hear panic evolving in her tone. She didn't know what to do or say. 'No, that can't be. I've done extensive study, and the Tagliabue family died out. They spent too much of their lives intent on revenge rather than building a future for themselves and their line petered out. I haven't been able to find a link to the Tagliabue line for almost a century.'

'But you couldn't find a link to the Visconti line either, could you?'

Paloma's voice reduced to a whisper. 'No. I couldn't.'

He threw himself into a seat, dropping his bag on the floor, strength sapped. 'So, they could still be out there. They could be after me, after my son?'

'Wait!' A new energy refreshed her words. 'No wait. In the play we showed Benedictine begging for mercy, and we left it like that, dramatic licence, but records show they did agree to grant some sort of leniency, for what it was worth at the time, from an endless timescale to ten generations. Even if the Tagliabue were still around, and the modern branch of the family were prepared to follow the judgement set down, it would have run out by now, surely?'

Tony grabbed at the sweet idea of reprieve, snatched his notebook from his bag and counted off the list of names. There was hope. 'Alessandro, Benedetto, Alessandro, Tonio, Leonardo, Leonard. That's six. Then there was Antonio, Robert, then me. I'm number nine.' The hope was gone. 'I'm only number nine. Jamie is ten. My son is number ten.'

'Tony. Tony, calm down. Don't panic. I'm sure your son is tucked up safe at home with your wife. I'm sure you're safe. This is history. It's not now, and even if it was, Jamie would be alright for the time being, as they'd want him alive to create another generation.'

'But if he's the last of the ten, it doesn't matter if there's another generation. They could kill him now. What if there's someone waiting to kill me, or him, right now?' He cast paranoid eyes across the departures lounge. Suddenly every single person in the building was a suspect.

'Let's get this into perspective. You have no reason to believe someone is out to get you right now, do you? Has there been any attempt on your life? Have you felt threatened in any way?' She sounded completely reasonable.

'I don't think so.' He racked his brains, thinking hard, but all he could think about was Jamie, hundreds of miles away, unprotected.

'Exactly! You're fine. Nothing has changed since this morning, except you've learned some history, and you felt safe this morning, right?'

'Right.'

'Good. Look, get your flight home. I'll email you all my research and if you're still worried, feel free to take it to the police. I'm guessing it'll all feel different after a night's sleep.'

'You think?' He was doubtful, but willing to be persuaded.

'I do think. Give me your email. I'll go crank up my laptop right now. All the research is in one file so I can get it to you in no time and you can read it through. Shall I ring you in a couple days?'

His breathing was starting to slow. 'Ok.' He relayed his contact details and rang off.

In the background, an Italian message was repeated in English, requesting passengers for his flight number. With one last look around, he hoisted his bag over his shoulder and headed for the boarding gate. More than anything, he needed to be back in the UK, back in surroundings he knew, where he felt comfortable; he needed to get back to his boy.

In the time he had been at the airport, a heavy mist had settled over the runway, making take-off impossible and passengers were held on the plane awaiting clearance for an hour and a half. It was the longest ninety minutes of Tony's life. He checked his phone for messages over and over, and when Paloma's email landed, he opened the file, desperately hoping something would stand out, making it clear there was nothing to worry about. The breadth of her research was impressive. She had obviously spent many hours scouring records for clues, building a picture, she was a knowledgeable woman, but there was nothing to reassure him.

When, finally, the flight was permitted to go, he switched the phone off and slipped it away, turning his face to the window and allowing his tired eyes to rest. On the inside of his lids, he replayed recent conversations, events which stood out, things in support or denial of his concerns. His trip to Wales; the conversation with his grandmother, his mentally incapacitated grandmother, he reminded himself; the chats with Howard and with Ruth, all dry dates and facts, nothing untoward. If he hadn't started working on his family tree, he would never have found out what he now knew. He would be living in blessed ignorance, no worries, nothing to lose sleep over. Was there someone out there, watching, waiting? If so, why had they waited so long? He had been completely unaware, unsuspecting, an open target until now. Now he would be alert to everybody and everything. Nothing would get past him. The whirr of the engines and dim lighting lulled him into a light, fractious sleep.

As the plane banked over France, his eyes flew open.

His heart was thumping out of his chest. Something had been floating around in his mind, something which suddenly forced him into full consciousness, something which had left him now, but was there, just beyond his reach.

It was Paloma's voice. Paloma had been talking to him. He had been replaying their earlier conversation, word for word. What had she said? What had been sufficient to slap him from semi-conscious to fully alert in a moment? She had said, "you're safe". She had said, "your son is safe", "safe at home with your wife". Vicky! All at once, the way in which Vicky died struck him. All the doubts and questions about what had happened that day were clear. She had been driving *his* car. The day she had died she had been at the wheel of *his* car. Why would witnesses have said they saw her racing down country lanes? Why would there be indications of another car on the scene? Unless there was another car. She hadn't been racing. She'd been trying to get away and whoever had been chasing her; had caused her to crash off the road; had caused her to die, had been after him. Vicky had died because of him. Jamie was in danger because of him.

Could it be someone he knew? Someone at work? A neighbour? He couldn't believe it. He knew them all so well; had known them for years. There was nobody new in his life, apart from Nina, and nobody he would suspect for a moment. Was there a stranger somewhere, someone he didn't know, but who knew him, watching from afar? No, that would be far too random. They would want to know all about him and his family, be observing his every move, biding their time. If someone was watching and waiting, they had to be closer to home.

Nothing had happened to raise his suspicions, he

had not felt threatened in any way … except that night at The Olive Branch, the night he got trapped in the storeroom, the night he went there with Nina. The police hadn't seemed at all bothered. High jinks, they'd called it. But he'd been bothered. It shook him up, rattled him, but he'd been prepared to put his fears to one side, because it was more comfortable that way. It confused him that Nina hadn't been aware of what was going on. She only went to the bathroom, but whoever it was had managed to trap him and set a fire in the time she was absent, then disappear before she came back. It all seemed a little too convenient now. On top of which, Nina was the only new figure in his life.

Nina had been present at the only time he'd felt threatened in recent times. She could so easily have slammed the door on him and set the fire, but then why did she release him? Another few minutes and he would have been done for. Perhaps, at the last minute, her conscience hadn't allowed her to go through with it. And Nina had connections to Southern Europe. She spoke Italian. It hurt his heart, but the answer suddenly shone out like a beacon. The woman he was in love with wanted him and his family dead. He had to stop her.

CHAPTER 32

The plane touched down in the early morning without further hitches, but Tony had counted off every second, desperate to speak to his son, to make sure he was alright and ensure he stayed that way. He didn't want to drag the Rossis out of their beds at some unearthly hour, but as soon as the clock reached a suitable time he would phone them, explain his predicament. He was hoping to be halfway along the motorway by then, halfway to seeing Jamie with his own eyes. The queue at arrivals snaked hundreds of metres and he shuffled impatiently, leaning one way, then another, to see the exit as he edged towards it. Rumours passed back the line that a security scare had resulted in tightened controls, and stern uniformed officers observed those entering closely to ensure everyone was abiding by the rules. There was no way he was getting anywhere quickly.

Tony half walked, half ran to the car park, threw his bag in the boot of his car and climbed wearily into the driver's seat. It was almost six. A little early to call, but, hell, he needed to get it done. He punched in Marco's number and waited, biting his lip, but after a few rings it went to voicemail. Swearing under his breath, he threw the phone to one side. There was a service station a few miles further on and he would fill up on fuel there and try again.

Three times he pulled over and dialled Marco's phone. Three times he was disappointed. By eight thirty he was within twenty-five miles of home, but it still felt like a world away. He couldn't understand why there was no answer. He knew Marco walked Max before work every day, so he should have been up and out by now. In desperation he tried Ruth's number, but that too offered up no response and he racked his brains to remember what it was they'd said they'd be doing that day. Maybe Marco wasn't working. He was sure they'd said something out of the ordinary was taking place, but for the life of him he couldn't recall what it was. His mind was too full of fear and violence and threats to remember anything.

The roads into town were heaving with traffic, morning rush hour well under way, as he left the motorway and joined the sea of vehicles heading for the centre. Tony was conscious he was intimidating the car in front, sitting on its bumper in his impatience, but for once he didn't care about driving etiquette.

When he turned into Marco's cul-de-sac, he was relieved to see their old Volkswagen on the drive and swerved in behind it, slamming his foot on the brakes at the last moment. Jumping out, he ran to the door, just as Marco stepped out. Max immediately picked up on Tony's agitation, barking excitedly, drawing Marco's attention from where he was locking up.

'Tony! We weren't expecting you 'til this afternoon. I thought we'd agreed Nina would drop Jamie back after the fair.'

The end of term School Fair. That was what was special about today. 'Sorry, my head's all over the place. Where's Jamie? Is he here? Can I see him?'

A frown brought Marco's eyebrows low. 'He's not here. Is something wrong?'

Tony didn't have time to answer questions. 'Where is he? Is he alright?'

'He was fine when they left twenty minutes ago.

Ruth volunteered to help set up at the park. She's rather taken with being a surrogate yummy mummy. And Jamie was more than happy to go early. Adrienne is part of the organising crew as I understand it, so the boys were going to get together to play while the ladies are busy.' Marco studied Tony's face. 'What's the problem, Tony? You don't seem at all yourself.'

Tony grabbed the knots at the back of his neck, not knowing what to do now he was here. He couldn't just go and grab Jamie and run, and if he did, where would they run to? He could take the information he had to the police, but they would probably laugh him out of the station. He had no physical evidence to prove anyone was threatening him, let alone Nina. All he had to go on was Paloma's research, his own calculation after putting two and two together and a gnawing gut feeling. It wasn't much. 'I don't know what to do.'

Marco turned the key in the lock in the opposite direction and pulled a disappointed Max back inside. 'Come on. I think you need to sit down before you fall down and explain exactly what's going on.'

A cup of coffee later, Tony had relayed the full story, and, in true Rossi style, Marco had broken it down, absorbed it and was rearranging the information into something more manageable. 'So, you think Nina is out to get you?'

In daylight, as Paloma had suggested, it sounded less plausible, but the facts still amounted to a serious threat in Tony's mind. 'It's got to be someone, and I can't see how it could be anyone else.'

Marco rubbed his chin in thought. 'I don't know, Tony. Maybe you're jumping the gun. It's a fine story you've been given, but stories can be bent and shaped to fit the facts, can't they? If you suspect foul play was involved with Vicky's accident, then you should definitely speak to the police, your contact, Matt, was it? I'm sure he would know who to pass the information to, but I don't think you should set too much store by it. As for Nina being at the bottom of it, she wasn't even around then.' He seemed to consider a new possibility; the possibility Tony had been seeing her before Vicky's death. 'Was she?'

Tony rapidly set the record straight. 'No. No, of course she wasn't. At least, I didn't know she was, but what if she was watching, waiting. She tried to kill me and got Vicky instead, so now she's moved in closer to be sure she gets it right this time.'

Marco pursed his lips but didn't respond, giving Tony time to think about what he'd just said and realise how mad it sounded.

'You think I'm crazy, don't you?' His confidence was waning, but in his heart, he was sure he was right.

'Not crazy. Not right, but not crazy. I think you need to talk to someone...'

Tony rolled his eyes and shrugged to the air, before rising to his feet. 'A shrink! You think I need to talk to a shrink. You do think I'm crazy.'

Marco was quick to reassure. 'That's not what I meant at all. I think you should talk to Nina. Before you start to throw accusations around; before you ruin what looks to me like the beginnings of a rather promising relationship, talk to her. Tell her what you've found out and see what her reaction is. If she's a part of this ... conspiracy. If there even is a conspiracy, she won't be able to hide it. You'll know straight away. If it's all news to her, then you'll know you've got it wrong.'

It was like light dawning over Tony's muddled brain. 'Of course! I'll talk to her. You're right. She won't be able to hide her guilt.'

Marco chuckled beneath his breath. 'The Rossi's

always right. You know that. Look, I'll come with you. Stop you jumping in with both feet. Max can have a trot round the park while we're there, kill two birds with one stone.'

'But, what if she's not guilty? What then?'

'Then, either it's all a big mistake, or you need to be watching your back in another direction. Come on. Let's sort this mess out, once and for all.'

They took separate vehicles to the fair and found parking spaces close together. Tony waited as Marco clipped the lead onto Max's collar, only the fear of making a fool of himself holding him back from running in to rescue Jamie. He couldn't let fear take over, because then he wouldn't be able to think straight and now, more than ever, he needed a clear head.

Marco marched on ahead, Max pulling on the lead in his eagerness to access the parkland. 'They're setting up on the green in front of the playground. Should be easy enough to spot, with all the gazebos and so forth. Go on Maxi, find Mummy.'

They strode down the main path, Max's tongue lolling out of his grinning mouth in wild enjoyment of the morning sun, smoothly side-stepping other visitors dawdling along the way. When they emerged from the trees, the whole green became visible, speckled with open fronted tents and tables, people milling around, getting things ready for the fair. Marco paused to scan the horizon for his wife and, when he spotted her amongst the circle, pointed her out to Tony.

'There's Ruth. Jamie can't be far away.'

They continued, Tony searching out the little boy with his eyes, between the tents, running around the centre with a huddle of children playing tag. There was no sign of him. 'Where is he? Can you see him?'

Marco was the voice of calm. ‘He’s here somewhere.’ Then he pointed to the play area. ‘There! By the fort. That’s Jamie, isn’t it? With the blue t-shirt?’

Relief washed over Tony, and he couldn’t stop himself running off the green, to the path running behind it, to the entrance of the wired off play area. Marco watched him go, a look of concern on his face, continuing to where his wife was busy laying out raffle prizes. She saw him coming and stood back, watching his progress.

Tony temporarily lost sight of the enclosure as he stuck to the path, circuiting tents and stalls, to get to it. As he got closer, he called Jamie’s name, but now there was no sign of him. Tony bent down to peer through the wire enclosure to the more obscured areas inside, but Jamie was nowhere to be seen.

He sped around to the entrance, checking every child’s face as he went, expecting the boy to appear at any moment, but he wasn’t there. Tony began to panic. He ran around the construction, poked his head inside. Nothing. A leg appeared, backing out of a tunnel, and Tony watched carefully. It was the right size and shape, but when the body emerged it wasn’t Jamie, it was Charlie.

‘Charlie. Where’s Jamie? I need to find him.’

Charlie stood up straight and scratched his blond tousled head. ‘He went with the lady.’ Clearly of the opinion he had fully answered the question, he folded himself in half to climb back inside.

Tony’s tone was urgent and loud and sent Charlie immediately bolt upright. ‘What lady? Where did he go?’

Charlie shot out a pointing finger to the path on the other side of the enclosure. ‘That lady. There he is.’

Tony could see his son, head down and wiping at his face, as if he was upset, next to a crouching Nina. He took off at full pelt to catch up with the pair. What had she done to him? Why was he crying? Whatever it was, he was darn sure he was going to put a stop to it right now, before it could go any further.

'Jamie. Jamie. Come here to me.'

The little boy looked back at his father, frowning. 'Daddy! Why are you here? I thought you wouldn't be home until later.' His face was grubby from playing in the mud and streaked with tears.

'I couldn't miss the fair, could I?' He held the boy by his shoulders, checking his body, eyeing Nina, who was standing to one side. 'What's wrong? What's happened to you?'

'I hurt my arm, and my knees.' Jamie looked over his shoulder. 'Charlie can go all the way to the top of the castle and down the other side in two minutes. I was trying to beat him.'

Tony pulled Jamie against him and turned his attention to Nina. 'What are you doing here? Where were you taking him?'

Nina looked askance at his tone. 'It's alright, Tony. I'd dropped the girls off for the majorettes' demonstration and happened to see Jamie was hurt. I was only going to take him to the First Aid tent. His knee is bleeding a little, that's all.'

'That's the story, is it?'

Nina shrugged. 'I don't understand. What do you mean, story? Look, you see? His knee is bleeding.'

'And that's it, is it? You've no ulterior motive for taking him away from his friends and his family?'

'Tony, you're making no sense. What are you talking about, taking him away? We were going to get a dressing, that's all. Why are you being like this?'

Jamie was looking up at his father's face, equally baffled. Tony ran a rough hand through his hair. He studied Nina's face, her movements, her demeanour, but she was the same Nina he'd known from the beginning. How could she be what he thought she was? How could she have committed the heinous crime of killing his wife? How could she be so loving with him, as she had been recently, with murder in her heart? Surely it would show somewhere about her person, it would leak out into her skin, her eyes, her character. He didn't know what to do.

Ruth wandered up next to them. 'Hi, can I help?' She looked Tony square in the eye, as if trying to convey a message. 'Marco has told me all about your trip. You've had an interesting time of it, I understand. Why don't I take Jamie to get that knee looked at while you two have a talk?'

'That's one word for it.' He thrust his hands into his pockets. On one hand, he didn't want to let Jamie out of his sight; on the other, he needed to tackle this with Nina before he went out of his mind.

CHAPTER 33

It had never occurred to Tony before how difficult it was to accuse someone of murder. Nina stood, gazing openly at him with such confusion, such wide-eyed innocence, he couldn't bring himself to begin.

'Tony, tell me what's wrong?'

He noticed the parallel lines which formed from the top of her nose, up past her eyebrows, when she frowned. 'I found something out while I was away, something shocking.'

'What is it?' She placed a hand on his arm and waited.

'I found out my family have been stalked and hunted and murdered by another Italian family with a grudge against them since the seventeen hundreds.'

'What? No!' Her face was a picture of doubtful horror and instantly Tony's confidence in her guilt waned.

'Yes. I have a file of evidence which links the deaths of my ancestors to the Tagliabue family, and I think they followed us to England. I have no absolute proof, but I think they killed my great grandfather, my grandfather and my parents too.' He maintained a steady tone.

Nina's mouth fell open. 'That's who pushed Robert in front of the train. Tony, that's horrific.'

'I'm pretty sure they killed Vicky too. She was driving my car, and witnesses said she had been racing with another driver, which frankly is unbelievable. I think they drove her off the road, thinking I was at the wheel.'

Nina's hand flew to her mouth. 'No! Tony, no! It can't be!'

'Can't it?' He looked deep into her eyes and read nothing but pain for him. This was all news to her. Nina was not the threat. 'I'm sure it's true, and if it is, it means both Jamie and I are still in danger.'

'They wouldn't hurt a child!'

'They would. He's the last in the line. They vowed to kill ten generations, and he is number ten, and from what I've seen, I don't think they would think twice about it.'

A heavy silence settled over them, Nina taking in what she'd been told, Tony floundering, at a loss. If it wasn't Nina, who was it? On top of which, he was now ashamed of ever suspecting her.

'Who are they? Do you know?' She searched his face for answers.

'I don't have any idea and I don't know how to find out. How can I keep Jamie safe?'

The frown suddenly cleared from her forehead. 'You thought I... Oh, Tony, no. You must know I would never...'

'I know. I can see that now.' He rested one hand on her shoulder. 'I'm sorry, It's just my brain has been all over the place since I found out. I don't know what to do.'

'You need to tell somebody. Have you reported it?'

He realised he couldn't allow another second to pass without taking action. He would collect Jamie, take him home and immediately phone Matt, and if Matt couldn't help, he would take it further. Beyond that, if it came to it, he'd bundle Jamie in the car and head far, far away, even it meant leaving everything and everybody else behind. Suddenly his own childhood made sense; the illogical relocation from one random town to another. His parents had been trying to protect him. 'You're right. I've got to go, right now.'

They hurried back to the circle of stalls, Nina almost running to keep up. 'I can't come with you. I've got to take the girls home after the parade. Can I come over later?'

He marched on ahead. 'I'll call you, let you know what's going on.' He couldn't make any commitments until this was sorted out.

Rounding the back of the tent where the Tombola was set up, he ran into Marco, hovering nervously behind the table. Max was prone under the canvas, tired by his walk. 'Marco, I'm heading off. I've got to get Jamie home and safe and phone the police. I need to get to the bottom of this.'

Marco eyed Nina warily. 'You haven't worked out who it is then?'

'No, I don't know who it is. Look, thanks for the last few days. Ruth's taken Jamie to get his knee looked at. I'll go and get him from there. I'll be in touch, ok?'

Nina stayed with Marco, watching Tony's retreating back as he hurried across to the First Aid tent and disappeared inside.

The tent was all but empty, and Tony quickly looked around for his son.

'Can I help you?' A short, bearded man in uniform stood up from behind a desk, clipboard in hand.

'I'm looking for my son, Jamie Viscount. He'd grazed his knees. My friend, Ruth, was bringing him over.

The man studied the clipboard. 'Not seen a Jamie. In fact, it's quiet this morning. Haven't seen anybody for the last twenty minutes. Are you sure they were coming here?'

'Definitely. This is the only first aid place, isn't it?'

'Yes. Sorry, he's not here.' The man shrugged. 'Perhaps they decided he didn't need our facilities after all. Probably gone back to the playground.'

'Ok. Thanks.'

Tony rushed out of the tent and back to the play area but couldn't see his son anywhere.

Adrienne walked up to the outside of the enclosure, spotting Tony's worried air. 'Looking for Jamie?'

'Yes. Have you seen him?'

'I saw him with Ruth. Only two minutes ago. I assumed you knew.'

This made no sense. Tony stood on the bottom rung of a nearby ladder for a better view of the surroundings, but there was no sign of the pair. 'Which way did they go?'

She clung to the netting with both hands. 'I'm not sure. I think they followed the path to the far gate, toward the river, but they may have cut across the grass to get back to the stalls. Is everything alright?'

He shook his head, unable to work it out. 'I'm sure it's fine, but I need to find him. If he comes back phone me, will you? Straight away?'

'Of course. I'll keep my eyes peeled.'

Tony rushed out of the enclosure and back to the Tombola. Marco and Nina were still standing over it.

'He's not there.' Tony explained. 'They said he left with Ruth. Where can she have gone?'

Marco shook his head. 'I don't know, but she can't be far.'

Tony's stomach clenched with fear. Something just wasn't right with this situation. 'Adrienne said she thought they were heading for the gate. I'm going to look for them.'

He set off at a jog, through the centre, past the perimeter of colourful canvas, circling the play area and through the gate, to a pathway which ran alongside a skate park to the riverbank. Why would she come this way? Why would she have taken Jamie at all? He stepped up onto a wooden bench seat so he could see into the skate park.

It was almost empty. A few young children were taking advantage of the fact the High Schools had not yet broken up for the summer, running up and down the ramps in their trainers while no bigger kids were there to interfere, but there was no sign of Jamie or Ruth.

In one direction, the path circuited past the skate park and some rough ground beyond and back into the park. It made no sense for them to have gone that way; it would have been quicker for them to go back the way they'd come. The other way, led to a path bordering a row of houses perched on the riverbank. Council offices blocked one end, though pedestrians could cut through the courtyard to a car park around the back, or there was a foot bridge part way along, spanning the fast-flowing river, to an industrial estate on the far side. None of the options seemed likely, but he had to make a choice. He ran around the skate park and through the narrow gap between the houses, so he had a good view of the length of the path. It was clear.

Tony grasped a handful of fringe with one hand in frustration. Think. Think. They'd left only minutes ahead of him. How far would they have got? They could have gone past the council buildings already. He sprinted along the path, braking hard to avoid colliding with a young woman, backing out of her garden gate with a small child in a buggy.

Apologising, he allowed her to pass in the opposite direction and was about to set off again when a flash of turquoise caught his eye, halfway across the footbridge. He squinted at the salty sea breeze, gusting in his face from the river. The flash was the same shade as Jamie's t-shirt and, as the scene came into focus, he realised it was Jamie and Ruth. He'd found them.

They had halted at the midpoint, looking down the river, towards him and as he watched, Ruth picked the wriggling boy up in her arms and manhandled him over the low metal railings of the bridge to a sliver of a platform on the other side. For a long-drawn-out moment, she stared right at Tony, then her head dipped and she climbed over to join the boy. Tony coughed a shocked sob. She couldn't hurt Jamie. Not his son. Jamie had been so proud when he brought home his swimming badge recently, ten metres, but in the powerful drag of the river he wouldn't last a minute.

CHAPTER 34

Digging deep inside himself, Tony found the energy to move; to run; to run like his life depended upon it; to run like his son's life depended upon it.

Breath ragged in his throat, Tony skidded on the gravel as he left the path and entered the footbridge, hollow metallic footsteps ringing out, as he mounted steps to their level. His eyes never left the pair, clinging precariously on the wrong side of the barrier. They were watching him too, waiting. He was close enough now to see Jamie crying, his eyes wide and round, his mouth moving as it formed words carried away by the air current, not to his father's ears. Tony slowed as he approached, not sure what to do when he got there, still not understanding.

'Stay there.' Ruth was shouting, her head flicking hair out of her face as it whipped in the wind. 'Don't come any closer or I'll drop him in.' She shook the boy by the arm to emphasise her point.

Tony pulled up short and gripped the ice-cold metal of the handrail desperately, trying to find his breath. 'What... What is all this Ruth? What are you doing?'

She let out a sad gulp of laughter. 'You know exactly what I'm doing. You found it all out in Puglia, didn't you! Any chance I had of getting rid of you and making it look like an accident disappeared then. After biding my time all these years, I saw you uncovering the old stories, murdered father, murdered grandfather, murdered great grandfather, but I still had time...until you decided to take yourself off to Italy.'

He tried to decipher what she was saying. 'What? You're... You're a Tagliabue?'

'No, I'm a Reynolds, and my father was a Reynolds, but my grandmother was a Tagliabue and so were her father and her uncles and her grandfather.'

Tony nudged forward, but she threw a hand up to halt him and shook her head. 'I knew a watered-down version of the story from such a young age, I can't ever remember not knowing it and, when my father died... He wasn't a violent man, but he was loyal, and Nonna had primed him from the minute he was born. He fulfilled his duty to our family by setting fire to your father's house, but it broke him. He couldn't live with what he'd done.' Her voice momentarily broke on the words, and she paused to cough and regain composure.

'I'll never know if it was the fact he had killed or the knowledge you'd escaped which made him take his own life. He didn't want the obligation to be passed to me, you see. When he died, my mother soon took up with somebody else and I was in the way, so she sent me to live with my grandmother. Then I understood the importance of it, the depth of the hatred. I was made to understand. The Kanun - that's what Albanians call it, this kind of vendetta, destroyed our family as much as it destroyed yours. You're the last of the Viscontis; I'm the last of the Tagliabues, but I must do my duty, even if it kills us both.'

Tony threw his arms wide and edged a step forward. 'No, Ruth, you don't. You don't have to do anything. It's all ancient history and it can stay that way. It's time for it all to end. We're friends.'

'Friends?' She threw her head back and laughed, and Jamie squealed, scrabbling to hold on to the rails as her body shook with mirth. 'We've never truly been friends. To begin with I thought, if I could get close enough to you, be part of your inner circle, I would find a way to get the job done and get away with it, still have a life of my own, but Vicky got in the way of that. I couldn't get anywhere near after she came along.'

A gust of wind bowed her sideways on her perch and Tony made to step forward, 'Ruth, please, you don't want to do this.'

'Don't even think about it!' She shouted, as she shuffled her feet, stabilising herself.

A metallic clang from the end of the bridge caused them all to swivel, only to see Marco and Max ascending to their level.

Ruth closed her eyes and muttered through clenched teeth, 'Merda! Merda! Merda!' before returning her attention to the man in front of her. 'This has nothing to do with what I want. It's never had anything to do with that, any more than it had anything to do with what my father wanted. It's about honour. I wish I'd never heard of the Kanun. I wish I'd been born to different parents, but I wasn't.'

Marco caught up with Tony and stalled, edging past him slowly. 'What the hell are you doing woman? Are you mad?'

She rolled her eyes, her tone weary. 'Go away, Marco. This has nothing to do with you. You're not needed here.'

'She's a Tagliabue. She's the one who wants to kill me, to kill Jamie.'

Marco stepped forward. 'Don't be ridiculous. We've been married nigh on ten years. How could she possibly be...'

'Stop right there, Marco, or he's going in the water.' She stood behind Jamie, gripping him between her body and the railings, holding on with one hand, waving at her husband with the other.

He stopped.

'Yes, we've been married for ten years, ten long years, but you know nothing. You don't know me. You don't know anything about me. All you're interested in is cricket and trips to the pub. You've never looked past the end of your nose.' She paused, briefly closing her eyes. 'Look, it doesn't matter now, does it? It's too late. It's all over for us, one way or another, so you might as well take the dog and go.'

She swiped hair out of her face. 'Tony, I don't want to prolong this any more than necessary. We've already got an audience.' She pointed roughly to the path, where Nina was hurrying, a small group following behind. 'My duty was to get rid of one generation, and heaven knows I tried my best, but it all went wrong.' She shook her head, muttering under her breath. 'But that was your fault. You never let her drive your car, never, so how was I supposed to know?'

'It was you who killed Vicky?'

'Yes, yes, it was me.' The group trailing Nina reached the steps, and a new urgency entered Ruth's voice. 'But if I can't get you, it will have to be Jamie. I don't feel good, killing a child. I tried when we were walking on the cliffs before but couldn't make myself go through with it. I never wanted to kill anyone really.' Her voice cracked, but she pulled herself together. 'I'm going in and I'm taking Jamie with me. There's nothing you can do to stop it, but I could have thrown him over before you got here, then I realised, this way we both get a chance to have the outcome we want. If you jump in the river yourself, maybe you'll save Jamie, or maybe I'll finally wipe out this branch of Viscontis in one swoop and the Kanun will be over.'

'Ruth, no. It's clear you don't want to do this, so don't. It's not too late.' Tony's only available course of action seemed to be to try and reason with her.

She looked beyond him to the trickle of onlookers

joining him on the bridge and chuckled. 'Oh, Tony, of course it is.' Grasping Jamie with one arm wrapped around his chest, she stepped back, into thin air. As she toppled backwards, Jamie yelled out in fear and grabbed at the railings, temporarily halting their descent with a jerk, but her body was too heavy, and he was pulled down after her.

In a second, Tony rushed to the spot where the boy had clung and threw himself over after them.

As Ruth and Jamie's bodies hit the water, Marco ran to the far side of the bridge, to see them both caught in the flow. 'The lifebelt! Someone throw the lifebelt,' he shouted to observers, watching from the shore.

Tony was only a moment behind his son. The shock of the icy water closing over him sent him floundering, but a sense of purpose returned, and he searched around him in the water for his son. Jamie was several metres away, his arms flailing in panic, having been separated from Ruth in the fall. At the sight of him, Tony struck out in the fastest front crawl he could manage and, aided by the momentum of the current, the gap between them shortened. He paused, lifting his head to again ensure he was going in the right direction, but Jamie had disappeared.

A voice shouted from the shoreline. 'There. He's there.' A stranger was pointing urgently to the left of where Tony was struggling to keep his head above the choppy water.

Tony turned and saw a flash of blue, just below the surface. He dived, his legs aching with the cold and the effort of propelling himself forward. Blind beneath the water, he reached out, waving his arms violently to find something, anything solid to grasp hold of. Just as he was about to give up hope, his fingers touched something cold and hard and he tugged it towards him, at the same time rising up to refill his lungs. It was Jamie's ankle and Tony pulled him in tight to his body, manoeuvring the boy's slippery torso until his head was held free of the water. Jamie coughed and spluttered in the unyielding grip of his father, and Tony, relieved by the sign of life, kicked back toward the edge.

Tony's muscles ached with the fatigue of keeping his son above water and fighting the current, but safety was tantalisingly close, and he knew he had to stay strong for just a little longer. The stranger who had shouted, was running along the shoreline and launched a lifebelt towards them, and Tony was glad to accept its support. Hooking one arm over the ring, as the other arm still gripped Jamie, the man held them fast, while he waited for others to join him to help pull them both out.

Tony lay gasping on the shore while a small crowd gathered around him with picnic blankets and jackets to ward off the cold. Jamie was crushed in his father's arms, whimpering but alive, and Tony never wanted to let him go again.

CHAPTER 35

Six Weeks Later

Tony stood at the foot of Vicky's grave. Her headstone was crisp and clean, yet to suffer the battering of the elements which had worn others nearby to more mellow tones. They looked like they belonged there, while Vicky's looked like an interloper.

He'd said all he needed to say, not convinced she could hear his explanations and his apologies, but he'd bared his soul and if felt right, if not good. He laid a dried flower arrangement by the stone, patted the marble once and turned away.

The gravel path took him the length of the graveyard to the main entrance, but at a junction with another path, just short of the gate, he paused. Breathing in and out three times, eyes still fixed in the direction he was supposed to be walking, with the last inhale, he clenched his teeth and turned. Several metres on, was a mound, unadorned and unmarked, except for a rectangle of twine, pinned around it to define the edges of the plot. Freshly dug and freshly filled in, covering what was left of Ruth.

Tony could never forgive her for the danger she'd put Jamie in. He'd never forgive her for killing Vicky, but he felt an intense sorrow that Ruth's life had been destroyed by the same vendetta which had infected his, and so many of his ancestors.

His mind was blighted by the final images of her, gripping Jamie, as she fell from the bridge, but they couldn't obliterate older, long-standing images of a woman who had been kind to him, supported him through challenging times. Even as he read the newspaper reports, vilifying her, describing her in evil terms, in complete contrast to the Ruth he thought he had known and loved, he couldn't help but question, which was the real Ruth? It left him angry and grief stricken. Even now he was confused.

'It won't do any good, you know?' Trish's voice interrupted his thoughts, as she joined him at the graveside. 'Sometimes there are no answers, and you're certainly not going to find any here. She did what she did, and we will never fully understand why.'

He nodded. He knew she was right but accepting that fact wasn't easy.

'Come on. Nina and Jamie will be waiting. His swimming lesson will be finished soon, and I believe you promised him ice cream and kite flying for being brave and getting back in the pool.' She patted his shoulder.

'He said he wants to see Max, but I don't think I'm ready. I don't know if I can face Marco just yet.'

'No, well, there's no rush. One step at a time, and I've been in touch with Marco and he's still feeling rather raw too. Give it a little while and perhaps you'll find your way back to the sort of friendship you used to have, but for now I think a respectful distance is probably best, to give you both space to heal.' She turned and walked away. 'I'll see you at the car.'

'I won't be long.' He watched her re-join the main path towards the exit, then returned his attention to Ruth's grave and sighed, it was time to look to the future, a very promising future with Jamie, Nina and

Trish.

'It's over.' There was no strength to his voice, and he coughed to clear his throat so he could give the words the power they required. 'For all of us, it's over.'

He noticed a small bouquet of flowers, laid a little inside the cordon. From Marco, he guessed, another victim of the Kanun. Who else was there to mourn her?

He turned and walked away. He was done with the past. It was time to get on with his life.

ABOUT THE AUTHOR

Sharon Francis

Born and bred in beautiful North Devon, Sharon is married with two grown up children. She studied Creative Writing with the Open University, completing her BA in 2017. She writes across a range of genres, including her romantic comedy Limbo Series, including titles, Girl Plans, God Laughs and What Might Have Been. Bloodline is her first crime novel.

For more information about Sharon, or her books, go to:-

Facebook.com/Sharon-Francis-Author-110933057304441/

Or

www.foursirenspress.co.uk/authors/sharon-francis

BOOKS BY THIS AUTHOR

Girl Plans, God Laughs

After a drunken New Year party goes bad, Violet is so desperate to sort out her love life, she makes a deal with God. Or does she?

A year of good deeds and personal sacrifices later and there should be some pay off, surely? But where's the man of her dreams? She's tired of waiting and will go to any length to get answers, but will it be the answer she's hoping for?

Sometimes it takes a bolt from the blue to see what's right in front of your nose.

BOOKS BY THIS AUTHOR

What Might Have Been

Life and love can be a rollercoaster, except for Lily Armitage, so far it's been more of a train crash. Perhaps it should be no surprise that she's decided to get off the ride and watch from the sidelines.

However, if Lily is to finally connect with her soulmate, she has no choice but to face whatever ups and downs life has to throw at her.

Can divine intervention give her the courage she needs to get back on the ride?

KEEP UP TO DATE

If you have enjoyed this book, please remember to leave a review on Amazon, so other readers can have the benefit of your thoughts.

You could be the first to know when Sharon's next novel is available to purchase and receive free additional content by signing up for the Four Sirens Press monthly newsletter at -

www.foursirenspress.co.uk

ACKNOWLEDGEMENT

No man is an island (and no woman either). Where would we be without family, friends and colleagues? I have no idea, but it certainly wouldn't be preparing for the publication of my third novel.

Thanks to the Four Sirens crew, not only for giving me the freedom to write in whatever genre I feel inspired to, but for the active encouragement to do so. Long may we support and motivate each other in the way we have been doing for the last three years. Thank you Denise, Sue & Beverley.

My family have had to put up with me, and my idiosyncrasies, for much longer, but they do so with much patience and understanding. Sometimes the going does get tough and it's only because of David, Shaun and Beth, that the tough is able to get going.

I always thank Clare and Christine for their unfaltering support and that stands once again, but there are many other friends I should mention but won't, because where would I stop? You know who you are.